A BOY WITH NO PAST . . .

Baslim was sure that Thorby had been taken from his parents so young that he had no conscious memory of them. The boy's notion of his life was a jumbled recollection of masters, some bad, some worse—all of whom had tried to break the spirit of a "bad boy."

Thorby had explicit memories of some of these masters, and he described them in gutter speech vivid and violent. But he was never sure of time or place—place was always some estate or household, never a particular planet or sun.

Although each planet has its day, its year, its own method of dating, it was impossible for an illiterate boy to date anything. To Thorby, therefore, a "day" was the time between two sleeps.

So Baslim could not begin to guess the lad's age. He looked like unmutated Earth stock and was preadolescent; but any guess would be based on unproved assumptions.

But all that was unimportant to Baslim. Thorby was a youngster who needed help!

Citizen
of the
Galaxy

Robert A. Heinlein

A Del Rey Book

BALLANTINE BOOKS • NEW YORK

TO FRITZ LEIBER

A Del Rey Book
Published by Ballantine Books

ISBN 0-345-26074-0

This edition published by arrangement
with Charles Scribner's Sons

Manufactured in the United States of America

First Ballantine Books Edition: July 1978

Cover art by Darrell Sweet

Chapter 1

"LOT NINETY-SEVEN," the auctioneer announced. "A boy."

The boy was dizzy and half sick from the feel of ground underfoot. The slave ship had come more than forty light-years; it carried in its holds the stink of all slave ships, a reek of crowded unwashed bodies, of fear and vomit and ancient grief. Yet in it the boy had been someone, a recognized member of a group, entitled to his meal each day, entitled to fight for his right to eat it in peace. He had even had friends.

Now he was again nothing and nobody, again about to be sold.

A lot had been knocked down on the auction block, matched blonde girls, alleged to be twins; the bidding had been brisk, the price high. The auctioneer turned with a smile of satisfaction and pointed at the boy. "Lot ninety-seven. Shove him up here."

The boy was cuffed and prodded onto the block, stood tense while his feral eyes darted around, taking in what he had not been able to see from the pen. The slave market lies on the spaceport side of the famous Plaza of Liberty, facing the hill crowned by the still more famous Praesidium of the Sargon, capitol of the Nine Worlds. The boy did not recognize it; he did not even know what planet he was on. He looked at the crowd.

Closest to the slave block were beggars, ready to wheedle each buyer as he claimed his property. Beyond them, in a semi-circle, were seats for the rich and privileged. On each flank of this elite group waited their slaves, bearers, and

5

bodyguards and drivers, idling near the ground cars of the rich and the palanquins and sedan chairs of the still richer. Behind the lords and ladies were commoners, idlers and curious, freedmen and pickpockets and vendors of cold drinks, an occasional commoner merchant not privileged to sit but alert for a bargain in a porter, a clerk, a mechanic, or even a house servant for his wives.

"Lot ninety-seven," the auctioneer repeated. "A fine, healthy lad, suitable as page or tireboy. Imagine him, my lords and ladies, in the livery of your house. Look at—" His words were lost in the scream of a ship, dopplering in at the spaceport behind him.

The old beggar Baslim the Cripple twisted his half-naked body and squinted his one eye over the edge of the block. The boy did not look like a docile house servant to Baslim; he looked a hunted animal, dirty, skinny, and bruised. Under the dirt, the boy's back showed white scar streaks, endorsements of former owners' opinions.

The boy's eyes and the shape of his ears caused Baslim to guess that he might be of unmutated Earth ancestry, but not much could be certain save that he was small, scared, male, and still defiant. The boy caught the beggar staring at him and glared back.

The din died out and a wealthy dandy seated in front waved a kerchief lazily at the auctioneer. "Don't waste our time, you rascal. Show us something like that last lot."

"Please, noble sir. I must dispose of the lots in catalog order."

"Then get on with it! Or cuff that starved varmint aside and show us merchandise."

"You are kind, my lord." The auctioneer raised his voice. "I have been asked to be quick and I am sure my noble employer would agree. Let me be frank. This beautiful lad is young; his new owner must invest instruction in him. There-fore—" The boy hardly listened. He knew only a smattering of this language and what was said did not matter anyhow. He looked over the veiled ladies and elegant men, wondering which one would be his new problem.

"—a low starting price and a quick turnover. A bargain! Do I hear twenty stellars?"

The silence grew awkward. A lady, sleek and expensive from sandaled feet to lace-veiled face, leaned toward the dandy, whispered and giggled. He frowned, took out a dagger and pretended to groom his nails. "I said to get on with it," he growled.

The auctioneer sighed. "I beg you to remember, gentlefolk, that I must answer to my patron. But we'll start still lower. Ten stellars—yes, I said, 'Ten.' Fantastic!"

He looked amazed. "Am I growing deaf? Did someone lift a finger and I fail to see it? Consider, I beg you. Here you have a fresh young lad like a clean sheet of paper; you can draw any design you like. At this unbelievably low price you can afford to make a mute of him, or alter him as your fancy pleases."

"Or feed him to the fish!"

" 'Or feed him—' Oh, you are witty, noble sir!"

"I'm bored. What makes you think that sorry item is worth anything? Your son, perhaps?"

The auctioneer forced a smile. "I would be proud if he were. I wish I were permitted to tell you this lad's ancestry—"

"Which means you don't know."

"Though my lips must be sealed, I can point out the shape of his skull, the perfectly rounded curve of his ears." The auctioneer nipped the boy's ear, pulled it.

The boy twisted and bit his hand. The crowd laughed.

The man snatched his hand away. "A spirited lad. Nothing a taste of leather won't cure. Good stock, look at his ears. The best in the Galaxy, some say."

The auctioneer had overlooked something; the young dandy was from Syndon IV. He removed his helmet, uncovering typical Syndonian ears, long, hairy, and pointed. He leaned forward and his ears twitched. "*Who is your noble protector?*"

The old beggar Baslim scooted near the corner of the block, ready to duck. The boy tensed and looked around, aware of trouble without understanding why. The auctioneer went white—no one sneered at Syndonians face to face . . . not more than once. "My lord," he gasped, "you misunderstood me."

"Repeat that crack about 'ears' and 'the best stock.'"

Police were in sight but not close. The auctioneer wet his lips. "Be gracious, gentle lord. My children would starve. I quoted a common saying—not *my* opinion. I was trying to hasten a bid for this chattel . . . as you yourself urged."

The silence was broken by a female voice saying, "Oh, let him go, Dwarol. It's not his fault how the slave's ears are shaped; he has to sell him."

The Syndonian breathed heavily. "Sell him, then!"

The auctioneer took a breath. "Yes, my lord." He pulled himself together and went on, "I beg my lords' and ladies' pardons for wasting time on a minor lot. I now ask for any bid at all."

He waited, said nervously, "I hear no bid, I see no bid. No bid once . . . if you do not bid, I am required to return this lot to stock and consult my patron before continuing. No bid twice. There are many beautiful items to be offered; it would be a shame not to show them. No bid three—"

"There's your bid," the Syndonian said.

"Eh?" The old begger was holding up two fingers. The auctioneer stared. "Are *you* offering a bid?"

"Yes," croaked the old man, "if the lords and ladies permit."

The auctioneer glanced at the seated circle. Someone in the crowd shouted, "Why not? Money is money."

The Syndonian nodded; the auctioneer said quickly, "You offer two stellars for this boy?"

"No, no, no, no, no!" Baslim screamed. "Two *minims!*"

The auctioneer kicked at him; the beggar jerked his head aside. The auctioneer shouted, "Get out! I'll teach you to make fun of your betters!"

"Auctioneer!"

"Sir? Yes, my lord?"

The Syndonian said, "Your words were 'any bid at all.' Sell him the boy."

"But—"

"You heard me."

"My lord, I *cannot* sell on one bid. The law is clear; one bid is not an auction. Nor even two unless the auctioneer has set a minimum. With no minimum, I am not allowed to sell with less than three bids. Noble sir, this law was given to protect the owner, not my unhappy self."

Someone shouted, "That's the law!"

The Syndonian frowned. "Then declare the bid."

"Whatever pleases my lords and ladies." He faced the crowd. "For lot ninety-seven: I heard a bid of two minims. Who'll make it four?"

"Four," stated the Syndonian.

"Five!" a voice called out.

The Syndonian motioned the beggar to him. Baslim moved on hands and one knee, with the stump of the other leg dragging and was hampered by his alms bowl. The auctioneer started droning, "Going at five minims once . . . five minims twice . . ."

"Six!" snapped the Syndonian, glanced into the beggar's bowl, reached in his purse and threw him a handful of change.

"I hear six. Do I hear seven?"

"Seven," croaked Baslim.

"I'm bid seven. You, over there, with your thumb up. You make it eight?"

"Nine!" interposed the beggar.

The auctioneer glared but put the bid. The price was approaching one stellar, too expensive a joke for most of the crowd. The lords and ladies neither wanted the worthless slave nor wished to queer the Syndonian's jest.

The auctioneer chanted, "Going once at nine . . . going twice at nine . . . going three times—*sold* at nine minims!" He shoved the boy off the block almost into the beggar's lap. "Take him and get out!"

"Softly," cautioned the Syndonian. "The bill of sale."

9

Restraining himself, the auctioneer filled in price and new owner on a form already prepared for lot ninety-seven. Baslim paid over nine minims—then had to be subsidized again by the Syndonian, as the stamp tax was more than the selling price. The boy stood quietly by. He knew that he had been sold again and he was getting it through his head that the old man was his new master—not that it mattered; he wanted neither of them. While all were busy with the tax, he made a break.

Without appearing to look the old beggar made a long arm, snagged an ankle, pulled him back. Then Baslim heaved himself erect, placed an arm across the boy's shoulders and used him for a crutch. The boy felt a bony hand clutch his elbow in a strong grip and relaxed himself to the inevitable—another time; they always got careless if you waited.

Supported, the beggar bowed with great dignity. "My lord," he said huskily, "I and my servant thank you."

"Nothing, nothing." The Syndonian flourished his kerchief in dismissal.

From the Plaza of Liberty to the hole where Baslim lived was less than a li, no more than a half mile, but it took them longer than such distance implies. The hopping progress the old man could manage using the boy as one leg was even slower than his speed on two hands and one knee, and it was interrupted frequently by rests for business—not that business ceased while they shuffled along, as the old man required the boy to thrust the bowl under the nose of every pedestrian.

Baslim accomplished this without words. He had tried Interlingua, Space Dutch, Sargonese, half a dozen forms of patois, thieves' kitchen, cant, slave lingo, and trade talk—even System English—without result, although he suspected that the boy had understood him more than once. Then he dropped the attempt and made his wishes known by sign language and a cuff or two. If the boy and he had no words in common, he would teach him—all in good time, all in good time. Baslim was in no hurry. Baslim was never in a hurry; he took the long view.

Baslim's home lay under the old amphitheater. When Sargon Augustus of imperial memory decreed a larger circus only part of the old one was demolished; the work was interrupted by the Second Cetan War and never resumed. Baslim led the boy into these ruins. The going was rough and it was necessary for the old man to resume crawling. But he never let go his grip. Once he had the boy only by breechclout; the boy almost wriggled out of his one bit of clothing before the beggar snatched a wrist. After that they went more slowly.

They went down a hole at the dark end of a ruined passage, the boy being forced to go first. They crawled over shards and rubble and came into a night-black but smooth corridor. Down again . . . and they were in the performers' barracks of the old amphitheater, under the old arena.

They came in the dark to a well-carpentered door. Baslim shoved the boy through, followed him and closed it, pressed his thumb to a personal lock, touched a switch; light came on. "Well, lad, we're home."

The boy stared. Long ago he had given up having expectations of any sort. But what he saw was not anything he could have expected. It was a modest decent small living room, tight, neat, and clean. Ceiling panels gave pleasant glareless light. Furniture was sparse but adequate. The boy looked around in awe; poor as it was, it was better than anything he remembered having lived in.

The beggar let go his shoulder, hopped to a stack of shelves, put down his bowl, and took up a complicated something. It was not until the beggar shucked his clout and strapped the thing in place that the boy figured out what it was: an artificial leg, so well articulated that it rivaled the efficiency of flesh and blood. The man stood up, took trousers from a chest, drew them on, and hardly seemed crippled. "Come here," he said, in Interlingua.

The boy did not move. Baslim repeated it in other languages, shrugged, took the boy by an arm, led him into a

11

room beyond. It was small, both kitchen and wash room; Baslim filled a pan, handed the boy a bit of soap and said, "Take a bath." He pantomimed what he wanted.

The boy stood in mute stubbornness. The man sighed, picked up a brush suitable for floors and started as if to scrub the boy. He stopped with stiff bristles touching skin and repeated, "Take a bath. Wash yourself," saying it in Interlingua and System English.

The boy hesitated, took off his clout and started slowly to lather himself.

Baslim said, "That's better," picked up the filthy breech clout, dropped it in a waste can, laid out a towel, and, turning to the kitchen side, started preparing a meal.

A few minutes later he turned and the boy was gone.

Unhurriedly he walked into the living room, found the boy naked and wet and trying very hard to open the door. The boy saw him but redoubled his futile efforts. Baslim tapped him on the shoulder, hooked a thumb toward the smaller room. "Finish your bath."

He turned away. The boy slunk after him.

When the boy was washed and dry, Baslim put the stew he had been freshening back on the burner, turned the switch to "simmer" and opened a cupboard, from which he removed a bottle and daubs of vegetable flock. Clean, the boy was a pattern of scars and bruises, unhealed sores and cuts and abrasions, old and new. "Hold still."

The stuff stung; the boy started to wiggle. "Hold still!" Baslim repeated in a pleasant firm tone and slapped him. The boy relaxed, tensing only as the medicine touched him. The man looked carefully at an old ulcer on the boy's knee, then, humming softly, went again to the cupboard, came back and injected the boy in one buttock—first acting out the idea that he would slap his head off his shoulders if he failed to take it quietly. That done, he found an old cloth, motioned the boy to wrap himself a clout, turned back to his cooking.

Presently Baslim placed big bowls of stew on the table in the living room, first moving chair and table so that the

12

boy might sit on the chest while eating. He added a handful of fresh green lentils and a couple of generous chunks of country bread, black and hard. "Soup's on, lad. Come and get it."

The boy sat down on the edge of the chest but remained poised for flight and did not eat.

Baslim stopped eating. "What's the matter?" He saw the boy's eyes flick toward the door, then drop. "Oh, so that's it." He got up, steadying himself to get his false leg under him, went to the door, pressed his thumb in the lock. He faced the boy. "The door is unlocked," he announced. "Either eat your dinner, or leave." He repeated it several ways and was pleased when he thought that he detected understanding on using the language he surmised might be the slave's native tongue.

But he let the matter rest, went back to the table, got carefully into his chair and picked up his spoon.

The boy reached for his own, then suddenly was off the chest and out the door. Baslim went on eating. The door remained ajar, light streaming into the labyrinth.

Later, when Baslim had finished a leisurely dinner, he became aware that the boy was watching him from the shadows. He avoided looking, lounged back, and started picking his teeth. Without turning, he said in the language he had decided might be the boy's own, "Will you come eat your dinner? Or shall I throw it away?"

The boy did not answer. "All right," Baslim went on, "if you won't, I'll have to close the door. I can't risk leaving it open with the light on." He slowly got up, went to the door, and started to close it. "Last call," he announced. "Closing up for the night."

As the door was almost closed the boy squealed, "Wait!" in the language Baslim expected, and scurried inside.

"Welcome," Baslim said quietly. "I'll leave it unlocked, in case you change your mind." He sighed. "If I had my way, no one would ever be locked in."

The boy did not answer but sat down, huddled himself over the food and began wolfing it as if afraid it might be snatched away. His eyes flicked from right to left. Baslim sat down and watched.

The extreme pace slowed but chewing and gulping never ceased until the last bit of stew had been chased with the last hunk of bread, the last lentil crunched and swallowed. The final bites appeared to go down by sheer will power, but swallow them he did, sat up, looked Baslim in the eye and smiled shyly. Baslim smiled back.

The boy's smile vanished. He turned white, then a light green. A rope of drool came willy-nilly from a corner of his mouth—and he was disastrously sick.

Baslim moved to avoid the explosion. "Stars in heaven, I'm an idiot!" he exclaimed, in his native language. He went into the kitchen, returned with rags and pail, wiped the boy's face and told him sharply to quiet down, then cleaned the stone floor.

After a bit he returned with a much smaller ration, only broth and a small piece of bread. "Soak the bread and eat it."

"I better not."

"Eat it. You won't be sick again. I should have known better, seeing your belly against your backbone, than to give you a man-sized meal. But eat slowly."

The boy looked up and his chin quivered. Then he took a small spoonful. Baslim watched while he finished the broth and most of the bread.

"Good," Baslim said at last. "Well, I'm for bed, lad. By the way, what's your name?"

The boy hesitated. "Thorby."

" 'Thorby'—a good name. You can call me 'Pop.' Good night." He unstrapped his leg, hopped to the shelf and put it away, hopped to his bed. It was a peasant bed, a hard mattress in a corner. He scrunched close to the wall to leave room for the boy and said, "Put out the light before you come to bed." Then he closed his eyes and waited.

There was long silence. He heard the boy go to the door; the light went out. Baslim waited, listening for noise of the

14

door opening. It did not come; instead he felt the mattress give as the boy crawled in. "Good night," he repeated.

"G'night."

He had almost dozed when he realized that the boy was trembling violently. He reached behind him, felt skinny ribs, patted them; the boy broke into sobs.

He turned over, eased his stump into a comfortable position, put an arm around the boy's shaking shoulders and pulled his face against his own chest. "It's all right, Thorby," he said gently, "it's all right. It's over now. It'll never happen again."

The boy cried out loud and clung to him. Baslim held him, speaking softly until the spasms stopped. Then he held still until he was sure that Thorby was asleep.

Chapter 2

THORBY'S WOUNDS healed, those outside quickly, those inside slowly. The old beggar acquired another mattress and stuck it in the other corner. But Baslim would sometimes wake to find a small warm bundle snuggled against his spine and know thereby that the boy had had another nightmare. Baslim was a light sleeper and hated sharing a bed. But he never forced Thorby to go back to his own bed when this happened.

Sometimes the boy would cry out his distress without waking. Once Baslim was jerked awake by hearing Thorby wail, "Mama, Mama!" Without making a light he crawled quickly to the boy's pallet and bent over him. "There, there, son, it's all right."

"Papa?"

"Go back to sleep, son. You'll wake Mama." He added, "I'll stay with you—you're safe. Now be quiet. We don't want to wake Mama . . . do we?"

"All right, Papa."

The old man waited, almost without breathing, until he was stiff and cold and his stump ached. When he was satisfied that the boy was asleep he crawled to his own bed.

That incident caused the old man to try hypnosis. A long time earlier, when Baslim had had two eyes, two legs, and no reason to beg, he had learned the art. But he had never liked hypnosis, even for therapy; he had an almost religious concept of the dignity of the individual; hypnotizing another person did not fit his basic evaluation.

But this was an emergency.

He was sure that Thorby had been taken from his parents so young that he had no conscious memory of them. The boy's notion of life was a jumbled recollection of masters, some bad, some worse, all of whom had tried to break the spirit of a "bad" boy. Thorby had explicit memories of some of these masters and described them in gutter speech vivid and violent. But he was never sure of time or place—"place" was some estate, or household, or factor's compound, never a particular planet or sun (his notions of astronomy were mostly wrong and he was innocent of galactography) and "time" was simply "before" or "after," "short" or "long." While each planet has its day, its year, its own method of dating, while they are reconciled for science in terms of the standard second as defined by radioactive decay, the standard year of the birthplace of mankind, and a standard reference date, the first jump from that planet, Sol III, to its satellite, it was impossible for an illiterate boy to date anything that way. Earth was a myth to Thorby and a "day" was the time between two sleeps.

Baslim could not guess the lad's age. The boy looked like unmutated Earth stock and was pre-adolescent, but any guess would be based on unproved assumption. Vandorians and Italo-Glyphs look like the original stock, but Vandorians take three times as long to mature—Baslim recalled the odd tale about the consular agent's daughter whose second husband was the great grandson of her first and she had outlived them both. Mutations do not necessarily show up in appearance.

It was conceivable that this boy was "older" in standard seconds than Baslim himself; space is deep and mankind adapted itself in many ways to many conditions. Never mind!—he was a youngster and he needed help.

Thorby was not afraid of hypnosis; the word meant nothing to him, nor did Baslim explain. After supper one evening the old man simply said, "Thorby, I want you to do something."

"Sure, Pop. What?"

"Lie down on your bed. Then I'm going to make you sleepy and we'll talk."

"Huh? You mean the other way around, don't you?"

"No. This is a different sort of sleep. You'll be able to talk."

Thorby was dubious but willing. The old man lighted a candle, switched off the glow plates. Using the flame to focus attention he started the ancient routines of monotonous suggestion, of relaxation, drowsiness . . . sleep.

"Thorby, you are asleep but you can hear me. You can answer."

"Yes, Pop."

"You will stay asleep until I tell you to wake. But you will be able to answer any question I ask."

"Yes, Pop."

"You remember the ship that brought you here. What was its name?"

"The *Merry Widow*. Only that wasn't what we called it."

"You remember getting into that ship. Now you are in it —you can see it. You remember all about it. Now go back to where you were when you went aboard."

The boy stiffened without waking. "I don't want to!"

"I'll be right with you. You'll be safe. Now what is the name of the place? Go back to it. Look at it."

An hour and a half later Baslim still squatted beside the sleeping boy. Sweat poured down wrinkles in his face and he felt badly shaken. To get the boy back to the time he wanted to explore it had been necessary to force him back through experiences disgusting even to Baslim, old and hardened as he was. Repeatedly Thorby had fought against it, nor could Baslim blame him—he felt now that he could count the scars on the boy's back and assign a villain to each.

But he had achieved his purpose: to delve farther back than the boy's waking memory ran, back into his very early childhood, and at last to the traumatic moment when the baby manchild had been taken from his parents.

He left the boy in deep coma while he collected his shattered thoughts. The last few moments of the quest had been so bad that the old man doubted his judgment in trying to dig out the source of the trouble.

Well, let's see . . . what had he found out?

The boy was born free. But he had always been sure of that.

The boy's native language was System English, spoken with an accent Baslim could not place; it had been blurred by baby speech. That placed him inside the Terran Hegemony; it was even possible (though not likely) that the boy had been born on Earth. That was a surprise; he had thought the boy's native language was Interlingua, since he spoke it better than he did the other three he knew.

What else? Well, the boy's parents were certainly dead, if the confused and terror-ridden memory he had pried out of the boy's skull could be trusted. He had been unable to dig out their family name nor any way of identifying them —they were just "Papa" and "Mama"—so Baslim gave up a half-formed plan of trying to get word to relatives of the boy.

Well, now to make this ordeal he had put the lad through worth the cost—

"Thorby?"

The boy moaned and stirred. "Yes, Pop?"

"You are asleep. You won't wake up until I tell you to."

"I won't wake up until you tell me to."

"When I tell you, you will wake at once. You will feel fine and you won't remember anything we've talked about."

"Yes, Pop."

"You will forget. But you will feel fine. About half an

hour later you will feel sleepy again. I'll tell you to go to bed and you will go to bed and go right to sleep. You'll sleep all night, good sleep and pleasant dreams. You won't have any more bad dreams. Say it."

"I won't have any more bad dreams."

"You won't ever have any more bad dreams. Not ever."

"Not ever."

"Papa and Mama don't want you to have any bad dreams. They're happy and they want you to be happy. When you dream about them, it will always be happy dreams."

"Happy dreams."

"Everything is all right now, Thorby. You are starting to wake. You're waking up and you can't remember what we've been talking about. But you'll never have bad dreams again. Wake up, Thorby."

The boy sat up, rubbed his eyes, yawned, and grinned. "Gee, I fell asleep. Guess I played out on you, Pop. Didn't work, huh?"

"Everything's all right, Thorby."

It took more than one session to lay those ghosts, but the nightmares dwindled and stopped. Baslim was not technician enough to remove the bad memories; they were still there. All he did was to implant suggestions to keep them from making Thorby unhappy. Nor would Baslim have removed memories had he been skilled enough; he had a stiff-necked belief that a man's experiences belonged to him and that even the worst should not be taken from him without his consent.

Thorby's days were as busy as his nights had become peaceful. During their early partnership Baslim kept the boy always with him. After breakfast they would hobble to the Plaza of Liberty, Baslim would sprawl on the pavement and Thorby would stand or squat beside him, looking starved and holding the bowl. The spot was always picked to obstruct foot traffic, but not enough to cause police to do more than growl. Thorby learned that none of the regular police in the Plaza would ever do more than growl; Baslim's arrangements with them were beneficial to underpaid police.

Thorby learned the ancient trade quickly—learned that men with women were generous but that the appeal should be made to the woman, that it was usually a waste of time to ask alms of unaccompanied women (except unveiled women), that it was an even bet between a kick and a gift in bracing a man alone, that spacemen hitting dirt gave handsomely. Baslim taught him to keep a little money in the bowl, neither smallest change nor high denominations.

At first Thorby was just right for the trade; small, half-starved, covered with sores, his appearance alone was enough. Unfortunately he soon looked better. Baslim repaired that with make-up, putting shadows under his eyes and hollows in his cheeks. A horrible plastic device stuck on his shinbone provided a realistic large "ulcer" in place of the sores he no longer had; sugar water made it attractive to flies—people looked away even as they dropped coins in the bowl.

His better-fed condition was not as easy to disguise but he shot up fast for a year or two and continued skinny, despite two hearty meals a day and a bed to doss on.

Thorby soaked up a gutter education beyond price. Jubbulpore, capital of Jubbul and of the Nine Worlds, residence in chief of the Great Sargon, boasts more than three thousand licensed beggars, twice that number of street vendors, more grog shops than temples and more temples than any other city in the Nine Worlds, plus numbers uncountable of sneak thieves, tattoo artists, griva pushers, doxies, cat burglars, back-alley money changers, pickpockets, fortune tellers, muggers, assassins, and grifters large and small. Its inhabitants brag that within a li of the pylon at the spaceport end of the Avenue of Nine anything in the explored universe can be had by a man with cash, from a starship to ten grains of stardust, from the ruin of a reputation to the robes of a senator with the senator inside.

Technically Thorby was not part of the underworld, since he had a legally recognized status, (slave) and a licensed profession (beggar). Nevertheless he was in it, with a worm's-eye view. There were no rungs below his on the social ladder.

As a slave he had learned to lie and steal as naturally as other children learn company manners, and much more quickly. But he discovered that these common talents were raised to high art in the seamy underside of the city. As he grew older, learned the language and the streets, Baslim began to send him out on his own, to run errands, to shop for food, and sometimes to make a pitch by himself while the old man stayed in. Thus he "fell into evil company" if one can fall from elevation zero.

He returned one day with nothing in his bowl. Baslim made no comment but the boy explained. "Look, Pop, I did all right!" From under his clout he drew a fancy scarf and proudly displayed it.

Baslim did not smile and did not touch it. "Where did you get that?"

"I inherited it!"

"Obviously. But from whom?"

"A lady. A nice lady, pretty.

"Let me see the house mark. Mmm . . . probably Lady Fascia. Yes, she is pretty, I suppose. But why aren't you in jail?"

"Why, gee, Pop, it was easy! Ziggie has been teaching me. He knows all the tricks. He's smooth—you should see him work."

Baslim wondered how one taught morals to a stray kitten? He did not consider discussing it in abstract ethical terms; there was nothing in the boy's background, nothing in his present environment, to make it possible to communicate on such a level.

"Thorby, why do you want to change trades? In our business you pay the police their commission, pay your dues to the guild, make an offering at the temple on holy day, and you've no worries. Have we ever gone hungry?"

"No, Pop—but look at it! It must have cost almost a stellar!"

"At least two stellars, I'd say. But a fence would give you

21

two minims—if he was feeling generous. You should have brought more than that back in your bowl."

"Well . . . I'll get better at it. And it's more fun than begging. You ought to see how Ziggie goes about it."

"I've seen Ziggie work. He's skillful."

"He's the best!"

"Still, I suppose he could do better with two hands."

"Well, maybe, though you only use one hand. But he's teaching me to use either hand."

"That's good. You might need to know—some day you might find yourself short one, the way Ziggie is. You know how Ziggie lost his hand?"

"Huh?"

"You know the penalty? If they catch you?"

Thorby did not answer. Baslim went on, "One hand for the first offense—that's what it cost Ziggie to learn his trade. Oh, he's good, for he's still around and plying his trade. You know what the second offense carries? Not just the other hand. You know?"

Thorby gulped. "I'm not sure."

"I think you must have heard; you don't want to remember." Baslim drew his thumb across his throat. "That's what Ziggie gets next time—they shorten him. His Serenity's justices figure that a boy who can't learn once won't learn twice, so they shorten him."

"But, Pop, I won't be caught! I'll be awful careful . . . just like today. I promise!"

Baslim sighed. The kid still believed that it couldn't happen to him. "Thorby, get your bill of sale."

"What for, Pop?"

"Get it."

The boy fetched it; Baslim examined it—"one male child, registered number (left thigh) 8XK40367"—nine minims and get out of here, you! He looked at Thorby and noted with surprise that he was a head taller than he had been that day. "Get my stylus. I'm going to free you. I've always meant to, but there didn't seem to be any hurry. But we'll do it now and tomorrow you go to the Royal Archives and register it."

Thorby's jaw dropped. "What for, Pop?"

"Don't you want to be free?"

"Uh . . . well . . . Pop, I *like* belonging to *you*."

"Thanks, lad. But I've got to do it."

"You mean you're kicking me out?"

"No. You can stay. But only as a freedman. You see, son, a master is responsible for his bondservant. If I were a noble and you did something, I'd be fined. But since I'm not . . . well, if I were shy a hand, as well as a leg and an eye, I don't think I could manage. So if you're going to learn Ziggie's trade, I had better free you; I can't afford the risk. You'll have to take your own chances; I've lost too much already. Any more and I'd be better off shortened."

He put it brutally, never mentioning that the law in application was rarely so severe—in practice, the slave was confiscated, sold, and his price used in restitution, if the master had no assets. If the master were a commoner, he might also get a flogging if the judge believed him to be actually as well as legally responsible for the slave's misdeed. Nevertheless Baslim had stated the law: since a master exercised high and low justice over a slave, he was therefore liable in his own person for his slave's acts, even to capital punishment.

Thorby started to sob, for the first time since the beginning of their relationship. "Don't turn me loose, Pop—please don't! I've *got* to belong to you"

"I'm sorry, son. I told you you don't have to go away."

"*Please*, Pop. I won't ever swipe another thing!"

Baslim took his shoulder. "Look at me, Thorby. I'll make you a bargain."

"Huh? Anything you say, Pop. As long as—"

"Wait till you hear it. I won't sign your papers now. But I want you to promise two things."

"Huh? Sure! What?"

"Don't rush. The first is that you promise never again

to steal anything, from anybody. Neither from fine ladies in sedan chairs, nor from poor people like ourselves—one is too dangerous and the other . . . well, it's disgraceful, though I don't expect you know what that means. The second is to promise that you will never lie to me about anything . . . *not anything.*"

Thorby said slowly, "I promise."

"I don't mean just lying about the money you've been holding out on me, either. I mean *anything.* By the way, a mattress is no place to hide money. Look at me, Thorby. You know I have connections throughout the city."

Thorby nodded. He had delivered messages for the old man to odd places and unlikely people. Baslim went on, "If you steal, I'll find out . . . eventually. If you lie to me, I'll catch you . . . eventually. Lying to other people is your business, but I tell you this: once a man gets a reputation as a liar, he might as well be struck dumb, for people do not listen to the wind. Never mind. The day I learn that you have stolen anything . . . or the day I catch you lying to me . . . I sign your papers and free you."

"Yes, Pop."

"That's not all. I'll kick you out with what you had when I bought you—a breechclout and a set of bruises. You and I will be finished. If I set eyes on you again, I'll spit on your shadow."

"Yes, Pop. Oh, I never will, Pop!"

"I hope not. Go to bed."

Baslim lay awake, worrying, wondering if he had been too harsh. But, confound it, it was a harsh world; he had to teach the kid to live in it.

He heard a sound like a rodent gnawing; he held still and listened. Presently he heard the boy get up quietly and go to the table; there followed a muted jingle of coins being placed on wood and he heard the boy return to his pallet.

When the boy started to snore he was able to drop off to sleep himself.

Chapter 3

BASLIM HAD LONG since taught Thorby to read and write Sargonese and Interlingua, encouraging him with cuffs and other inducements since Thorby's interest in matters intellectual approached zero. But the incident involving Ziggie and the realization that Thorby was growing up reminded Baslim that time did not stand still, not with kids.

Thorby was never able to place the time when he realized that Pop was not exactly (or not entirely) a beggar. The extremely rigorous instruction he now received, expedited by such unlikely aids as a recorder, a projector, and a sleep instructor, would have told him, but by then nothing Pop could do or say surprised him—Pop knew everything and could manage anything. Thorby had acquired enough knowledge of other beggars to see discrepancies; he was not troubled by them—Pop was Pop, like the sun and the rain.

They never mentioned outside their home anything that happened inside, nor even where it was; no guest was ever there. Thorby acquired friends and Baslim had dozens or even hundreds and seemed to know the whole city by sight. No one but Thorby had access to Baslim's hideaway. But Thorby was aware that Pop had activities unconnected with begging. One night they went to sleep as usual; Thorby awakened about dawn to hear someone stirring and called out sleepily, "Pop?"

"Yes. Go back to sleep."

Instead the boy got up and switched on the glow plates. He knew it was hard for Baslim to get around in the dark without his leg; if Pop wanted a drink of water or anything, he'd fetch it. "You all right, Pop?" he asked, turning away from the switch.

Then he gasped in utter shock. This was a stranger, a *gentleman!*

"It's all right, Thorby," the stranger said with Pop's voice. "Take it easy, son."

"Pop?"

"Yes, son. I'm sorry I startled you—I should have changed before I came back. Events pushed me." He started stripping off fine clothing.

When Baslim removed the evening head dress, he looked more like Pop . . except for one thing. "Pop . . . your eye."

"Oh, that. It comes out as easily as it went in. I look better with two eyes, don't I?"

"I don't know." Thorby stared at it worriedly. "I don't think I like it."

"So? Well, you won't often see me wear it. As long as you are awake you can help."

Thorby was not much help; everything Pop did was new to him. First Baslim dug tanks and trays from a food cupboard which appeared to have an extra door in its back. Then he removed the false eye and, handling it with great care, unscrewed it into two parts and removed a tiny cylinder, using tweezers.

Thorby watched the processing that followed but did not understand, except that he could see that Pop was working with extreme care and exact timing. At last Baslim said, "All done. Now we'll see if I got any pictures."

Baslim inserted the spool in a microviewer, scanned it, smiled grimly and said, "Get ready to go out. Skip breakfast. You can take along a piece of bread."

"Huh?"

"Get moving. No time to waste."

Thorby put on his make-up and clout and dirtied his face. Baslim was waiting with a photograph and a small flat cylinder about the size of a half-minim bit. He shoved the photo at Thorby. "Look at it. Memorize it."

"Why?"

Baslim pulled it back. "Would you recognize that man?"

"Uh . . . let me see it again."

"You've *got* to know him. Look at it well this time."

Thorby did so, then said, "All right, I'll know him."

26

"He'll be in one of the taprooms near the port. Try Mother Shaum's first, then the Supernova and the Veiled Virgin. If you don't hit, work both sides of Joy Street until you do. You've *got* to find him before the third hour."

"I'll find him, Pop."

"When you do, put this thing in your bowl along with a few coins. Then tell him the tale but be sure to mention that you are the son of Baslim the Cripple."

"Got it, Pop."

"Get going."

Thorby wasted no time getting down to the port. It was the morning following the Feast of the Ninth Moon and few were stirring; he did not bother to pretend to beg en route, he simply went the most direct way, through back courts, over fences, or down streets, avoiding only the sleepy night patrol. But, though he reached the neighborhood quickly, he had the Old One's luck in finding his man; he was in none of the dives Baslim had suggested, nor did the rest of Joy Street turn him up. It was pushing the deadline and Thorby was getting worried when he saw the man come out of a place he had already tried.

Thorby ducked across the street, came up behind him. The man was with another man—not good. But Thorby started in:

"Alms, gentle lords! Alms for mercy on your souls!"

The wrong man tossed him a coin; Thorby caught it in his teeth. "Bless you, my lord!" He turned to the other. "Alms, gentle sir. A small gift for the unfortunate. I am the son of Baslim the Cripple and—"

The first man aimed a kick at him. "Get out."

Thorby rolled away from it. "—son of Baslim the Cripple. Poor old Baslim needs soft foods and medicines. I am all alone—"

The man of the picture reached for his purse. "Don't do it," his companion advised. "They're all liars and I've paid him to let us alone."

" 'Luck for the jump,' " the man answered. "Now let me

see . . ." He fumbled in his purse, glanced into the bowl, placed something in it.

"Thank you, my lords. May your children be sons." Thorby moved on before he looked. The tiny flat cylinder was gone.

He worked on up Joy Street, doing fairly well, and checked the Plaza before heading home. To his surprise Pop was in his favorite pitch, by the auction block and facing the port. Thorby slipped down beside him. "Done."

The old man grunted.

"Why don't you go home, Pop? You must be tired. I've made us a few bits already."

"Shut up. Alms, my lady! Alms for a poor cripple."

At the third hour a ship took off with a *whoosh!* that dopplered away into subsonics; the old man seemed to relax. "What ship was that?" Thorby asked. "Not the Syndon liner."

"Free Trader *Romany Lass,* bound for the Rim . . . and your friend was in her. You go home now and get your breakfast. No, go buy your breakfast, for a treat."

Baslim no longer tried to hide his extraprofessional activities from Thorby, although he never explained the why or how. Some days only one of them would beg, in which case the Plaza of Liberty was always the pitch, for it appeared that Baslim was especially interested in arrivals and departures of ships and most especially movements of slave ships and the auction that always followed the arrival of one.

Thorby was more use to him after his education had progressed. The old man seemed to think that everyone had a perfect memory and he was stubborn enough to impress his belief despite the boy's grumbles.

"Aw, Pop, how do you expect me to remember? You didn't give me a chance to *look* at it!"

"I projected that page at least three seconds. Why didn't you read it?"

"Huh? There wasn't time."

"I read it. You can, too. Thorby, you've seen jugglers

in the Plaza. You've seen old Mikki stand on his head and keep nine daggers in the air while he spins four hoops with his feet?"

"Uh, sure."

"Can you do that?"

"No."

"Could you learn to?"

"Uh . . . I don't know."

"*Anyone* can learn to juggle . . . with enough practice and enough beatings." The old man picked up a spoon, a stylus, and a knife and kept them in the air in a simple fountain. Presently he missed and stopped. "I used to do a little, just for fun. This is juggling with the mind . . . and anyone can learn *it*, too."

"Show me how you did that, Pop."

"Another time, if you behave yourself. Right now you are learning to use your eyes. Thorby, this mind-juggling was developed a long time ago by a wise man, a Doctor Renshaw, on the planet Earth. You've heard of Earth."

"Well . . . sure, I've heard of it."

"Mmm . . . meaning you don't believe in it?"

"Uh, I don't know . . . but all that stuff about frozen water falling from the sky, and cannibals ten feet tall, and towers higher than the Praesidium, and little men no bigger than dolls that live in trees—well, I'm not a fool, Pop."

Baslim sighed and wondered how many thousands of times he had sighed since saddling himself with a son. "Stories get mixed up. Someday—when you've learned to read—I'll let you view books you trust."

"But I can read now."

"You just think you can. Thorby, there is such a place as Earth and it truly is strange and wonderful—a most unlikely planet. Many wise men have lived and died there—along with the usual proportion of fools and villains—and some of their wisdom has come down to us. Samuel Renshaw was one such wise man. He proved that most people go all their lives only half awake; more than that, he showed how a man could wake up and live—see with his eyes, hear with his ears, taste with his tongue, think with his mind, and remember perfectly what he saw, heard, tasted, thought." The old man shoved his stump out. "This doesn't make me a cripple. I see more with my one eye than you do with two. I am growing deaf . . . but not as deaf as you are, because what I hear, I remember. Which one of us is the cripple? But, son, you aren't going to stay crippled, for I am going to renshaw you if I have to beat your silly head in!"

As Thorby learned to use his mind, he found that he liked to; he developed an insatiable appetite for the printed page, until, night after night, Baslim would order him to turn off the viewer and go to bed. Thorby didn't see any use in much of what the old man forced him to learn—languages, for example, that Thorby had never heard. But they were not hard, with his new skill in using his mind, and when he discovered that the old man had spools and reels which could be read or listened to only in these "useless" tongues, he suddenly found them worth knowing. History and galactography he loved; his personal world, light-years wide in physical space, had been in reality as narrow as a slave factor's pen. Thorby reached for wider horizons with the delight of a baby discovering its fist.

But mathematics Thorby saw no use in, other than the barbaric skill of counting money. But presently he learned that mathematics need not have use; it was a game, like chess but more fun.

The old man wondered sometimes what use it all was? That the boy was even brighter than he had thought, he now knew. But was it fair to the boy? Was he simply teaching him to be discontented with his lot? What chance on Jubbul had the slave of a beggar? Zero raised to the nth power remained zero.

"Thorby."

"Yeah, Pop. Just a moment, I'm in the middle of a chapter."

"Finish it later. I want to talk with you."

"Yes, my lord. Yes, master. Right away, boss."

"And keep a civil tongue in your head."

"Sorry, Pop. What's on your mind?"

"Son, what are you going to do when I'm dead?"

Thorby looked stricken. "Are you feeling bad, Pop?"

"No. So far as I know, I'll last for years. On the other hand, I may not wake up tomorrow. At my age you never know. If I don't, what are you going to do? Hold down my pitch in the Plaza?"

Thorby didn't answer; Baslim went on, "You can't and we both know it. You're already so big that you can't tell the tale convincingly. They don't give the way they did when you were little."

Thorby said slowly, "I haven't meant to be a burden, Pop."

"Have I complained?"

"No." Thorby hesitated. "I've thought about it . . . some. Pop, you could hire me out to a labor company."

The old man made an angry gesture. "That's no answer! No, son, I'm going to send you away."

"Pop! You promised you wouldn't."

"I promised nothing."

"But I don't want to be freed, Pop. If you free me—well, if you do, I won't leave!"

"I didn't exactly mean that."

Thorby was silent for a long moment. "You're going to sell me, Pop?"

"Not exactly. Well . . . yes and no."

Thorby's face held no expression. At last he said quietly, "It's one or the other, so I know what you mean . . . and I guess I oughtn't to kick. It's your privilege and you've been the best . . . master . . . I ever had."

"*I'm not your master!*"

"Paper says you are. Matches the number on my leg."

"Don't talk that way! Don't *ever* talk that way."

"A slave had better talk that way, or else keep his mouth shut."

"Then, for Heaven's sake, keep it shut! Listen, son, let me explain. There's nothing here for you and we both know

31

it. If I die without freeing you, you revert to the Sargon—"

"They'll have to catch me!"

"They will. But manumission solves nothing. What guilds are open to freedmen? Begging, yes—but you'd have to poke out your eyes to do well at it, after you're grown. Most freedmen work for their former masters, as you know, for the free-born commoners leave mighty slim pickings. They resent an ex-slave; they won't work with him."

"Don't worry, Pop. I'll get by."

"I do worry. Now you listen. I'm going to arrange to sell you to a man I know, who will ship you away from here. Not a slave ship, just a ship. But instead of shipping you where the bill of lading reads, you'll—"

"No!"

"Hold your tongue. You'll be dropped on a planet where slavery is against the law. I can't tell you which one, because I am not sure of the ship's schedule, nor even what ship; the details have to be worked out. But in any free society I have confidence you can get by." Baslim stopped to mull a thought he had had many times. Should he send the kid to Baslim's own native planet? No, not only would it be extremely difficult to arrange but it was not a place to send a green immigrant . . . get the lad to any frontier world, where a sharp brain and willingness to work were all a man needed; there were several within trading distance of the Nine Worlds. He wished tiredly that there were some way of knowing the boy's own home world. Possibly he had relatives there, people who would help him. Confound it, there ought to be a galaxy-wide method of identification!

Baslim went on, "That's the best I can do. You'll have to behave as a slave between the sale and being shipped out. But what's a few weeks against a chance—"

"No!"

"Don't be foolish, son."

"Maybe I am. But I won't do it. I'm staying."

"So? Son . . . I hate to remind you—but you can't stop me."

"Huh?"

"As you pointed out, there's a paper that says I can."

"Oh."

"Go to bed, son."

Baslim did not sleep. About two hours after they had put out the light he heard Thorby get up very quietly. He could follow every move the lad made by interpreting muffled sounds. Thorby dressed (a simple matter of wrapping his clout), he went into the adjoining room, fumbled in the bread safe, drank deeply, and left. He did not take his bowl; he did not go near the shelf where it was kept.

After he was gone, Baslim turned over and tried to sleep, but the ache inside him would not permit. It had not occurred to him to speak the word that would keep the boy; he had too much self-respect not to respect another person's decision.

Thorby was gone four days. He returned in the night and Baslim heard him but again said nothing. Instead he went quietly and deeply asleep for the first time since Thorby had left. But he woke at the usual time and said, "Good morning, son."

"Uh, good morning, Pop."

"Get breakfast started. I have something to attend to."

They sat down presently over bowls of hot mush. Baslim ate with his usual careful disinterest; Thorby merely picked at his. Finally he blurted out, "Pop, when are you going to sell me?"

"I'm not."

"Huh?"

"I registered your manumission at the Archives the day you left. You're a free man, Thorby."

Thorby looked startled, then dropped his eyes to his food. He busied himself building little mountains of mush that slumped as soon as he shaped them. Finally he said, "I wish you hadn't."

"If they picked you up, I didn't want you to have 'escaped slave' against you."

33

"Oh." Thorby looked thoughtful. "That's 'F&B,' isn't it? Thanks, Pop. I guess I acted kind of silly."

"Possibly. But it wasn't the punishment I was thinking of. Flogging is over quickly, and so is branding. I was thinking of a possible second offense. It's better to be shortened than to be caught again after a branding."

Thorby abandoned his mush entirely. "Pop? Just what does a lobotomy do to you?"

"Mmm . . . you might say it makes the thorium mines endurable. But let's not go into it, not at meal times. Speaking of such, if you are through, get your bowl and let's not dally. There's an auction this morning."

"You mean I can stay?"

"This is your home."

Baslim never again suggested that Thorby leave him. Manumission made no difference in their routine or relationship. Thorby did go to the Royal Archives, paid the fee and the customary gift and had a line tattooed through his serial number, the Sargon's seal tattooed beside it with book and page number of the record which declared him to be a free subject of the Sargon, entitled to taxes, military service, and starvation without let or hindrance. The clerk who did the tattooing looked at Thorby's serial number and said, "Doesn't look like a birthday job, kid. Your old man go bankrupt? Or did your folks sell you just to get shut of you?"

"None of your business!"

"Don't get smart, kid, or you'll find that this needle can hurt even more. Now give me a civil answer. I see it's a factor's mark, not a private owner's, and from the way it has spread and faded, you were maybe five or six. When and where was it?"

"I don't know. Honest I don't."

"So? That's what I tell my wife when she asks personal questions. Quit wiggling; I'm almost through. There . . . congratulations and welcome to the ranks of free men. I've been free a parcel of years now and I predict that you will find it looser but not always more comfortable."

Chapter 4

THORBY'S LEG HURT for a couple of days; otherwise manumission left his life unchanged. But he really was becoming inefficient as a beggar; a strong healthy youth does not draw the alms that a skinny child can. Often Baslim would have Thorby place him on his pitch, then send him on errands or tell him to go home and study. However, one or the other was always in the Plaza. Baslim sometimes disappeared, with or without warning; when this happened it was Thorby's duty to spend daylight hours on the pitch, noting arrivals and departures, keeping mental notes of slave auctions, and picking up information about both traffics through contacts around the port, in the wineshops, and among the unveiled women.

Once Baslim was gone for a double nineday; he was simply missing when Thorby woke up. It was much longer than he had ever been away before; Thorby kept telling himself that Pop could look out for himself, while having visions of the old man dead in a gutter. But he kept track of the doings at the Plaza, including three auctions, and recorded everything that he had seen and had been able to pick up.

Then Baslim returned. His only comment was, "Why didn't you memorize it instead of recording?"

"Well, I did. But I was afraid I would forget something, there was so much."

"Hummph!"

After that Baslim seemed even quieter, more reserved, than he had always been. Thorby wondered if he had displeased him, but it was not the sort of question Baslim answered. Finally one night the old man said, "Son, we never did settle what you are to do after I'm gone."

"Huh? But I thought we had decided that, Pop. It's my problem."

35

"No, I simply postponed it . . . because of your thick-headed stubbornness. But I can't wait any longer. I've got orders for you and you are going to carry them out."

"Now, wait a minute, Pop! If you think you can bully me into leaving you—"

"Shut up! I said, 'After I'm gone.' When I'm dead, I mean; not one of these little business trips . . . you are to look up a man and give him a message. Can I depend on you? Not goof off and forget it?"

"Why, of course, Pop. But I don't like to hear you talk that way. You're going to live a long time—you might even outlive me."

"Possibly. But will you shut up and listen, then do as I tell you?"

"Yes, sir."

"You'll find this man—it may take a while—and deliver this message. Then he will have something for you to do . . . I think. If he does, I want you to do exactly what he tells you to. Will you do that also?"

"Why, of course, Pop, if that's what you want."

"Count it as one last favor to an old man who tried to do right by you and would have done better had he been able. It's the very last thing I want from you, son. Don't bother to burn an offering for me at the temple, just do these two things: deliver a message and one more thing, whatever the man suggests that you do."

"I will, Pop," Thorby answered solemnly.

"All right. Let's get busy."

The "man" turned out to be any one of five men. Each was skipper of a starship, a tramp trader, not of the Nine Worlds but occasionally picking up cargoes from ports of the Nine Worlds. Thorby thought over the list. "Pop, there's only one of these ships I recall ever putting down here."

"They all have, one time or another."

"It might be a long time before one showed up."

"It might be years. But when it happens, I want the message delivered exactly."

"To any of them? Or all of them?"

36

"The first one who shows up."

The message was short but not easy, for it was in three languages, depending on who was to receive it, and none of the languages was among those Thorby knew. Nor did Baslim explain the words; he wanted it learned by rote in all three.

After Thorby had stumbled through the first version of the message for the seventh time Baslim covered his ears. "No, no! It won't do, son. That accent!"

"I'm doing my best," Thorby answered sullenly.

"I know. But I want the message understood. See here, do you remember a time when I made you sleepy and talked to you?"

"Huh? I get sleepy every night. I'm sleepy now."

"So much the better." Baslim put him into a light trance—with difficulty as Thorby was not as receptive as he had been as a child. But Baslim managed it, recorded the message in the sleep instructor, set it running and let Thorby listen, with post-hypnotic suggestion that he would be able to say it perfectly when he awakened.

He was able to. The second and third versions were implanted in him the following night. Baslim tested him repeatedly thereafter, using the name of a skipper and a ship to bring each version forth.

Baslim never sent Thorby out of the city; a slave required a travel permit and even a freedman was required to check in and out. But he did send him all over the metropolis. Three ninedays after Thorby had learned the messages Baslim gave him a note to deliver in the shipyard area, which was a reserve of the Sargon rather than part of the city. "Carry your freedman's tag and leave your bowl behind. If a policeman stops you, tell him you're looking for work in the yards."

"He'll think I'm crazy."

"But he'll let you through. They do use freedmen, as sweepers and such. Carry the message in your mouth. Who are you looking for?"

"A short, red-haired man," Thorby repeated, "with a big

wart on the left side of his nose. He runs a lunch stand across from the main gate. No beard. I'm to buy a meat pie and slip him the message with the money."

"Right."

Thorby enjoyed the outing. He did not wonder why Pop didn't viewphone messages instead of sending him a half day's journey; people of their class did not use such luxuries. As for the royal mails, Thorby had never sent or received a letter and would have regarded the mails as a most chancy way to send a note.

His route followed one arc of the spaceport through the factory district. He relished that part of the city; there was always so much going on, so much life and noise. He dodged traffic, with truck drivers cursing him and Thorby answering with interest; he peered in each open door, wondering what all the machines were for and why commoners would stand all day in one place, doing the same thing over and over—or were they slaves? No, they couldn't be; slaves weren't allowed to touch power machinery except on plantations—that was what the riots had been about last year and the Sargon had lifted his hand in favor of the commoners.

Was it true that the Sargon never slept and that his eye could see anything in the Nine Worlds? Pop said that was nonsense, the Sargon was just a man, like anybody. But if so, how did he get to be Sargon?

He left the factories and skirted the shipyards. He had never been this far before. Several ships were in for overhaul and two small ships were being built, cradled in lacy patterns of steel. Ships made his heart lift and he wished he were going somewhere. He knew that he had traveled by starship twice—or was it three times?—but that was long ago and he didn't mean traveling in the hold of a slaver, that wasn't traveling!

He got so interested that he almost walked past the lunch stand. The main gate reminded him; it was twice as big as the others, had a guard on it, and a big sign curving over it with the seal of the Sargon on top. The lunch stand was across from it; Thorby dodged traffic pouring through the gate and went to it.

The man behind the counter was not the right man; what little hair he had was black and his nose had no wart.

Thorby walked up the road, killed a half-hour and came back. There was still no sign of his man. The counterman noticed the inspection, so Thorby stepped forward and said, "Do you have sunberry crush?"

The man looked him over. "Money?"

Thorby was used to being required to prove his solvency; he dug out the coin. The man scooped it up, opened a bottle for him. "Don't drink at the counter, I need the stools."

There were plenty of stools, but Thorby was not offended; he knew his social status. He stood back but not so far as to be accused of trying to abscond with the bottle, then made the drink last a long time. Customers came and went; he checked each, on the chance that the red-headed man might have picked this time to eat. He kept his ears cocked.

Presently the counterman looked up. "You trying to wear that bottle out?"

"Just through, thanks." Thorby came up to put the bottle down and said, "Last time I was over this way a red-headed chap was running this place."

The man looked at him. "You a friend of Red?"

"Well, not exactly. I just used to see him here, when I'd stop for a cold drink, or—"

"Let's see your permit."

"What? I don't need—" The man grabbed at Thorby's wrist. But Thorby's profession had made him adept at dodging kicks, cuffs, canes, and such; the man clutched air.

The man came around the counter, fast; Thorby ducked into traffic. He was halfway across the street and had had two narrow escapes before he realized that he was running toward the gate—and that the counterman was shouting for the guard there.

Thorby turned and started dodging traffic endwise. Fortunately it was dense; this road carried the burden of the yards. He racked up three more brushes with death, saw a side street that dead-ended into the throughway, ducked between two trucks, down the side street as fast as he could go, turned into the first alley, ran down it, hid behind an outbuilding and waited.

He heard no pursuit.

He had been chased many times before, it did not panic him. A chase was always two parts: first breaking contact, second the retiring action to divorce oneself from the incident. He had accomplished the first; now he had to get out of the neighborhood without being spotted—slow march and no suspicious moves. In losing himself he had run away from the city, turned left into the side street, turned left again into the alley; he was now almost behind the lunch stand—it had been a subconscious tactic. The chase always moved away from the center; the lunch stand was one place where they would not expect him to be. Thorby estimated that in five minutes, or ten, the counterman would be back at his job and the guard back at the gate; neither one could leave his post unwatched. Shortly, Thorby could go on through the alley and head home.

He looked around. The neighborhood was commercial land not yet occupied by factories, jumble of small shops, marginal businesses, hovels, and hopeless minor enterprise. He appeared to be in back of a very small hand laundry; there were poles and lines and wooden tubs and steam came out a pipe in the outbuilding. He knew his location now—two doors from the lunch stand; he recalled a homemade sign: "MAJESTIC HOME LAUNDRY—*Lowest Prices.*"

He could cut around this building and—but better check first. He dropped flat and stuck an eye around the corner of the outbuilding, sighted back down the alley.

Oh, oh!—two patrolmen moving up the alley . . . he had been wrong, wrong! They hadn't dropped the matter, they had sent out the alarm. He pulled back and looked around. The laundry? No. The outbuilding? The patrol would check it. Nothing but to run for it—right into the arms of another patrol. Thorby knew how fast the police could put a cordon around a district. Near the Plaza he could go through their nets, but here he was in strange terrain.

His eye lit on a worn-out washtub . . . then he was under it. It was a tight fit, with knees to his chin and splinters in his spine. He was afraid that his clout was sticking out but it was too late to correct it; he heard someone coming.

Footsteps came toward the tub and he stopped breathing. Someone stepped on the tub and stood on it.

"Hi there, mother!" It was a man's voice. "You been out here long?"

"Long enough. Mind that pole, you'll knock the clothes down."

"See anything of a boy?"

"What boy?"

"Youngster, getting man-tall. Fuzz on his chin. Breech clout, no sandals."

"Somebody," the woman's voice above him answered indifferently, "came running through here like his ghost was after him. I didn't really see him—I was trying to get this pesky line up."

"That's our baby! Where'd he go?"

"Over that fence and between those houses."

"Thanks, mother! Come on, Juby."

Thorby waited. The woman continued whatever she was doing; her feet moved and the tub creaked. Then she stepped down and sat on the tub. She slapped it gently. "Stay where you are," she said softly. A moment later he heard her go away.

Thorby waited until his bones ached. But he resigned himself to staying under that tub until dark. It would be chancy, as the night patrol questioned everyone but nobles after curfew, but leaving this neighborhood in daylight had become impossible. Thorby could not guess why he had been honored by a turn-out of the guard, but he did not want to find out. He heard someone—the woman?—moving around the yard from time to time.

At least an hour later he heard the creak of ungreased

wheels. Someone tapped on the tub. "When I lift the tub, get into the cart, fast. It's right in front of you."

Thorby did not answer. Daylight hit his eyes, he saw a small pushcart—and was in it and trying to make himself small. Laundry landed on him. But before that blanked out his sight he saw that the tub was no longer nakedly in the open; sheets had been hung on lines so that it was screened.

Hands arranged bundles over him and a voice said, "Hold still until I tell you to move."

"Okay . . . and thanks a million! I'll pay you back someday."

"Forget it." She breathed heavily. "I had a man once. Now he's in the mines. I don't care what you've done—I don't turn anybody over to the patrol."

"Oh. I'm sorry."

"Shut up."

The little cart bumped and wobbled and presently Thorby felt the change to pavement. Occasionally they stopped; the woman would remove a bundle, be gone a few minutes, come back and dump dirty clothes into the cart. Thorby took it with the long patience of a beggar.

A long time later the cart left pavement. It stopped and the woman said in a low voice, "When I tell you, get out the righthand side and keep going. Make it fast."

"Okay. And thanks again!"

"Shut up." The cart bumped along a short distance, slowed without stopping, and she said, "Now!"

Thorby threw off his covering, bounced out and landed on his feet, all in one motion. He was facing a passage between two buildings, a serviceway from alley to street. He started down it fast but looked back over his shoulder.

The cart was just disappearing. He never did see her face.

Two hours later he was back in his own neighborhood. He slipped down beside Baslim. "No good."

"Why not?"

"Snoopies. Squads of 'em."

"Alms, gentle sir! You swallowed it? Alms for the sake of your parents!"

"Of course."

"Take the bowl." Baslim got to hands and knee, started away.

"Pop! Don't you want me to help you?"

"You stay here."

Thorby stayed, irked that Pop had not waited for a full report. He hurried home as soon as it was dark, found Baslim in the kitchen-washroom, paraphernalia spread around him and using both recorder and book projector. Thorby glanced at the displayed page, saw that he could not read it and wondered what language it was—an odd one; the words were all seven letters, no more, no less. "Hi, Pop. Shall I start supper?"

"No room . . . and no time. Eat some bread. What happened today?"

Thorby told him, while munching bread. Baslim simply nodded. "Lie down. I've got to use hypnosis on you again. We've got a long night ahead."

The material Baslim wanted him to memorize consisted of figures, dates, and endless three-syllable nonsense words. The light trance felt dreamily pleasant and the droning of Baslim's voice coming out of the recorder was pleasant, too.

During one of the breaks, when Baslim had commanded him to wake up, he said, "Pop, who's this message for?"

"If you ever get a chance to deliver it, you'll know; you won't have any doubts. If you have trouble remembering it, tell him to put you into a light trance; it'll come back."

"Tell whom?"

"Him. Never mind. You are going to sleep. You are asleep." Baslim snapped his fingers.

While the recorder was droning Thorby was vaguely aware once that Baslim had just come in. He was wearing his false leg, which affected Thorby with dreamy surprise; Pop ordinarily wore it only indoors. Once Thorby smelled smoke and thought dimly that something must be burning in the kitchen and he should go check. But he was unable

43

to move and the nonsense words kept droning into his ears.

He became aware that he was droning back to Pop the lesson he had learned. "Did I get it right?"

"Yes. Now go to sleep. Sleep the rest of the night."

Baslim was gone in the morning. Thorby was not surprised; Pop's movements had been even less predictable than usual lately. He ate breakfast, took his bowl and set out for the Plaza. Business was poor—Pop was right; Thorby now looked too healthy and well fed for the profession. Maybe he would have to learn to dislocate his joints like Granny the Snake. Or buy contact lenses with cataracts built into them.

Midafternoon an unscheduled freighter grounded at the port. Thorby started the usual inquiries, found that it was the Free Trader *Sisu*, registered home port New Finlandia, Shiva III.

Ordinarily this would have been a minor datum, to be reported to Pop when he saw him. But Captain Krausa of the *Sisu* was one of the five persons to whom Thorby was someday to deliver a message, if and when.

It fretted Thorby. He knew that he was not to look up Captain Krausa—that was the distant future, for Pop was alive and well. But maybe Pop would be anxious to know that this ship had arrived. Tramp freighters came and went, nobody knew when, and sometimes they were in port only a few hours.

Thorby told himself that he could get home in five minutes—and Pop might thank him. At worst he would bawl him out for leaving the Plaza, but, shucks, he could pick up anything he missed, through gossip.

Thorby left.

The ruins of the old amphitheater extend around one third of the periphery of the new. A dozen holes lead down into the labyrinth which had served the old slave barracks; an unlimited number of routes ran underground from these informal entrances to that part which Baslim had preempted as a home. Thorby and he varied their route in random fashion and avoided being seen entering or leaving.

This time, being in a hurry, Thorby went to the nearest —and on past; there was a policeman at it. He continued as if his destination had been a tiny greengrocer's booth on the street rimming the ruins. He stopped and spoke to the proprietress. "Howdy, Inga. Got a nice ripe melon you're going to have to throw away?"

"No melons."

He displayed money. "How about that big one? Half price and I won't notice the rotten spot." He leaned closer. "What's burning?"

Her eyes flicked toward the patrolman. "Get lost."

"Raid?"

"Get lost, I said."

Thorby dropped a coin on the counter, picked up a bell-fruit and walked away, sucking the juice. He did not hurry.

A cautious reconnaissance showed him that police were staked out all through the ruins. At one entrance a group of ragged troglodytes huddled sadly under the eye of a patrolman. Baslim had estimated that at least five hundred people lived in the underground ruins. Thorby had not quite believed it, as he had rarely seen anyone else enter or heard them inside. He recognized only two faces among the prisoners.

A half-hour later and more worried every minute Thorby located an entrance which the police did not seem to know. He scanned it for several minutes, then darted from behind a screen of weeds and was down it. Once inside he got quickly into total darkness, then moved cautiously, listening. The police were supposed to have spectacles which let them see in the dark. Thorby wasn't sure this was true as he had always found darkness helpful in evading them. But he took no chances.

There were indeed police down below; he heard two of them and saw them by hand torches they carried—if snoopies could see in the dark these two did not seem equipped for it. They were obviously searching, stun guns drawn. But they were in strange territory whereas Thorby was playing his home field. A specialized speleologist, he knew these corridors the way his tongue knew his teeth; he had been finding his way through them in utter blackness twice a day for years.

At the moment they had him trapped; he kept just far enough ahead to avoid their torches, skirted a hole that reached down into the next level, went beyond it, ducked into a doorway and waited.

They reached the hole, eyed the narrow ledge Thorby had taken so casually in the dark, and one of them said, "We need a ladder."

"Oh, we'll find stairs or a chute." They turned back. Thorby waited, then went back and down the hole.

A few minutes later he was close to his home doorway. He looked and listened and sniffed and waited until he was certain that no one was close, then crept to the door and reached for the thumbhole in the lock. Even as he reached he knew that something was wrong.

The door was gone; there was just a hole.

He froze, straining every sense. There was an odor of strangers but it wasn't fresh and there was no sound of breathing. The only sound was a faint drip-drip in the kitchen.

Thorby decided that he just had to see. He looked behind him, saw no glimmer, reached inside for the light switch and turned it to "dim."

Nothing happened. He tried the switch in all positions, still no light. He went inside, avoided something cluttering Baslim's neat living room, on into the kitchen, and reached for candles. They were not where they belonged but his hand encountered one nearby; he found the match safe and lit the candle.

Ruin and wreckage!

Most of the damage seemed the sort that results from a search which takes no account of cost, aiming solely at speed and thoroughness. Every cupboard, every shelf had been spilled, food dumped on the floor. In the large room the mattresses had been ripped open, stuffing spilled out. But some of it looked like vandalism, unnecessary, pointless.

Thorby looked around with tears welling up and his chin quivering. But when he found, near the door, Pop's false leg, lying dead on the floor with its mechanical perfection smashed as if trampled by boots, he broke into sobs and had to put the candle down to keep from dropping it. He picked up the shattered leg, held it like a doll, sank to the floor and cradled it, rocking back and forth and moaning.

Chapter 5

THORBY SPENT THE next several hours in the black corridors outside their ruined home, near the first branching, where he would hear Pop if he came back but where Thorby would have a chance to duck if police showed up.

He caught himself dozing, woke with a start, and decided that he had to find out what time it was; it seemed as if he had been keeping vigil a week. He went back into their home, found a candle and lit it. But their only clock, a household "Eternal," was smashed. No doubt the radioactive capsule was still reckoning eternity but the works were mute. Thorby looked at it and forced himself to think in practical terms.

If Pop were free, he would come back. But the police had taken Pop away. Would they simply question him and turn him loose?

No, they would not. So far as Thorby knew, Pop had never done anything to harm the Sargon—but he had known for a long time that Pop was not simply a harmless old beggar. Thorby did not know why Pop had done the many things which did not fit the idea of "harmless old beggar" but it was clear that the police knew or suspected. About once a year the police had "cleaned out" the ruins by dropping a few retch-gas bombs down the more conspicuous holes; it simply meant having to sleep somewhere else for a couple of nights. But this was a raid in force. They had intended to arrest Pop and they had been searching for something.

The Sargon's police operated on a concept older than justice; they assumed that a man was guilty, they questioned him by increasingly strong methods until he talked . . . methods so notorious that an arrested person was usually anxious to tell all before questioning started. But Thorby was certain that the police would get nothing out of Pop which the old man did not wish to admit.

Therefore the questioning would go on a long time.

They were probably working on Pop this very minute. Thorby's stomach turned over.

He had to get Pop away from them.

How? How does a moth attack the Praesidium? Thorby's chances were not much better. Baslim might be in a back room of the district police barracks, the logical place for a petty prisoner. But Thorby had an unreasoned conviction that Pop was not a petty prisoner . . . in which case he might be anywhere, even in the bowels of the Praesidium.

Thorby could go to the district police office and ask where his patron had been taken—but such was the respect in which the Sargon's police were held that this solution did not occur to him; had he presented himself as next of kin of a prisoner undergoing interrogation Thorby would have found himself in another closed room being interviewed by the same forceful means as a check on the answers (or lack of them) which were being wrung out of Baslim.

Thorby was not a coward; he simply knew that one does not dip water with a knife. Whatever he did for Pop would have to be done indirectly. He could not demand his "rights" because he had none; the idea never entered his head. Bribery was possible—for a man with a poke full of stellars. Thorby had less than two minims. Stealth was all that was left and for that he needed information.

He reached this conclusion as soon as he admitted that there was no reasonable chance that the police would turn

Pop loose. But, on the wild chance that Baslim might talk his way free, Thorby wrote a note, telling Pop that he would check back the next day, and left it on a shelf they used as a mail drop. Then he left.

It was night when he stuck his head above ground. He could not decide whether he had been down in the ruins for half a day or a day and a half. It forced him to change plans; he had intended to go first to Inga the greengrocer and find out what she knew. But at least there were no police around now; he could move freely as long as he evaded the night patrol. But where? Who could, or would, give him information?

Thorby had dozens of friends and knew hundreds by sight. But his acquaintances were subject to curfew; he saw them only in daylight and in most cases did not know where they slept. But there was one neighborhood which was not under curfew; Joy Street and its several adjoining courts never closed. In the name of commerce and for the accommodation of visiting spacemen taprooms and gaming halls and other places of hospitality to strangers in that area near the spaceport never closed their doors. A commoner, even a freedman, might stay up all night there, although he could not leave between curfew and dawn without risking being picked up.

This risk did not bother Thorby; he did not intend to be seen and, although it was patrolled inside, he knew the habits of the police there. They traveled in pairs and stayed on lighted streets, leaving their beats only to suppress noisy forms of lawbreaking. But the virtue of the district, for Thorby's purpose, was that the gossip there was often hours ahead of the news as well as covering matters ignored or suppressed by licensed news services.

Someone on Joy Street would know what had happened to Pop.

Thorby got into the honky-tonk neighborhood by scrambling over roof tops. He went down a drain into a dark court, moved along it to Joy Street, stopped short of the street lights, looked up and down for police and tried to spot someone he knew. There were many people about but most of them were strangers on the town. Thorby knew every proprietor and almost every employee up and down the street but he hesitated to walk into one of the joints; he might walk into the arms of police. He wanted to spot someone he trusted, whom he could motion into the darkness of the court.

No police but no friendly faces, either—just a moment; there was Auntie Singham.

Of the many fortunetellers who worked Joy Street Auntie Singham was the best; she never purveyed anything but good fortune. If these things failed to come to pass, no customer ever complained; Auntie's warm voice carried conviction. Some whispered that she improved her own fortunes by passing information to the police, but Thorby did not believe it because Pop did not. She was a likely source of news and Thorby decided to chance it—the most she could tell the police was that he was alive and on the loose . . . which they knew.

Around the corner to Thorby's right was the Port of Heaven cabaret; Auntie was spreading her rug on the pavement there, anticipating customers spilling out at the end of a performance now going on.

Thorby glanced each way and hurried along the wall almost to the cabaret. "Psst! Auntie!"

She looked around, looked startled, then her face became expressionless. Through unmoving lips she said, loud enough to reach him, "Beat it, son! Hide! Are you crazy?"

"Auntie . . . *where have they got him?*"

"Crawl in a hole and pull it in after you. There's a reward out!"

"For *me?* Don't be silly, Auntie; nobody would pay a reward for me. Just tell me where they're holding him. Do you know?"

"They're not."

" 'They're not' what?"

"You don't know? Oh, poor lad! They've shortened him."

Thorby was so shocked that he was speechless. Although

Baslim had talked of the time when he would be dead, Thorby had never really believed in it; he was incapable of imagining Pop dead and gone.

He missed her next words; she had to repeat. "Snoopers! Get out!"

Thorby glanced over his shoulder. Two patrolmen, moving this way—time to leave! But he was caught between street and blank wall, with no bolt hole but the entrance to the cabaret . . . if he ducked in there, dressed as he was, being what he was, the management would simply shout for the patrol.

But there was nowhere else to go. Thorby turned his back on the police and went inside the narrow foyer of the cabaret. There was no one there; the last act was in progress and even the hawker was not in sight. But just inside was a ladder-stool and on it was a box of transparent letters used to change signs billing the entertainers. Thorby saw them and an idea boiled up that would have made Baslim proud of his pupil—Thorby grabbed the box and stool and went out again.

He paid no attention to the approaching policemen, placed the ladder-stool under the little lighted marquee that surmounted the entrance and jumped up on it, with his back to the patrolmen. It placed most of his body in bright light but his head and shoulders stuck up into the shadow above the row of lights. He began methodically to remove letters spelling the name of the star entertainer.

The two police reached a point right behind him. Thorby tried not to tremble and worked with the steady listlessness of a hired hand with a dull job. He heard Auntie Singham call out, "Good evening, Sergeant."

"Evening, Auntie. What lies are you telling tonight?"

"Lies indeed! I see a sweet young girl in your future, with hands graceful as birds. Let me see your palm and perhaps I can read her name."

"What would my wife say? No time to chat tonight, Auntie." The sergeant glanced at the workman changing the sign, rubbed his chin and said, "We've got to stay on the prowl for Old Baslim's brat. You haven't seen him?" He looked again at the work going on above him and his eyes widened slightly.

"Would I sit here swapping gossip if I had?"

"Hmm . . ." He turned to his partner. "Roj, move along and check Ace's Place, and don't forget the washroom. I'll keep an eye on the street."

"Okay, Sarge."

The senior patrolman turned to the fortuneteller as his partner moved away. "It's a sad thing, Auntie. Who would have believed that old Baslim could have been spying against the Sargon and him a cripple?"

"Who indeed?" She rocked forward. "Is it true that he died of fright before they shortened him?"

"He had poison ready, knowing what was coming. But dead he was, before they pulled him out of his hole. The captain was furious."

"If he was dead already, why shorten him?"

"Come, come, Auntie, the law must be served. Shorten him they did, though it's not a job I'd relish." The sergeant sighed. "It's a sad world, Auntie. Think of that poor boy, led astray by that old rascal . . . and now the captain and the commandant both want to ask the lad questions they meant to ask the old man."

"What good will that do them?"

"None, likely." The sergeant poked gutter filth with the butt of his staff. "But if I were the lad, knowing the old man is dead and not knowing any answers to difficult questions, I'd be far, far from here already. I'd find me a farmer a long way from the city, one who needed willing hands cheap and took no interest in the troubles of the city. But since I'm not, why then, as soon as I clap eyes on him, if I do, I'll arrest him and haul him up before the captain."

"He's probably hiding between rows in a bean field this minute, trembling with fright."

"Likely. But that's better than walking around with no head on your shoulders." The police sergeant looked down the street, called out, "Okay, Roj. Right with you." As he started away he glanced again at Thorby and said, "Night, Auntie. If you see him, shout for us."

"I'll do that. Hail to the Sargon."

"Hail."

Thorby continued to pretend to work and tried not to shake, while the police moved slowly away. Customers trickled out of the cabaret and Auntie took up her chant, promising fame, fortune, and a bright glimpse of the future, all for a coin. Thorby was about to get down, stick the gear back into the entranceway and get lost, when a hand grabbed his ankle.

"What are you doing!"

Thorby froze, then realized it was just the manager of the place, angry at finding his sign disturbed. Without looking down Thorby said, "What's wrong? You paid me to change this blinker."

"*I* did?"

"Why, sure, you did. You told me—" Thorby glanced down, looked amazed and blurted, "You're not the one."

"I certainly am not. Get down from there."

"I can't. You've got my ankle."

The man let go and stepped back as Thorby climbed down. "I don't know what silly idiot could have told you—" He broke off as Thorby's face came into light. "Hey, it's that beggar boy!"

Thorby broke into a run as the man grabbed for him. He went ducking in and out between pedestrians as the shout of, "Patrol! Patrol! *Police!*" rose behind him. Then he was in the dark court again and, charged with adrenalin, was up a drainpipe as if it had been level pavement. He did not stop until he was several dozen roofs away.

He sat down against a chimney pot, caught his breath and tried to think.

Pop was dead. He couldn't be but he was. Old Poddy wouldn't have said so if he hadn't known. Why . . . why, Pop's head must be on a spike down at the pylon this minute, along with the other losers. Thorby had one grisly flash of visualization, and at last collapsed, wept uncontrollably.

After a long time he raised his head, wiped his face with knuckles, and straightened up.

Pop was dead. All right, what did he do now?

Anyhow, Pop had beat them out of questioning him. Thorby felt bitter pride. Pop was always the smart one; they had caught him but Pop had had the last laugh.

Well, what *did* he do now?

Auntie Singham had warned him to hide. Poddy had said, plain as anything, to get out of town. Good advice—if he wanted to stay as tall as he was, he had better be outside the city before daylight. Pop would expect him to put up a fight, not sit still and wait for the snoopies, and there was nothing left that he could do for Pop, now that Pop was dead—*hold it!*

"When I'm dead, you are to look up a man and give him a message. Can I depend on you? Not goof off and forget it?"

Yes, Pop, you can! I didn't forget—I'll deliver it! Thorby recalled for the first time in more than a day why he had come home early: Starship *Sisu* was in port; her skipper was on Pop's list. *"The first one who shows up"*—that's what Pop had said. I didn't goof, Pop; I almost did but I remembered. I'll do it, I'll do it! Thorby decided with fierce resurgence that this message must be the final, important thing that Pop had to get out—since they said he was a spy. All right, he'd help Pop finish his job. I'll do it, Pop. You'll have the best of them yet!

Thorby felt no twinge at the "treason" he was about to attempt; shipped in as a slave against his will, he felt no loyalty to the Sargon and Baslim had never tried to instill any. His strongest feeling toward the Sargon was superstitious fear and even that washed away in the violence of his need for revenge. He feared neither police nor Sargon himself; he simply wanted to evade them long enough to carry out Baslim's wishes. After that . . . well, if they caught him, he hoped to have finished the job before they shortened him.

If the *Sisu* were still in port . . .

Oh, she had to be! But the first thing was to find out for sure that the ship had not left, then—no, the *first* thing was to get out of sight before daylight. It was a million times more important to stay clear of the snoopies now that he had it through his thick head that there was something he could do for Pop.

Get out of sight, find out if the *Sisu* was still dirtside, get a message to her skipper . . . and do all this with every patrolman in the district looking for him—

Maybe he had better work his way over to the shipyards, where he was not known, sneak inside and back the long way to the port and find the *Sisu*. No, that was silly; he had almost been caught over that way just from not knowing the layout. Here, at least, he knew every building, most of the people.

But he had to have help. He couldn't go on the street, stop spacemen and ask. Who was a close enough friend to help . . . at risk of trouble with police? Ziggie? Don't be silly; Ziggie would turn him in for the reward, for two minims Ziggie would sell his own mother—Ziggie thought that anyone who didn't look out for number one first, last, and always was a sucker.

Who else? Thorby came up against the hard fact that most of his friends were around his age and as limited in resources. Most of them he did not know how to find at night, and he certainly could not hang around in daylight and wait for one to show up. As for the few who lived with their families at known addresses, he could not think of one who could both be trusted and could keep parents concerned from tipping off the police. Most honest citizens at Thorby's level went to great lengths to mind their own business and stay on the right side of the police.

It had to be one of Pop's friends.

He ticked off this list almost as quickly. In most cases he could not be sure how binding the friendship was, blood brotherhood or merely acquaintance. The only one whom he could possibly reach and who might possibly help was Mother Shaum. She had sheltered them once when they were driven out of their cave with retch gas and she had always had a kind word and a cold drink for Thorby.

He got moving; daylight was coming.

Mother Shaum's place was a taproom and lodging house, on the other side of Joy Street and near the crewmen's gate to the spaceport. Half an hour later, having crossed many roofs, twice been up and down in side courts and once having ducked across the lighted street, Thorby was on the roof of her place. He had not dared walk in her door; too many witnesses would force her to call the patrol. He had considered the back entrance and had squatted among garbage cans before deciding that there were too many voices in the kitchen.

But when he did reach her roof, he was almost caught by daylight; he found the usual access to the roof but he found also that its door and lock were sturdy enough to defy bare-handed burglary.

He went to the rear with the possibility in mind of going down, trying the back door anyhow; it was almost dawn and becoming urgent to get under cover. As he looked down the back he noticed ventilation holes for the low attic, one at each side. They were barely as wide as his shoulders, as deep as his chest—but they led inside.

They were screened but a few minutes and many scratches later he had one kicked in. Then he tried the unlikely task of easing himself over the edge feet first and snaking into the hole. He got in as far as his hips, his clout caught on raw edges of screening and he stuck like a cork, lower half inside the house, chest and head and arms sticking out like a gargoyle. He could not move and the sky was getting lighter.

With a drag from his heels and sheer force of will the cloth parted and he moved inside, almost knocking himself out by banging his head. He lay still and caught his breath, then pushed the screening untidily back into place. It would no longer stop vermin but it might fool the eye from four stories down. It was not until then that he realized that he had almost fallen those four stories.

The attic was no more than a crawl space; he started to explore on hands and knees for the fixture he believed must be here: a scuttle hole for repairs or inspection. Once he started looking and failed to find it, he was not sure that there was such a thing—he knew that some houses had them but he did not know much about houses; he had not lived in them much.

He did not find it until sunrise striking the vent holes gave illumination. It was all the way forward, on the street side.

And it was bolted from underneath.

But it was not as rugged as the door to the roof. He looked around, found a heavy spike dropped by a workman and used it to dig at the wooden closure. In time he worked a knot loose, stopped and peered through the knot-hole.

There was a room below; he saw a bed with one figure in it.

Thorby decided that he could not expect better luck; only one person to cope with, to persuade to find Mother Shaum without raising an alarm. He took his eye away, put a finger through and felt around; he touched the latch, then gladly broke a fingernail easing the bolt back. Silently he lifted the trap door.

The figure in the bed did not stir.

He lowered himself, hung by his fingertips, dropped the remaining short distance and collapsed as noiselessly as possible.

The person in bed was sitting up with a gun aimed at him. "It took you long enough," she said. "I've been listening to you for the past hour."

"Mother Shaum! Don't shoot!"

She leaned forward, looked closely. "Baslim's kid!" She shook her head. "Boy, you're a mess . . . and you're hotter than a fire in a mattress, too. What possessed you to come here?"

"I didn't know where else to go."

She frowned. "I suppose that's a compliment . . . though

57

I had ruther have had a plague of boils, if I'd uv had my druthers." She got out of bed in her nightdress, big bare feet slapping on the floor, and peered out the window at the street below. "Snoopies here, snoopies there, snoopies checking every joint in the street three times in one night and scaring my customers . . . boy, you've caused more hooraw than I've seen since the factory riots. Why didn't you have the kindness to drop dead?"

"You won't hide me, Mother?"

"Who said I wouldn't? I've never gone out of my way to turn anybody in yet. But I don't have to like it." She glowered at him. "When did you eat last?"

"Uh, I don't remember."

"I'll scare you up something. I don't suppose you can pay for it?" She looked at him sharply.

"I'm not hungry. Mother Shaum, is the *Sisu* still in port?"

"Huh? I don't know. Yes, I do; she is—a couple of her boys were in earlier tonight. Why?"

"I've got to get a message to her skipper. I've got to see him, I've just *got* to!"

She gave a moan of utter exasperation. "First he wakes a decent working woman out of her first sleep of the night, he plants himself on her at rare risk to her life and limb and license. He's filthy dirty and scratched and bloody and no doubt will be using my clean towels with laundry prices the way they are. He hasn't eaten and can't pay for his tucker . . . and now he adds insult to injury by demanding that I run *errands* for him!"

"I'm not hungry . . . and it doesn't matter whether I wash or not. But I've *got* to see Captain Krausa."

"Don't be giving me orders in my own bedroom. Overgrown and unspanked, you are, if I knew that old scamp you lived with. You'll have to wait until one of the *Sisu's* lads shows up later in the day, so's I can get a note out to the Captain." She turned toward the door. "Water's in the jug, towel's on the rack. Mind you get clean." She left.

Washing did feel good and Thorby found astringent powder on her dressing table, dusted his scratches. She came

58

back, slapped two slices of bread with a generous slab of meat between them in front of him, added a bowl of milk, left without speaking. Thorby hadn't thought that it was possible to eat, with Pop dead, but found that it was—he had quit worrying when he first saw Mother Shaum.

She came back. "Gulp that last bite and in you go. The word is they're going to search every house."

"Huh? Then I'll get out and run for it."

"Shut up and do as I say. In you go now."

"In where?"

"In there," she answered, pointing.

"In *that*?" It was a built-in window seat and chest, in a corner; its shortcoming lay in its size, it being as wide as a man but less than a third as long. "I don't think I can fold up that small."

"And that's just what the snoopies will think. Hurry." She lifted the lid, dug out some clothing, lifted the far end of the box at the wall adjoining the next room as if it were a sash, and disclosed thereby that a hole went on through the wall. "Scoot your legs through—and don't think you are the only one who has ever needed to lie quiet."

Thorby got into the box, slid his legs through the hole, lay back; the lid when closed would be a few inches above his face. Mother Shaum threw clothing on top of him, concealing him. "You okay?"

"Yeah, sure. Mother Shaum? Is he really dead?"

Her voice became almost gentle. "He is, lad. A great shame it is, too."

"You're sure?"

"I was bothered by the same doubt, knowing him so well. So I took a walk down to the pylon to see. He is. But I can tell you this, lad, he's got a grin on his face like he'd outsmarted them . . . and he had, too. They don't like it when a man doesn't wait to be questioned." She sighed again. "Cry now, if you need, but be quiet. If you hear anyone, don't even breathe."

The lid slammed. Thorby wondered whether he would be able to breathe at all, but found that there must be air holes; it was stuffy but bearable. He turned his head to get his nose clear of cloth resting on it.

Then he did cry, after which he went to sleep.

He was awakened by voices and footsteps, recalled where he was barely in time to keep from sitting up. The lid above his face opened, and then slammed, making his ears ring; a man's voice called out, "Nothing in this room, Sarge!"

"We'll see." Thorby recognized Poddy's voice. "You missed that scuttle up there. Fetch the ladder."

Mother Shaum's voice said, "Nothing up there but the breather space, Sergeant."

"I said, 'We'd see.'"

A few minutes later he added, "Hand me the torch. Hmm . . . you're right, Mother . . . but he has been here."

"Huh?"

"Screen broken back at the end of the house and dust disturbed. I think he got in this way, came down through your bedroom, and out."

"Saints and devils! I could have been murdered in my bed! Do you call that police protection?"

"You're not hurt. But you'd better have that screen fixed, or you'll have snakes and all their cousins living with you." He paused. "It's my thought he tried to stay in the district, found it too hot, and went back to the ruins. If so, no doubt we'll gas him out before the day is over."

"Do you think I'm safe to go back to my bed?"

"Why should he bother an old sack of suet like you?"

"What a nasty thing to say! And just when I was about to offer you a drop to cut the dust."

"You were? Let's go down to your kitchen, then, and we'll discuss it. I may have been wrong." Thorby heard them leave, heard the ladder being removed. At last he dared breathe.

Later she came back, grumbling, and opened the lid. "You can stretch your legs. But be ready to jump back in. Three pints of my best. Policemen!"

Chapter 6

THE SKIPPER of the *Sisu* showed up that evening. Captain Krausa was tall, fair, rugged and had the worry wrinkles and grim mouth of a man used to authority and responsibility. He was irked with himself and everyone for having allowed himself to be lured away from his routine by nonsense. His eye assayed Thorby unflatteringly. "Mother Shaum, is *this* the person who insisted that he had urgent business with me?"

The captain spoke Nine Worlds trade lingo, a degenerate form of Sargonese, uninflected and with a rudimentary positional grammar. But Thorby understood it. He answered, "If you are Captain Fjalar Krausa, I have a message for you, noble sir."

"Don't call me 'noble sir'; I'm Captain Krausa, yes."

"Yes, nob—yes, Captain."

"If you have a message, give it to me."

"Yes, Captain." Thorby started reciting the message he had memorized, using the Suomish version to Krausa. " 'To Captain Fjalar Krausa, master of Starship *Sisu* from Baslim the Cripple: Greetings, old friend! Greetings to your family, clan, and sib, and my humblest respects to your revered mother. I am speaking to you through the mouth of my adopted son. He does not understand Suomic; I address you privately. When you receive this message, I am already dead—"

Krausa had started to smile; now he let out an exclamation. Thorby stopped. Mother Shaum interrupted with, "What's he saying? What language is that?"

Krausa brushed it aside. "It's my language. Is what he says true?"

"Is what true? How would I know? I don't understand that yammer."

61

"Uh . . . sorry, sorry! He tells me that an old beggar who used to hang around the Plaza—'Baslim' he called himself—is dead. Is this true?"

"Eh? Of course it is. I could have told you, if I had known you were interested. Everybody knows it."

"Everybody but me, apparently. What happened to him?"

"He was shortened."

"Shortened? *Why?*"

She shrugged. "How would I know? The word is, he died or poisoned himself, or something, before they could question him—so how would I know? I'm just a poor old woman, trying to make an honest living, with prices getting higher every day. The Sargon's police don't confide in *me.*"

"But if—never mind. He managed to cheat them, did he? It sounds like him." He turned to Thorby. "Go on. Finish your message."

Thorby, thrown off stride, had to go back to the beginning. Krausa waited impatiently until he reached: "—I am already dead. My son is the only thing of value of which I die possessed; I entrust him to your care. I ask that you succor and admonish him as if you were I. When opportunity presents, I ask that you deliver him to the commander of any vessel of the Hegemonic Guard, saying that he is a distressed citizen of the Hegemony and entitled as such to their help in locating his family. If they will bestir themselves, they can establish his identity and restore him to his people. All the rest I leave to your good judgment. I have enjoined him to obey you and I believe that he will; he is a good lad, within the limits of his age and experience, and I entrust him to you with a serene heart. Now I must depart. My life has been long and rich; I am content. Farewell."

The Captain chewed his lip and his face worked in the fashion of a grown man who is busy not crying. Finally he said gruffly, "That's clear enough. Well, lad, are you ready?"

"Sir?"

"You're coming with me. Or didn't Baslim tell you?"

"No, sir. But he told me to do whatever you told me to. I'm to come with you?"

"Yes. How soon can you leave?"

Thorby gulped. "Right now, sir."

"Then come on. I want to get back to my ship." He looked Thorby up and down. "Mother Shaum, can we put some decent clothes on him? That outlandish rig won't do to come aboard in. Or never mind; there's a slop shop down the street; I'll pick him up a kit."

She had listened with growing amazement. Now she said, "You're taking him to your ship?"

"Any objections?"

"Huh? Not at all . . . if you don't care if they rack him apart."

"What do you mean?"

"Are you crazy? There are six snoopers between here and the spaceport gate . . . and each one anxious to pick up the reward."

"You mean he's wanted?"

"Why do you think I've hidden him in my own bedroom? He's as hot as bubbling cheese."

"But why?"

"Again, how would I know? He is."

"You don't really think that a lad like this would know enough about what old Baslim was doing to make it worth—"

"Let's not speak of what Baslim was doing or did. I'm a loyal subject of the Sargon . . . with no wish to be shortened. You say you want to take the boy into your ship. I say, 'Fine!' I'll be happy to be quit of the worry. But *how?*"

Krausa cracked his knuckles one by one. "I had thought," he said slowly, "that it would be just a matter of walking him down to the gate and paying his emigration tax."

"It's not, so forget it. Is there any way to get him aboard without passing him through the gate?"

Captain Krausa looked worried. "They're so strict about smuggling here that if they catch you, they confiscate the ship. You're asking me to risk my ship . . . and myself . . . and my whole crew."

"I'm not asking you to risk anything. I've got myself to worry about. I was just telling you the straight score. If you ask me, I'd say you were crazy to attempt it."

Thorby said, "Captain Krausa—"

"Eh? What is it, lad?"

"Pop told me to do as you said . . . but I'm sure he never meant you to risk your neck on my account." He swallowed. "I'll be all right."

Krausa sawed the air impatiently. "No, no!" he said harshly. "Baslim wanted this done . . . and debts are paid. Debts are always paid!"

"I don't understand."

"No need for you to. But Baslim wanted me to take you with me, so that's how it's got to be." He turned to Mother Shaum. "The question is, how? Any ideas?"

"Mmm . . . possibly. Let's go talk it over." She turned. "Get back in your hide-away, Thorby, and be careful. I may have to go out for a while."

Shortly before curfew the next day a large sedan chair left Joy Street. A patrolman stopped it and Mother Shaum stuck her head out. He looked surprised. "Going out, Mother? Who'll take care of your customers?"

"Mura has the keys," she answered. "But keep an eye on the place, that's a good friend. She's not as firm with them as I am." She put something in his hand and he made it disappear.

"I'll do that. Going to be gone all night?"

"I hope not. Perhaps I had better have a street pass, do you think? I'd like to come straight home if I finish my business."

"Well, now, they've tightened up a little on street passes."

"Still looking for the beggar's boy?"

"As a matter of fact, yes. But we'll find him. If he's fled to the country, they'll starve him out; if he's still in town, we'll run him down."

"Well, you could hardly mistake me for him. So how about a short pass for an old woman who needs to make a private call?" She rested her hand on the door; the edge of a bill stuck out.

He glanced at it and glanced away. "Is midnight late enough?"

"Plenty, I should think."

He took out his book and started writing, tore out the form and handed it to her. As she accepted it the money disappeared. "Don't make it later than midnight."

"Earlier, I hope."

He glanced inside the sedan chair, then looked over her entourage. The four bearers had been standing patiently, saying nothing—which was not surprising, since they had no tongues. "Zenith Garage?"

"I always trade there."

"I thought I recognized them. Well matched."

"Better look them over. One of them might be the beggar's boy."

"Those great hairy brutes! Get along with you, Mother."

"Hail, Shol."

The chair swung up and moved away at a trot. As they rounded the corner she slowed them to a walk and drew all curtains. Then she patted the cushions billowing around her. "Doing all right?"

"I'm squashed," a voice answered faintly.

"Better squashed than shortened. I'll ease over a bit. Your lap is bony."

For the next mile she was busy modifying her costume, and putting on jewels. She veiled her face until only her live, black eyes showed. Finished, she stuck her head out and called instructions to the head porter; the chair swung right toward the spaceport. When they reached the road girdling its high, impregnable fence it was almost dark.

The gate for spacemen is at the foot of Joy Street, the gate for passengers is east of there in the Emigration Control Building. Beyond that, in the warehouse district, is Traders' Gate—freight and outgoing customs. Miles beyond are shipyard gates. But between the shipyards and Traders'

Gate is a small gate reserved for nobles rich enough to own space yachts.

The chair reached the spaceport fence short of Traders' Gate, turned and went along the fence toward it. Traders' Gate is several gates, each a loading dock built through the barrier, so that a warehouse truck can back up, unload; the Sargon's inspectors can weigh, measure, grade, prod, open, and ray the merchandise, as may be indicated, before it slides across the dock into spaceport trucks on the other side, to be delivered to waiting ships.

This night dock-three of the gate had its barricade open; Free Trader *Sisu* was finishing loading. Her master watched, arguing with inspectors, and oiling their functioning in the immemorial fashion. A ship's junior officer helped him, keeping tally with pad and pencil.

The sedan chair weaved among waiting trucks and passed close to the dock. The master of the *Sisu* looked up as the veiled lady in the chair peered out at the activity. He glanced at his watch and spoke to his junior officer. "One more load, Jan. You go in with the loaded truck and I'll follow with the last one."

"Aye aye, sir." The young man climbed on the tail of the truck and told the driver to take it away. An empty truck pulled into its place. It loaded quickly as the ship's master seemed to find fewer things to argue about with the inspectors. Then he was not satisfied and demanded that it be done over. The boss stevedore was pained but the master soothed him, glanced at his watch again and said, "There's time. I don't want these crates cracked before we get them into the ship; the stuff costs money. So let's do it right."

The sedan chair had moved on along the fence. Shortly it was dark; the veiled lady looked at the glowing face of her finger watch and urged her bearers into a trot.

They came at last to the gate reserved for nobles. The veiled lady leaned her head out and snapped, "Open up!"

There were two guards on the gate, one in a little watch room, the other lounging outside. The one outside opened the gate, but placed his staff across it when the sedan chair started to go through. Stopped, the bearers lowered it to the ground with the righthand or door side facing into the gate.

The veiled lady called out, "Clear the way, you! Lord Marlin's yacht."

The guard blocking the gate hesitated. "My lady has a pass?"

"Are you a fool?"

"If my lady has no pass," he said slowly, "perhaps my lady will suggest some way to assure the guard that My Lord Marlin is expecting her?"

The veiled lady was a voice in the dark—the guard had sense enough not to shine the light in her face; he had long experience with nobles and fumed. "If you insist on being a fool, call my lord at his yacht! Phone him—and I trust you'll find you've pleased him!"

The guard in the watch room came out. "Trouble, Sean?"

"Uh, no." They held a whispered consultation. The junior went inside to phone Lord Marlin's yacht, while the other waited outside.

But it appeared that the lady had had all the nonsense she was willing to endure. She threw open the door of the chair, burst out, and stormed into the watch room with the other startled guard after her. The one making the call stopped punching keys with connection uncompleted and looked up . . . and felt sick. This was even worse than he had thought. This was no flighty young girl, escaped from her chaperones; this was an angry dowager, the sort with enough influence to break a man to common labor or worse —with a temper that made her capable of it. He listened open-mouthed to the richest tongue-lashing it had been his misfortune to endure in all the years he had been checking lords and ladies through their gate.

While the attention of both guards was monopolized by Mother Shaum's rich rhetoric, a figure detached itself from the sedan chair, faded through the gate and kept going, until it was lost in the gloom of the field. As Thorby ran, even as he expected the burning tingle of a stun gun bolt in his guts, he watched for a road on the right joining the one from the gate. When he came to it he threw himself down and lay panting.

Back at the gate, Mother Shaum stopped for breath. "My lady," one of them said placatingly, "if you will just let us complete the call—"

"Forget it! No, *remember* it!—for tomorrow you'll hear from My Lord Marlin." She flounced back to her chair.

"Please, my lady!"

She ignored them, spoke sharply to the slaves; they swung the chair up, broke into a trot. One guard's hand went to his belt, as a feeling of something badly wrong possessed him. But his hand stopped. Right or wrong, knocking down a lady's bearer was not to be risked, no matter what she might be up to.

And, after all, she hadn't actually done anything wrong.

When the master of the *Sisu* finally okayed the loading of the last truck, he climbed onto its bed, waved the driver to start, then worked his way forward. "Hey, there!" He knocked on the back of the cab.

"Yes, Captain?" The driver's voice came through faintly.

"There's a stop sign where this road joins the one out to the ships. I notice most of you drivers don't bother with it."

"That one? There's never any traffic on that road. That road is a stop just because the nobles use it."

"That's what I mean. One of them might pop up and I'd miss my jump time just for a silly traffic accident with one of your nobles. They could hold me here for many nine-days. So come to a full stop, will you?"

"Whatever you say, Captain. You're paying the bill."

"So I am." A half-stellar note went through a crack in the cab.

When the truck slowed, Krausa went to the tail gate. As it stopped he reached down and snaked Thorby inside. "Quiet!" Thorby nodded and trembled. Krausa took tools from his pockets, attacked one of the crates. Shortly he had one side open, burlap pulled back, and he started dumping verga leaves, priceless on any other planet. Soon he had a largish hole and a hundred pounds of valuable leaves were scattered over the plain. "Get in!"

Thorby crawled into the space, made himself small. Krausa pulled burlap over him, sewed it, crimped slats back into place, and finished by strapping it and sealing it with a good imitation of the seal used by the inspectors—it was a handcrafted product of his ship's machine shop. He straightened up and wiped sweat from his face. The truck was turning into the loading circle for the *Sisu*.

He supervised the final loads himself, with the Sargon's field inspector at his elbow, checking off each crate, each bale, each carton as it went into the sling. Then Krausa thanked the inspector appropriately and rode the sling up instead of the passenger hoist. Since a man was riding it, the hoist man let down the sling with more than usual care. The hold was almost filled and stowed for jump; 'there was very little head room. Crewmen started wrestling crates free of the sling and even the Captain lent a hand, at least to the extent of one crate. Once the sling was dragged clear, they closed the cargo door and started dogging it for space. Captain Krausa reached into his pocket again and started tearing open that crate.

Two hours later Mother Shaum stood at her bedroom window and looked out across the spaceport. She glanced at her watch. A green rocket rose from the control tower; seconds later a column of white light climbed to the sky. When the noise reached her, she smiled grimly and went downstairs to supervise the business—Mura couldn't really handle it properly alone.

Chapter 7

INSIDE THE FIRST few million miles Thorby was unhappily convinced that he had made a mistake.

He passed out from inhaling fumes of verga leaves and

awakened in a tiny, one-bunk stateroom. Waking was painful; although the *Sisu* maintained one standard gravity of internal field throughout a jump his body had recognized both the slight difference from Jubbul-surface gravity and the more subtle difference between an artificial field and the natural condition. His body decided that he was in the hold of a slaver and threw him into the first nightmare he had had in years.

Then his tired, fume-sodden brain took a long time struggling up out of the horror.

At last he was awake, aware of his surrounding, and concluded that he was aboard the *Sisu* and safe. He felt a glow of relief and gathering excitement that he was traveling, going somewhere. His grief over Baslim was pushed aside by strangeness and change. He looked around.

The compartment was a cube, only a foot or so higher and wider than his own height. He was resting on a shelf that filled half the room and under him was a mattress strangely and delightfully soft, of material warm and springy and smooth. He stretched and yawned in surprised wonder that traders lived in such luxury. Then he swung his feet over and stood up.

The bunk swung noiselessly up and fitted itself into the bulkhead. Thorby could not puzzle out how to open it again. Presently he gave up. He did not want a bed then; he did want to look around.

When he woke the ceiling was glowing faintly. When he stood up it glowed brightly and remained so. But the light did not show where the door was. There were vertical metal panels on three sides, any of which might have been a door, save that none displayed thumb slot, hinge, or other familiar mark.

He considered the possibility that he had been locked in, but was not troubled. Living in a cave, working in the Plaza, he was afflicted neither with claustrophobia nor agoraphobia; he simply wanted to find the door and was annoyed that he could not recognize it. If it were locked, he did not think that Captain Krausa would let it stay locked unduly long. But he could not find it.

He did find a pair of shorts and a singlet, on the deck. When he woke he had been bare, the way he usually slept. He picked up these garments, touched them timidly, wondered at their magnificence. He recognized them as being the sort of thing most spacemen wore and for a moment let himself be dazzled at the thought of wearing such luxuries. But his mind shied away from such impudence.

Then he recalled Captain Krausa's distaste at his coming aboard in the clothes he normally wore—why, the Captain had even intended to take him to a tailoring shop in Joy Street which catered to spacemen! He had *said* so.

Thorby concluded that these clothes must be for him. For *him!* His breech clout was missing and the Captain certainly had not intended him to appear in the *Sisu* naked. Thorby was not troubled by modesty; the taboo was spotty on Jubbul and applied more to the upper classes. Nevertheless clothes were worn.

Marveling at his own daring, Thorby tried them on. He got the shorts on backwards, figured out his mistake, and put them on properly. He got the pullover shirt on backwards, too, but the error was not as glaring; he left it that way, thinking that he had it right. Then he wished mightily that he could see himself.

Both garments were of simple cut, undecorated light green, and fashioned of strong, cheap material; they were working clothes from the ship's slop chest, a type of garment much used by both sexes on many planets through many centuries. Yet Solomon in all his glory was not arrayed as Thorby! He smoothed the cloth against his skin and wanted someone to see him in his finery. He set about finding the door with renewed eagerness.

It found him. While running his hands over the panels on one bulkhead he became aware of a breeze, turned and found that one panel had disappeared. The door let out into a passageway.

A young man dressed much as Thorby was (Thorby was

overjoyed to find that he had dressed properly for the occasion) was walking down the curved corridor toward Thorby. Thorby stepped out and spoke a greeting in Sargonese trade talk.

The man's eyes flicked toward Thorby, then he marched on past as if no one was there. Thorby blinked, puzzled and a little hurt. Then he called out to the receding back in Interlingua.

No answer and the man disappeared before he could try other languages.

Thorby shrugged and let it roll off; a beggar does not gain by being touchy. He set out to explore.

In twenty minutes he discovered many things. First, the *Sisu* was much larger than he had imagined. He had never before seen a starship close up, other than from the doubtful vantage of a slaver's hold. Ships in the distance, sitting on the field of Jubbul's port, had seemed large but not this enormous. Second, he was surprised to find so many people. He understood that the Sargon's freighters operating among the Nine Worlds were usually worked by crews of six or seven. But in his first few minutes he encountered several times that number of both sexes and all ages.

Third, he became dismally aware that he was being snubbed. People did not look at him, nor did they answer when he spoke; they walked right through him if he did not jump. The nearest he accomplished to social relations was with a female child, a toddler who regarded him with steady, grave eyes in answer to his overtures—until snatched up by a woman who did not even glance at Thorby.

Thorby recognized the treatment; it was the way a noble treated one of Thorby's caste. A noble could not see him, he did not exist—even a noble giving alms usually did so by handing it through a slave. Thorby had not been hurt by such treatment on Jubbul; that was natural, that was the way things had always been. It had made him neither lonely nor depressed; he had had plenty of warm company in his misery and had not known that it was misery.

But had he known ahead of time that the entire ship's

ompany of the *Sisu* would behave like nobles he would
ever have shipped in her, snoopies or not. But he had not
xpected such treatment. Captain Krausa, once Baslim's mes-
age had been delivered, had been friendly and gruffly
paternal; Thorby had expected the crew of the *Sisu* to re-
lect the attitude of her master.

He wandered the steel corridors, feeling like a ghost among
living, and at last decided sadly to go back to the cubicle
in which he had awakened. Then he discovered that he
was lost. He retraced what he thought was the route—and
in fact was; Baslim's renshawing had not been wasted—
but all he found was a featureless tunnel. So he set out
again, uncomfortably aware that whether he found his own
room or not, he must soon find where they hid the washroom,
even if he had to grab someone and shake him.

He blundered into a place where he was greeted by
squeals of female indignation; he retreated hastily and heard
a door slam behind him.

Shortly thereafter he was overtaken by a hurrying man
who spoke to him, in Interlingua: "What the dickens are
you doing wandering around and butting into things?"

Thorby felt a wave of relief. The grimmest place in the
world, lonelier than being alone, is Coventry, and even a
reprimand is better than being ignored. "I'm lost," he said
meekly.

"Why didn't you stay where you were?"

"I didn't know I was supposed to—I'm sorry, noble sir—
and there wasn't any washroom."

"Oh. But there is, right across from your bunkie."

"Noble sir, I did not know."

"Mmm . . . I suppose you didn't. I'm not 'noble sir';
I'm First Assistant Power Boss—see that you remember it.
Come along." He grabbed Thorby by an arm, hurried him
back through the maze, stopped in the same tunnel that had
stumped Thorby, ran his hand down a seam in the metal.
"Here's your bunkie." The panel slid aside.

The man turned, did the same on the other side. "Here's
the starboard bachelors' washroom." The man advised him

scornfully when Thorby was confused by strange fixtures, then chaperoned him back to his room. "Now stay here. Your meals will be fetched."

"First Assistant Power Boss, sir?"

"Eh?"

"Could I speak with Captain Krausa?"

The man looked astonished. "Do you think the Skipper has nothing better to do than talk to *you*?"

"But—"

The man had left; Thorby was talking to a steel panel.

Food appeared eventually, served by a youngster who behaved as if he were placing a tray in an empty room. More food appeared later and the first tray was removed. Thorby almost managed to be noticed; he hung onto the first tray and spoke to the boy in Interlingua. He detected a flicker of understanding, but he was answered by one short word. The word was "Fraki!" and Thorby did not recognize it . . . but he could recognize the contempt with which it was uttered. A fraki is a small, shapeless, semi-saurian scavenger of Alpha Centaura Prime III, one of the first worlds populated by men. It is ugly, almost mindless, and has disgusting habits. Its flesh can be eaten only by a starving man. Its skin is unpleasant to touch and leaves a foul odor.

But "fraki" means more than this. It means a groundhog, an earthcrawler, a dirt dweller, one who never goes into space, not of our tribe, not human, a goy, an auslander, a savage, beneath contempt. In Old Terran cultures almost every animal name has been used as an insult: pig, dog, sow, cow, shark, louse, skunk, worm—the list is endless. No such idiom carries more insult than "fraki."

Fortunately all Thorby got was the fact that the youngster did not care for him . . . which he knew.

Presently Thorby became sleepy. But, although he had mastered the gesture by which doors were opened, he still could not find any combination of swipes, scratches, punches, or other actions which would open the bed; he spent that night on the floorplates. His breakfast appeared next morning but he was unable to detain the person serving it, even to be insulted again. He did encounter other boys and young men in the washroom across the corridor; while he was still ignored, he learned one thing by watching— he could wash his clothing there. A gadget would accept a garment, hold it a few minutes, spew it forth dry and fresh. He was so delighted that he laundered his new finery three times that day. Besides, he had nothing else to do. He again slept on the floor that night.

He was squatting in his bunkie, feeling a great aching loneliness for Pop and wishing that he had never left Jubbul, when someone scratched at his door. "May I come in?" a voice inquired in careful, badly-accented Sargonese.

"Come in!" Thorby answered eagerly and jumped up to open the door. He found himself facing a middle-aged woman with a pleasant face. "Welcome," he said in Sargonese, and stood aside.

"I thank you for your gracious—" she stumbled and said quickly, "Do you speak Interlingua?"

"Certainly, madam."

She muttered in System English, "Thank goodness for that—I've run out of Sargonese," then went on in Interlingua, "Then we will speak it, if you don't mind."

"As you wish, madam," Thorby answered in the same language, then added in System English, "unless you would rather use another language."

She looked startled. "How many languages do you speak?"

Thorby thought. "Seven, ma'am. I can puzzle out some others, but I cannot say that I speak them."

She looked even more surprised and said slowly, "Perhaps I have made a mistake. But—correct me if I am wrong and forgive my ignorance—I was told that you were a beggar's son in Jubbulpore."

"I am the son of Baslim the Cripple," Thorby said proudly, "a licensed beggar under the mercy of the Sargon. My late father was a learned man. His wisdom was famous from one side of the Plaza to the other."

"I believe it. Uh . . . are all beggars on Jubbul linguists?"

"What, ma'am? Most of them speak only gutter argot. But

my father did not permit me to speak it . . . other than professionally, of course."

"Of course." She blinked. "I wish I could have met your father."

"Thank you, ma'am. Will you sit down? I am ashamed that I have nothing but the floor to offer . . . but what I have is yours."

"Thank you." She sat on the floor with more effort than did Thorby, who had remained thousands of hours in lotus seat, shouting his plea for alms.

Thorby wondered whether to close the door, whether this lady—in Sargonese he thought of her as "my lady" even though her friendly manner made her status unclear—had left it open on purpose. He was floundering in a sea of unknown customs, facing a social situation totally new to him. He solved it with common sense; he asked, "Do you prefer the door open or closed, ma'am?"

"Eh? It doesn't matter. Oh, perhaps you had better leave it open; these are bachelor quarters of the starboard moiety and I'm supposed to live in port purdah, with the unmarried females. But I'm allowed some of the privileges and immunities of . . . well, of a pet dog. I'm a tolerated 'fraki.' " She spoke the last word with a wry smile.

Thorby had missed most of the key words. "A 'dog'? That's a wolf creature?"

She looked at him sharply. "You learned this language on Jubbul?"

"I have never been off Jubbul, ma'am—except when I was very young. I'm sorry if I do not speak correctly. Would you prefer Interlingua?"

"Oh, no. You speak System English beautifully . . . a better Terran accent than mine—I've never been able to get my birthplace out of my vowels. But it's up to me to make myself understood. Let me introduce myself. I'm not a trader; I'm an anthropologist they are allowing to travel with them. My name is Doctor Margaret Mader."

Thorby ducked his head and pressed his palms together. "I am honored. My name is Thorby, son of Baslim."

"The pleasure is mine, Thorby. Call me 'Margaret.' My title doesn't count here anyhow, since it is not a ship's title. Do you know what an anthropologist is?"

"Uh, I am sorry, ma'am—Margaret."

"It's simpler than it sounds. An anthropologist is a scientist who studies how people live together."

Thorby looked doubtful. "This is a science?"

"Sometimes I wonder. Actually, Thorby, it is a complicated study, because the patterns that men work out to live together seem unlimited. There are only six things that all men have in common with all other men and not with animals—three of them part of our physical makeup, the way our bodies work, and three of them are learned. Everything else that a man does, or believes, all his customs and economic practices, vary enormously. Anthropologists study those variables. Do you understand 'variable'?"

"Uh," Thorby said doubtfully, "the x in an equation?"

"Correct!" she agreed with delight. "We study the x's in the human equations. That's what I'm doing. I'm studying the way the Free Traders live. They have worked out possibly the oddest solutions to the difficult problem of how to be human and survive of any society in history. They are unique." She moved restlessly. "Thorby, would you mind if I sat in a chair? I don't bend as well as I used to."

Thorby blushed. "Ma'am . . . I have none. I am dis—"

"There's one right behind you. And another behind me." She stood up and touched the wall. A panel slid aside; an upholstered armchair - unfolded from the space disclosed.

Seeing his face she said, "Didn't they show you?" and did the same on the other wall; another chair sprang out.

Thorby sat down cautiously, then let his weight relax into cushions as the chair felt him out and adjusted itself to him. A big grin spread over his face. "Gosh!"

"Do you know how to open your work table?"

"Table?"

"Good heavens, didn't they show you anything?"

"Well . . . there was a bed in here once. But I've lost it."

Doctor Mader muttered something, then said, "I might

have known it. Thorby, I admire these Traders. I even like them. But they can be the most stiff-necked, self-centered, contrary, self-righteous, uncooperative—but I should not criticize our hosts. Here." She reached out both hands, touched two spots on the wall and the disappearing bed swung down. With the chairs open, there remained hardly room for one person to stand. "I'd better close it. You saw what I did?"

"Let me try."

She showed Thorby other built-in facilities of what had seemed to be a bare cell: two chairs, a bed, clothes cupboards. Thorby learned that he owned, or at least had, two more work suits, two pairs of soft ship's shoes, and minor items, some of which were strange, bookshelf and spool racks (empty, except for the Laws of *Sisu*), a drinking fountain, a bed reading light, an intercom, a clock, a mirror, a room thermostat, and gadgets which were useless to him as his background included no need. "What's that?" he asked at last.

"That? Probably the microphone to the Chief Officer's cabin. Or it may be a dummy with the real one hidden. But don't worry; almost no one in this ship speaks System English and she isn't one of the few. They talk their 'secret language'—only it isn't secret; it's just Finnish. Each Trader ship has its own language—one of the Terran tongues. And the culture has an over-all 'secret' language which is merely degenerate Church Latin—and at that they don't use it; 'Free Ships' talk to each other in Interlingua."

Thorby was only half listening. He had been excessively cheered by her company and now, in contrast, he was brooding over his treatment from others. "Margaret . . . why won't they *speak* to people?"

"Eh?"

"You're the first person who's spoken to me!"

"Oh." She looked distressed. "I should have realized it. You've been ignored."

"Well . . . they feed me."

"But they don't talk with you. Oh, you poor dear! Thorby,

78

they don't speak to you because you are *not* 'people.' Nor am I."

"They don't talk to you either?"

"They do now. But it took direct orders from the Chief Officer and much patience on my part." She frowned. "Thorby, every excessively clannish culture—and I know of none more clannish than this—every such culture has the same key word in its language . . . and the word is 'people' however they say it. It means themselves. 'Me and my wife, son John and his wife, us four and no more'—cutting off their group from all others and denying that others are even human. Have you heard the word 'fraki' yet?"

"Yes. I don't know what it means."

"A fraki is just a harmless, rather repulsive little animal. But when they say it, it means 'stranger.' "

"Uh, well, I guess I am a stranger."

"Yes, but it also means you can never be anything else. It means that you and I are subhuman breeds outside the law—*their* law."

Thorby looked bleak. "Does that mean I have to stay in this room and never, ever talk to anybody?"

"Goodness! I don't know. *I'll* talk to you—"

"Thanks!"

"Let me see what I can find out. They're not cruel; they're just pig-headed and provincial. The fact that you have feelings never occurs to them. I'll talk to the Captain; I have an appointment with him as soon as the ship goes irrational." She glanced at her anklet. "Heavens, look at the time! I came here to talk about Jubbul and we haven't said a word about it. May I come back and discuss it with you?"

"I wish you would."

"Good. Jubbul is a well-analyzed culture, but I don't think any student has ever had opportunity to examine it from the perspective you had. I was delighted when I heard that you were a professed mendicant."

"Excuse me?"

"A beggar. Investigators who have been allowed to live

there have all been guests of the upper classes. That forces them to see . . . well, the way slaves live for example, from the outside, not the inside. You see?"

"I guess so." Thorby added, "If you want to know about slaves, I was one."

"You *were?*"

"I'm a freedman. Uh, I should have told you," he added uncomfortably, afraid that his new-found friend would scorn him, now that she knew his class.

"No reason to, but I'm overjoyed that you mentioned it. Thorby, you're a treasure trove! Look, dear, I've got to run; I'm late now. But may I come back soon?"

"Huh? Why, surely, Margaret." He added honestly, "I really don't have much else to do."

Thorby slept in his wonderful new bed that night. He was left alone the next morning but he was not bored, as he had so many toys to play with. He opened things out and caused them to fold up again, delighted at how each gadget folded in on itself to occupy minimum space. He concluded that it must be witchcraft. Baslim had taught him that magic and witchcraft were nonsense but the teaching had not fully stuck—Pop had known everything but just the same, how could you fly in the face of experience? Jubbul had plenty of witches and if they weren't practicing magic, what were they doing?

He had just opened his bed for the sixth time when he was almost shocked out of the shoes he had dared to try on by an unholy racket. It was the ship's alarm, calling all hands to General Quarters, and it was merely a drill, but Thorby did not know that. When he reswallowed his heart, he opened the door and looked out. People were running at breakneck speed.

Shortly the corridors were empty. He went back into his bunkie, waited and tried to understand. Presently his sharp ears detected the absence of the soft sigh of the ventilation system. But there was nothing he could do about it. He should have mustered in the innermost compartment, along with children and other noncombatants, but he did not know.

So he waited.

The alarm rang again, in conjunction with a horn signal, and again there were running people in the passageways. Again it was repeated, until the crew had run through General Quarters, Hull Broach, Power Failure, Air Hazard, Radiation Hazard, and so forth—all the general drills of a taut ship. Once the lights went out and once for frightening moments Thorby experienced the bewildering sensation of free fall as the ship's artificial field cut off.

After a long time of such inexplicable buffoonery he heard the soothing strains of recall and the ventilation system whispered back to normal. No one bothered to look for him; the old woman who mustered nonparticipants hadn't noticed the absence of the fraki although she had counted the animal pets aboard.

Immediately thereafter Thorby was dragged up to see the Chief Officer.

A man opened his door, grabbed his shoulder and marched him away. Thorby put up with it for a short distance, then he rebelled; he had his bellyful of such treatment.

The gutter fighting he had learned in order to survive in Jubbulpore was lacking in rules. Unfortunately this man had learned in a school equally cold-blooded but more scientific; Thorby got in one swipe, then found himself pinned against the bulkhead with his left wrist in danger of breaking. "Cut out the nonsense!"

"Quit pushing me around!"

"I said, 'Cut out the nonsense.' You're going up to see the Chief Officer. Don't give me trouble, Fraki, or I'll stuff your head in your mouth."

"I want to see Captain Krausa!"

The man relaxed the pressure and said, "You'll see him. But the Chief Officer has ordered you to report . . . and she can't be kept waiting. So will you go quietly? Or shall I carry you there in pieces?"

Thorby went quietly. Pressure on a wrist joint combined with pressure on a nerve between the bones of the palm carries its own rough logic. Several decks up he was shoved through an open door. "Chief Officer, here's the fraki."

"Thank you, Third Deck Master. You may go."

Thorby understood only the word "fraki." He picked himself up and found himself in a room many times as large as his own. The most prominent thing in it was an imposing bed, but the small figure in the bed dominated the room. Only after he had looked at her did he notice that Captain Krausa stood silent on one side of the bed and that a woman perhaps the Captain's age stood on the other.

The woman in bed was shrunken with age but radiated authority. She was richly dressed—the scarf over her thin hair represented more money than Thorby had ever seen at one time—but Thorby noticed only her fierce, sunken eyes. She looked at him. "So! Oldest Son, I have much trouble believing it." She spoke in Suomic.

"My Mother, the message could not have been faked." She sniffed.

Captain Krausa went on with humble stubbornness, "Hear the message yourself, My Mother." He turned to Thorby and said in Interlingua, "Repeat the message from your father."

Obediently, not understanding but enormously relieved to be in the presence of Pop's friend, Thorby repeated the message by rote. The old woman heard him through, then turned to Captain Krausa. "What is this? He speaks our language! A *fraki!*"

"No, My Mother, he understands not a word. That is Baslim's voice."

She looked back at Thorby, spilled a stream of Suomic on him. He looked questioningly at Captain Krausa. She said, "Have him repeat it again."

The Captain gave the order; Thorby, confused but willing, did so. She lay silent after he had concluded while the other waited. Her face screwed up in anger and exasperation. At last she rasped, "Debts must be paid!"

"That was my thought, My Mother."

"But why should the draft be drawn on us?" she answered angrily.

The Captain said nothing. She went on more quietly, "The message is authentic. I thought surely it must be faked. Had I known what you intended I would have forbidden it. But, Oldest Son, stupid as you are, you were right. And debts must be paid." Her son continued to say nothing; she added angrily, "Well? Speak up! What coin do you propose to tender?"

"I have been thinking, My Mother," Krausa said slowly. "Baslim demands that we care for the boy only a limited time . . . until we can turn him over to a Hegemonic military vessel. How long will that be? A year, two years. But even that presents problems. However, we have a precedent—the fraki female. The Family has accepted her—oh, a little grumbling, but they are used to her now, even amused by her. If My Mother intervened for this lad in the same way—"

"Nonsense!"

"But, My Mother, we are obligated. Debts must—"

"Silence!"

Krausa shut up.

She went on quietly, "Did you not listen to the wording of the burden Baslim placed on you? '—succor and admonish him as if you were I.' What was Baslim to this fraki?"

"Why, he speaks of him as his adopted son. I thought—"

"You didn't think. If you take Baslim's place, what does that make you? Is there more than one way to read the words?"

Krausa looked troubled. The ancient went on, "Sisu pays debts in full. No half-measures, no short weights—in full. The fraki must be adopted . . . by you."

Krausa's face was suddenly blank. The other woman, who had been moving around quietly with make-work, dropped a tray.

The Captain said, "But, My Mother, what will the Family—"

"I am the Family!" She turned suddenly to the other

woman. "Oldest Son's Wife, have all my senior daughters attend me."

"Yes, Husband's Mother." She curtsied and left.

The Chief Officer looked grimly at the overhead, then almost smiled. "This is not all bad, Oldest Son. What will happen at the next Gathering of the People?"

"Why, we will be thanked."

"Thanks buy no cargo." She licked her thin lips. "The People will be in debt to *Sisu* . . . and there will be a change in status of ships. We won't suffer."

Krausa smiled slowly. "You always were a shrewd one, My Mother."

"A good thing for *Sisu* that I am. Take the fraki boy and prepare him. We'll do this quickly."

Chapter 8

THORBY HAD TWO choices: be adopted quietly, or make a fuss and be adopted anyhow. He chose the first, which was sensible, as opposing the will of the Chief Officer was unpleasant and almost always futile. Besides, while he felt odd and rather unhappy about acquiring a new family so soon after the death of Pop, nevertheless he could see that the change was to his advantage. As a fraki, his status had never been lower. Even a slave has equals.

But most important, Pop had told him to do what Captain Krausa said for him to do.

The adoption took place in the dining saloon at the evening meal that day. Thorby understood little of what went on and none of what was said, since the ceremonies were in the "secret language," but the Captain had coached him in what to expect. The entire ship's company was there, except those on watch. Even Doctor Mader was there, inside the main door and taking no part but where she could see and hear.

The Chief Officer was carried in and everyone stood. She was settled on a lounge at the head of the officers' table, where her daughter-in-law, the Captain's wife attended her. When she was comfortable, she made a gesture and they sat down, the Captain seating himself on her right. Girls from the port moiety, the watch with the day's duty, then served all hands with bowls of thin mush. No one touched it. The Chief Officer banged her spoon on her bowl and spoke briefly and emphatically.

Her son followed her. Thorby was surprised to discover that he recognized a portion of the Captain's speech as being identical with part of the message Thorby had delivered; he could spot the sequence of sounds.

The Chief Engineer, a man older than Krausa, answered, then several older people, both men and women, spoke. The Chief Officer asked a question and was answered in chorus—a unanimous assent. The old woman did not ask for dissenting votes.

Thorby was trying to catch Doctor Mader's eye when the Captain called to him in Interlingua. Thorby had been seated on a stool alone and was feeling conspicuous, especially as persons he caught looking at him did not seem very friendly.

"Come here!"

Thorby looked up, saw both the Captain and his mother looking at him. She seemed irritated or it may have been the permanent set of her features. Thorby hurried over.

She dipped her spoon in his dish, barely licked it. Feeling as if he were doing something horribly wrong but having been coached, he dipped his spoon in her bowl, timidly took a mouthful. She reached up, pulled his head down and pecked him with withered lips on both cheeks. He returned the symbolic caress and felt gooseflesh.

Captain Krausa ate from Thorby's bowl; he ate from the Captain's. Then Krausa took a knife, held the point between thumb and forefinger and whispered in Interlingua, "Mind you don't cry out." He stabbed Thorby in his upper arm.

Thorby thought with contempt that Baslim had taught

him to ignore ten times that much pain. But blood flowed freely. Krausa led him to a spot where all might see, said something loudly, and held his arm so that a puddle of blood formed on the deck. The Captain stepped on it, rubbed it in with his foot, spoke loudly again—and a cheer went up. Krausa said to Thorby in Interlingua, "Your blood is now in the steel; our steel is in your blood."

Thorby had encountered sympathetic magic all his life and its wild, almost reasonable logic he understood. He felt a burst of pride that he was now part of the ship.

The Captain's wife slapped a plaster over the cut. Then Thorby exchanged food and kisses with her, after which he had to do it right around the room, every table, his brothers and his uncles, his sisters and his cousins and his aunts. Instead of kissing him, the men and boys grasped his hands and then clapped him across the shoulders. When he came to the table of unmarried females he hesitated— and discovered that they did not kiss him; they giggled and squealed and blushed and hastily touched forefingers to his forehead.

Close behind him, girls with the serving duty cleared away the bowls of mush—purely ritualistic food symbolizing the meager rations on which the People could cross space if necessary—and were serving a feast. Thorby would have been clogged to his ears with mush had he not caught onto the trick: don't eat it, just dip the spoon, then barely taste it. But when at last he was seated, an accepted member of the Family, at the starboard bachelors' table, he had no appetite for the banquet in his honor. Eighty-odd new relatives were too much. He felt tired, nervous, and let down.

But he tried to eat. Presently he heard a remark in which he understood only the word "fraki." He looked up and saw a youth across the table grinning unpleasantly.

The president of the table, seated on Thorby's right, rapped for attention. "We'll speak nothing but Interlingua tonight," he announced, "and thereafter follow the customs in allowing a new relative gradually to acquire our language." His eye rested coldly on the youngster who had sneered at Thorby. "As for you, Cross-Cousin-in-Law by Marriage, I'll remind you—just once—that my Adopted Younger Brother is senior to you. And I'll see you in my bunkie after dinner."

The younger boy looked startled. "Aw, Senior Cousin, I was just saying—"

"Drop it." The young man said quietly to Thorby, "Use your fork. People do not eat meat with fingers."

"Fork?"

"Left of your plate. Watch me; you'll learn. Don't let them get you riled. Some of these young oafs have yet to learn that when Grandmother speaks, she means business."

Thorby was moved from his bunkie into a less luxurious larger room intended for four bachelors. His roommates were Fritz Krausa, who was his eldest unmarried foster brother and president of the starboard bachelor table, Chelan Krausa-Drotar, Thorby's foster ortho-second-cousin by marriage, and Jeri Kingsolver, his foster nephew by his eldest married brother.

It resulted in his learning Suomic rapidly. But the words he needed first were not Suomish; they were words borrowed or invented to describe family relationships in great detail. Languages reflect cultures; most languages distinguish brother, sister, father, mother, aunt, uncle, and link generations by "great" or "grand." Some languages make no distinction between (for example) "father" and "uncle" and the language reflects tribal custom. Contrariwise, some languages (e.g., Norwegian) split "uncle" into maternal and paternal ("morbror" and "farbror").

The Free Traders can state a relationship such as "my maternal foster half-stepuncle by marriage, once removed and now deceased" in *one* word, one which means that relationship and no other. The relation between any spot on a family tree and any other spot can be so stated. Where most cultures find a dozen titles for relatives sufficient the Traders use more than two thousand. The languages name discreetly and quickly such variables as generation, lineal or collateral, natural or adopted, age within generation, sex of speaker, sex of relative referred to, sexes of relatives forming linkage, consanguinity or affinity, and vital status.

Thorby's first task was to learn the word and the relationship defined by it with which he must address each of more than eighty new relatives; he had to understand the precise flavor of relationship, close or distant, senior or junior; he had to learn other titles by which he would be addressed by each of them. Until he had learned all this, he could not talk because as soon as he opened his mouth he would commit a grave breach in manners.

He had to associate five things for each member of the *Sisu*'s company, a face, a full name (his own name was now Thorby Baslim-Krausa), a family title, that person's family title for him, and that person's ship's rank (such as "Chief Officer" or "Starboard Second Assistant Cook"). He learned that each person must be addressed by family title in family matters, by ship's rank concerning ship's duties, and by given names on social occasions if the senior permitted it—nicknames hardly existed, since the nickname could be used only down, *never* up.

Until he grasped these distinctions, he could not be a functioning member of the family even though he was legally such. The life of the ship was a caste system of such complex obligations, privileges and required reactions to obligatory actions, as to make the stratified, protocol-ridden society of Jubbul seem like chaos. The Captain's wife was Thorby's "mother" but she was also Deputy Chief Officer; how he addressed her depended on what he had to say. Since he was in bachelor quarters, the mothering phase ceased before it started; nevertheless she treated him warmly as a son and offered her cheek for his kiss just as she did for Thorby's roommate and elder brother Fritz.

But as Deputy Chief Officer she could be as cold as a tax collector.

Not that her status was easier; she would not be Chief Officer until the old woman had the grace to die. In the meantime she was hand and voice and body servant for her mother-in-law. Theoretically senior officers were elective; practically it was a one-party system with a single slate. Krausa was captain because his father had been; his wife was deputy chief officer because she was his wife, and she would someday become chief officer—and boss him and his ship as his mother did—for the same reason. Meanwhile his wife's high rank carried with it the worst job in the ship, with no respite, for senior officers served for life . . . unless impeached, convicted, and expelled—onto a planet for unsatisfactory performance, into the chilly thinness of space for breaking the ancient and pig-headed laws of *Sisu*.

But such an event was as scarce as a double eclipse; Thorby's mother's hope lay in heart failure, stroke, or other hazard of old age.

Thorby as adopted youngest son of Captain Krausa, senior male of the Krausa sept, titular head of *Sisu* clan (the Captain's mother being the real head), was senior to three-fourths of his new relatives in clan status (he had not yet acquired ship's rank). But seniority did not make life easier. With rank goeth privileges—so it ever shall be. But also with it go responsibility and obligation, always more onerous than privileges are pleasant.

It was easier to learn to be a beggar.

He was swept up in his new problems and did not see Doctor Margaret Mader for days. He was hurrying down the trunk corridor of fourth deck—he was always hurrying now—when he ran into her.

He stopped. "Hello, Margaret."

"Hello, Trader. I thought for a moment that you were no longer speaking to fraki."

"Aw, Margaret!"

She smiled. "I was joking. Congratulations, Thorby. I'm happy for you—it's the best solution under the circumstances."

"Thanks. I guess so."

She shifted to System English and said with motherly

concern, "You seem doubtful, Thorby. Aren't things going well?"

"Oh, things are all right." He suddenly blurted the truth. "Margaret, I'm never going to understand these people!"

She said gently, "I've felt the same way at the beginning of every field study and this one has been the most puzzling. What is bothering you?"

"Uh . . . I don't know. I never know. Well, take Fritz—he's my elder brother. He's helped me a lot—then I miss something that he expects me to understand and he blasts my ears off. Once he hit me. I hit back and I thought he was going to explode."

"Peck rights," said Margaret.

"What?"

"Never mind. It isn't scientifically parallel; humans aren't chickens. What happened?"

"Well, just as quickly he went absolutely cold, told me he would forget it, wipe it out, because of my ignorance."

"*Noblesse oblige.*"

"Huh?"

"Sorry. My mind is a junk yard. And did he?"

"Completely. He was sweet as sugar. I don't know why he got sore . . . and I don't know why he quit being sore when I hit him." He spread his hands. "It's not natural."

"No, it isn't. But few things are. Mmm . . . Thorby, I might be able to help. It's possible that I know how Fritz works better than he knows. Because I'm *not* one of the 'People.'"

"I don't understand."

"I do, I think. It's my job to. Fritz was born into the People; most of what he knows—and he is a very sophisticated young man—is subconscious. He can't explain it because he doesn't know he knows it; he simply functions. But what I have learned these past two years I have learned consciously. Perhaps I can advise you when you are shy about asking one of them. You can speak freely with me; I have no status."

"Gee, Margaret, would you?"

"Whenever you have time. I haven't forgotten that you promised to discuss Jubbul with me, either. But don't let me hold you; you seemed in a hurry."

"I wasn't, not really." He grinned sheepishly. "When I hurry I don't have to speak to as many people . . . and I usually don't know *how*."

"Ah, yes. Thorby, I have photographs, names, family classification, ship's job, on everyone. Would it help?"

"Huh? I should say so! Fritz thinks it's enough just to point somebody out once and say who he is."

"Then come to my room. It's all right; I have a dispensation to interview anyone there. The door opens into a public corridor; you don't cross purdah line."

Arranged by case cards with photographs, the data Thorby had had trouble learning piecemeal he soaked up in half an hour—thanks to Baslim's training and Doctor Mader's orderliness. In addition, she had prepared a family tree for the *Sisu*; it was the first he had seen; his relatives did not need diagrams, they simply knew.

She showed him his own place. "The plus mark means that while you are in the direct sept, you were not born there. Here are a couple more, transferred from collateral branches to sept . . . to put them into line of command I suspect. You people call yourselves a 'family' but the grouping is a phratry."

"A what?"

"A related group without a common ancestor which practices exogamy—that means marrying outside the group. The exogamy taboo holds, modified by rule of moiety. You know how the two moieties work?"

"They take turns having the day's duty."

"Yes, but do you know why the starboard watch has more bachelors and the port watch more single women?"

"Uh, I don't think so."

"Females adopted from other ships are in port moiety; native bachelors are starboard. Every girl in your side must be exchanged . . . unless she can find a husband among a very few eligible men. You should have been adopted on this side, but that would have required a different foster father. See the names with a blue circle-and-cross? One of those girls is your future wife . . . unless you find a bride on another ship."

Thorby felt dismayed at the thought. "Do I *have* to?"

"If you gain ship's rank to match your family rank, you'll have to carry a club to beat them off."

It fretted him. Swamped with family, he felt more need for a third leg than he did for a wife.

"Most societies," she went on, "practice both exogamy and endogamy—a man must marry outside his family but inside his nation, race, religion, or some large group, and you Free Traders are no exception; you must cross to another moiety but you can't marry fraki. But your rules produce an unusual setup; each ship is a patrilocal matriarchy."

"A what?"

" 'Patrilocal' means that wives join their husbands' families; a matriarchy . . . well, who bosses this ship?"

"Why, the Captain."

"He does?"

"Well, Father listens to Grandmother, but she is getting old and—"

"No 'buts.' The Chief Officer is boss. It surprised me; I thought it must be just this ship. But it extends all through the People. Men do the trading, conn the ship and mind its power plant—but a woman always is boss. It makes sense within its framework; it makes your marriage customs tolerable."

Thorby wished she would not keep referring to marriage.

"You haven't seen ships trade daughters. Girls leaving weep and wail and almost have to be dragged . . . but girls arriving have dried their eyes and are ready to smile and flirt, eyes open for husbands. If a girl catches the right man and pushes him, someday she can be sovereign of an independent state. Until she leaves her native ship, she isn't anybody—which is why her tears dry quickly. But if men were boss, girl-swapping would be slavery; as it is, it's a girl's big chance."

Doctor Mader turned away from the chart. "Human customs that help people live together are almost never planned. But they *are* useful, or they don't survive. Thorby, you have been fretted about how to behave toward your relatives."

"I certainly have!"

"What's the most important thing to a Trader?"

Thorby thought. "Why, the Family. Everything depends on who you are in the Family."

"Not at all. His ship."

"Well, when you say 'ship' you mean 'family.'"

"Just backwards. If a Trader becomes dissatisfied, where can he go? Space won't have him without a ship around him; nor can he imagine living on a planet among fraki, the idea is disgusting. His ship is his life, the air he breathes comes from his ship; somehow he must learn to live in it. But the pressure of personalities is almost unbearable and there is no way to get away from each other. Pressure could build up until somebody gets killed . . . or until the ship itself is destroyed. But humans devise ways to adjust to any conditions. You people lubricate with rituals, formalism, set patterns of speech, obligatory actions and responses. When things grow difficult you hide behind a pattern. That's why Fritz didn't stay angry."

"Huh?"

"He couldn't. You had done something wrong . . . but the fact itself showed that you were ignorant. Fritz had momentarily forgotten, then he remembered and his anger disappeared. The People do not permit themselves to be angry with a child; instead they set him back on the proper path . . . until he follows your complex customs as automatically as Fritz does."

"Uh, I think I see." Thorby sighed. "But it isn't easy."

"Because you weren't born to it. But you'll learn and it will be no more effort than breathing—and as useful. Customs tell a man who he is, where he belongs, what he must do. Better illogical customs than none; men cannot live together without them. From an anthropologist's view, 'justice' is a search for workable customs."

"My father—my other father, I mean; Baslim the Cripple —used to say the way to find justice is to deal fairly with other people and not worry about how they deal with you."

"Doesn't that fit what I said?"

"Uh, I guess so."

"I think Baslim the Cripple would regard the People as just." She patted his shoulder. "Never mind, Thorby. Do your best and one day you'll marry one of those nice girls. You'll be happy."

The prophecy did not cheer Thorby.

Chapter 9

By THE TIME *Sisu* approached Losian Thorby had a battle station worthy of a man. His first assignment had been to assist in the central dressing station, an unnecessary job. But his background in mathematics got him promoted.

He had been attending the ship's school. Baslim had given him a broad education, but this fact did not stand out to his instructors, since most of what they regarded as necessary—the Finnish language as they spoke it, the history of the People and of *Sisu*, trading customs, business practices, and export and import laws of many planets, hydroponics and ship's economy, ship safety and damage control—were subjects that Baslim had not even touched; he had emphasized languages, science, mathematics, galactography and history. The new subjects Thorby gobbled with a speed possible only to one renshawed by Baslim's strenuous methods. The Traders needed applied mathematics—bookkeeping and accounting, astrogation, nucleonics for a hydrogen-fusion-powered n-ship. Thorby splashed through the first, the second was hardly more difficult, but as for the third, the ship's schoolmaster was astounded that this ex-fraki had already studied multi-dimensional geometries.

So he reported to the Captain that they had a mathematical genius aboard.

· This was not true. But it got Thorby reassigned to the starboard fire-control computer.

The greatest hazard to trading ships is in the first and last legs of each jump, when a ship is below speed-of-light. It is theoretically possible to detect and intercept a ship going many times speed-of-light, when it is irrational to the four-dimensional space of the senses; in practice it is about as easy as hitting a particular raindrop with a bow and arrow during a storm at midnight. But it is feasible to hunt down a ship moving below speed-of-light if the attacker is fast and the victim is a big lumbering freighter.

The *Sisu* had acceleration of one hundred standard gravities and used it all to cut down the hazard time. But a ship which speeds up by a kilometer per second each second will take three and one half standard days to reach speed-of-light.

Half a week is a long, nervous time to wait. Doubling acceleration would have cut danger time by half and made the *Sisu* as agile as a raider—but it would have meant a hydrogen-fission chamber eight times as big with parallel increase in radiation shielding, auxiliary equipment, and paramagnetic capsule to contain the hydrogen reaction; the added mass would eliminate cargo capacity. Traders are working people; even if there were no parasites preying on them they could not afford to burn their profits in the inexorable workings of an exponential law of multi-dimensional physics. So the *Sisu* had the best legs she could afford—but not long enough to outrun a ship unburdened by cargo.

Nor could *Sisu* maneuver easily. She had to go precisely in the right direction when she entered the trackless night of n-space, else when she came out she would be too far from market; such a mistake could turn the ledger from black to red. Still more hampering, her skipper had to be prepared to cut power entirely, or risk having his in-ship artificial gravity field destroyed—and thereby make strawberry jam of the Family as soft bodies were suddenly exposed to one hundred gravities.

This is why a captain gets stomach ulcers; it isn't dickering for cargoes, figuring discounts and commissions, and trying to guess what goods will show the best return. It's not long jumps through the black—that is when he can relax and dandle babies. It is starting and ending a jump that kills him off, the long aching hours when he may have to make a split-second decision involving the lives—or freedom—of his family.

If raiders wished to destroy merchant ships, *Sisu* and her sisters would not stand a chance. But the raider wants loot and slaves; it gains nothing simply to blast a ship.

Merchantmen are limited by no qualms; an attacking ship's destruction is the ideal outcome. Atomic target-seekers are dreadfully expensive, and using them up is rough on profit-and-loss—but there is no holding back if the computer says the target can be reached—whereas a raider will use destruction weapons only to save himself. His tactic is to blind the trader, burn out her instruments so that he can get close enough to paralyze everyone aboard—or, failing that, kill without destroying ship and cargo.

The trader runs if she can, fights if she must. But when she fights, she fights to kill.

Whenever *Sisu* was below speed-of-light, she listened with artificial senses to every disturbance in multi-space, the whisper of n-space communication or the "white" roar of a ship boosting at many gravities. Data poured into the ship's astrogational analog of space and the questions were: Where is this other ship? What is its course? speed? acceleration? Can it catch us before we reach n-space?

If the answers were threatening, digested data channeled into port and starboard fire-control computers and *Sisu* braced herself to fight. Ordnancemen armed A-bomb target seekers, caressed their sleek sides and muttered charms; the Chief Engineer unlocked the suicide switch which could let the power plant become a hydrogen bomb of monstrous size and prayed that, in final extremity, he would have the courage to deliver his people into the shelter of death; the Captain sounded the clangor calling the ship from watch-and-watch to General Quarters. Cooks switched off fires; auxiliary engineers closed down air circulation; farmers said good-by to their green growing things and hurried to fighting stations; mothers with babies mustered, then strapped down and held those babies tightly.

Then the waiting started.

But not for Thorby—not for those assigned to fire-control computers. Sweating into their straps, for the next minutes or hours the life of *Sisu* is in their hands. The fire-control computer machines, chewing with millisecond meditation data from the analog, decide whether or not torpedoes can reach the target, then offer four answers: ballistic "possible" or "impossible" for projected condition, yes or no for condition changed by one ship, or the other, or both, through cutting power. These answers automatic circuits could handle alone, but machines do not think. Half of each computer is designed to allow the operator to ask what the situation might be in the far future of five minutes or so from now if variables change . . . and whether the target might be reached under such changes.

Any variable can be shaded by human judgment; an intuitive projection by a human operator can save his ship —or lose it. A paralysis beam travels at speed-of-light; torpedoes never have time to get up to more than a few hundred kilometers per second—yet it is possible for a raider to come within beaming range, have his pencil of paralyzing radiation on its way, and the trader to launch a target-seeker before the beam strikes . . . and still be saved when the outlaw flames into atomic mist a little later.

But if the operator is too eager by a few seconds, or overly cautious by the same, he can lose his ship. Too eager, the missile will fail to reach target; too cautious, it will never be launched.

Seasoned oldsters are not good at these jobs. The perfect firecontrolman is an adolescent, or young man or woman, fast in thought and action, confident, with intuitive grasp of mathematical relations beyond rote and rule, and not afraid of death he cannot yet imagine.

The traders must be always alert for such youngsters; Thorby seemed to have the feel for mathematics; he might have the other talents for a job something like chess played under terrific pressure and a fast game of spat ball. His mentor was Jeri Kingsolver, his nephew and roommate. Jeri was junior in family rank but appeared to be older; he called Thorby "Uncle" outside the computer room; on the job Thorby called him "Starboard Senior Firecontrolman" and added "Sir."

During long weeks of the dive through dark toward Losian, Jeri drilled Thorby. Thorby was supposed to be training for hydroponics and Jeri was the Supercargo's Senior Clerk, but the ship had plenty of farmers and the Supercargo's office was never very busy in space; Captain Krausa directed Jeri to keep Thorby hard at it in the computer room.

Since the ship remained at battle stations for half a week while boosting to speed-of-light, each fighting station had two persons assigned watch-and-watch. Jeri's junior controlman was his younger sister Mata. The computer had twin consoles, either of which could command by means of a selector switch. At General Quarters they sat side by side, with Jeri controlling and Mata ready to take over.

After a stiff course in what the machine could do Jeri put Thorby at one console, Mata at the other and fed them problems from the ship's control room. Each console recorded; it was possible to see what decisions each operator had made and how these compared with those made in battle, for the data were from records, real or threatened battles in the past.

Shortly Thorby became extremely irked; Mata was enormously better at it than he was.

So he tried harder and got worse. While he sweated, trying to outguess a slave raider which had once been on

Sisu's screens, he was painfully aware of a slender, dark, rather pretty girl beside him, her swift fingers making tiny adjustments among keys and knobs, changing a bias or modifying a vector, herself relaxed and unhurried. It was humiliating afterwards to find that his pacesetter had "saved the ship" while he had failed.

Worse still, he was aware of her as a girl and did not know it—all he knew was that she made him uneasy.

After one run Jeri called from ship's control, "End of drill. Stand by." He appeared shortly and examined their tapes, reading marks on sensitized paper as another might read print. He pursed his lips over Thorby's record. "Trainee, you fired three times . . . and not a one of your beasts got within fifty thousand kilometers of the enemy. We don't mind expense—it's merely Grandmother's blood. But the object is to blast him, not scare him into a fit. You have to wait until you can hit."

"I did my best!"

"Not good enough. Let's see yours, Sis."

The nickname irritated Thorby still more. Brother and sister were fond of each other and did not bother with titles. So Thorby had tried using their names . . . and had been snubbed; he was "Trainee," they were "Senior Controlman" and "Junior Controlman." There was nothing he could do; at drill he was junior. For a week, Thorby addressed Jeri as "Foster Ortho-Nephew" outside of drills and Jeri had carefully addressed him by family title. Then Thorby decided it was silly and went back to calling him Jeri. But Jeri continued to call him "Trainee" during drill, and so did Mata.

Jeri looked over his sister's record and nodded. "Very nice, Sis! You're within a second of post-analyzed optimum, and three seconds better than the shot that got the so-and-so. I have to admit that's sweet shooting . . . because the real run is my own. That raider off Ingstel . . . remember?"

"I certainly do." She glanced at Thorby.

Thorby felt disgusted. "It's not fair!" He started hauling at safety-belt buckles.

Jeri looked surprised. "What, Trainee?"

"I said it's not fair! You send down a problem, I tackle it cold—and get bawled out because I'm not perfect. But all she had to do is to fiddle with controls to get an answer she already knows ... to make me look cheap!"

Mata was looking stricken. Thorby headed for the door. "I never asked for this! I'm going to the Captain and ask for another job."

"*Trainee!*"

Thorby stopped. Jeri went on quietly. "Sit down. When I'm through, you can see the Captain—if you think it's advisable."

Thorby sat down.

"I've two things to say," Jeri continued coldly. "First—" He turned to his sister. "Junior Controlman, did you know what problem this was when you were tracking?"

"No, Senior Controlman."

"Have you worked it before?"

"I don't think so."

"How was it you remembered it?"

"What? Why, you said it was the raider off Ingstel. I'll never forget because of the dinner afterwards—you sat with Great Grandmo—with the Chief Officer."

Jeri turned to Thorby. "You see? She tracked it cold ... as cold as I had to when it happened. And she did even better than I did; I'm proud to have her as my junior tracker. For your information, Mister Stupid Junior Trainee, this engagement took place before the Junior Controlman became a trainee. She hasn't even run it in practice. She's just better at it than you are."

"All right," Thorby said sullenly. "I'll probably never be any good. I said I wanted to quit."

"I'm talking. Nobody asks for this job; it's a headache. Nobody quits it, either. After a while the job quits him, when post-analysis shows that he is losing his touch. Maybe I'm beginning to. But I promise you this: you'll either learn, or *I* will go to the Captain and tell him you don't measure up. In the meantime ... if I have any lip out of you, I'll haul you before the Chief Officer!" He snapped, "Extra drill run. Battle stations. Cast loose your equipment." He left the room.

Moments later his voice reached them. "Bogie! Starboard computer room, report!"

The call to dinner sounded; Mata said gravely, "Starboard tracker manned. Data showing, starting run." Her fingers started caressing keys. Thorby bent over his own controls; he wasn't hungry anyhow. For days Thorby spoke with Jeri only formally. He saw Mata at drill, or across the lounge at meals; he treated her with cold correctness and tried to do as well as she did. He could have seen her at other times; young people associated freely in public places. She was taboo to him, both as his niece and because they were of the same moiety, but that was no bar to social relations.

Jeri he could not avoid; they ate at the same table, slept in the same room. But Thorby could and did throw up a barrier of formality. No one said anything—these things happened. Even Fritz pretended not to notice.

But one afternoon Thorby dropped into the lounge to see a story film with a Sargonese background; Thorby sat through it to pick it to pieces. But when it was over he could not avoid noticing Mata because she walked over, stood in front of him, addressed him humbly as her uncle and asked if he would care for a game of spat ball before supper?

He was about to refuse when he noticed her face; she was watching him with tragic eagerness. So he answered, "Why, thanks, Mata. Work up an appetite."

She broke into smiles. "Good! I've got Ilsa holding a table. Let's!"

Thorby beat her three games and tied one . . . a remarkable score, since she was female champion and was allowed only one point handicap when playing the male champion. But he did not think about it; he was enjoying himself.

His performance picked up, partly through the grimness with which he worked, partly because he did have feeling for complex geometry, and partly because the beggar's boy had had his brain sharpened by an ancient discipline. Jeri never again compared aloud the performances of Mata and Thorby and gave only brief comments on Thorby's results: "Better," or "Coming along," and eventually, "You're getting there." Thorby's morale soared; he loosened up and spent more time socially, playing spat ball with Mata rather frequently.

Toward the end of journey through darkness they finished the last drill one morning and Jeri called out, "Stand easy! I'll be a few minutes." Thorby relaxed from pleasant strain. But after a moment he fidgeted; he had a hunch that he had been in tune with his instruments. "Junior Controlman . . . do you suppose he would mind if I looked at my tape?"

"I don't think so," Mata answered. "I'll take it out; then it's my responsibility."

"I don't want to get you in trouble."

"You won't," Mata answered serenely. She reached back of Thorby's console, pulled out the strip record, blew on it to keep it from curling, and examined it. Then she pulled her own strip, compared the two.

She looked at him gravely. "That's a very good run, Thorby."

It was the first time she had ever spoken his name. But Thorby hardly noticed. "Really? You mean it?"

"It's a *very* good run . . . Thorby. We both got hits. But yours is optimum between 'possible' and 'critical limit' —whereas mine is too eager. See?"

Thorby could read strips only haltingly, but he was happy to take her word for it. Jeri came in, took both strips, looked at Thorby's, then looked more closely. "I dug up the post-analysis before I came down," he said.

"Yes, sir?" Thorby said eagerly.

"Mmm . . . I'll check it after chow—but it looks as if your mistakes had cancelled out."

Mata said, "Why, Bud, that's a perfect run and you know it!"

"Suppose it is?" Jeri grinned. "You wouldn't want our star pupil to get a swelled head, would you?"

"Pooh!"

"Right back to you, small and ugly sister. Let's go to chow."

They went through a narrow passage into trunk corridor of second deck, where they walked abreast. Thorby gave a deep sigh.

"Trouble?" his nephew asked.

"Not a bit!" Thorby put an arm around each of them. "Jeri, you and Mata are going to make a marksman out of me yet."

It was the first time Thorby had addressed his teacher by name since the day he had received the scorching. But Jeri accepted his uncle's overture without stiffness. "Don't get your hopes up, bunkmate. But I think we've got it licked." He added, "I see Great Aunt Tora is giving us her famous cold eye. If anybody wants my opinion, I think Sis can walk unassisted—I'm sure Great Aunt thinks so."

"Pooh to her, too!" Mata said briskly. "Thorby just made a perfect run."

Sisu came out of darkness, dropping below speed-of-light. Losian's sun blazed less than fifty billion kilometers away; in a few days they would reach their next market. The ship went to watch-and-watch battle stations.

Mata took her watch alone; Jeri required the trainee to stand watches with him. The first watch was always free from strain; even if a raider had accurate information via n-space communicator of *Sisu*'s time of departure and destination, it was impossible in a jump of many light-years to predict the exact time and place where she would poke her nose out into rational space.

Jeri settled in his chair some minutes after Thorby had strapped down with that age-old tense feeling that this time it was not practice. Jeri grinned at him. "Relax. If you get your blood stream loaded, your back will ache, and you'll never last."

Thorby grinned feebly. "I'll try."

"That's better. We're going to play a game." Jeri pulled a boxlike contrivance out of a pocket, snapped it open.

"What is that?"

"A 'killjoy.' It fits here." Jeri slipped it over the switch that determined which console was in command. "Can you see the switch?"

"Huh? No."

"Hand the man the prize." Jeri fiddled with the switch behind the screen. "Which of us is in control in case we have to launch a bomb now?"

"How can I tell? Take that off, Jeri; it makes me nervous."

"That's the game. Maybe I'm controlling and you are just going through motions; maybe *you* are the man at the trigger and I'm asleep in my chair. Every so often I'll fiddle with the switch—but you won't know how I've left it. So when a flap comes—and one will; I feel it in my bones—you can't assume that good old Jeri, the man with the micrometer fingers, has the situation under control. You might have to save the firm. *You.*"

Thorby had a queasy vision of waiting men and bombs in the missile room below—waiting for him to solve precisely an impossible problem of life and death, of warped space and shifting vectors and complex geometry. "You're kidding," he said feebly. "You wouldn't leave me in control. Why, the Captain would skin you alive."

"Ah, that's where you're wrong. There always comes a day when a trainee makes his first real run. After that, he's a controlman . . . or an angel. But we don't let you worry at the time. Oh no! we just keep you worried all the time. Now here's the game. Any time I say, 'Now!' you guess who has control. You guess right, I owe you one dessert; you guess wrong, you owe me one. *Now!*"

Thorby thought quickly. "I guess I've got it."

"Wrong." Jeri lifted the killjoy. "You owe me one dessert—and it's berry tart tonight; my mouth is watering. But faster; you're supposed to make quick decisions. Now!"

"You've still got it!"

"So I have. Even. Now!"

"You!"

"Nope. See? And I eat your tart—I ought to quit while I'm ahead. Love that juice! Now!"

When Mata relieved them, Jeri owned Thorby's desserts for the next four days. "We start again with that score," Jeri said, "except that I'm going to collect that berry tart. But I forgot to tell you the big prize."

"Which is?"

"Comes the real thing, we bet three desserts. After it's over, you guess and we settle. Always bet more on real ones."

Mata sniffed. "Bud, are you trying to make him nervous?"

"Are you nervous, Thorby?"

"Nope!"

"Quit fretting, Sis. Got it firmly in your grubby little hands?"

"I relieve you, sir."

"Come on, Thorby; let's eat. Berry tarts—aaah!"

Three days later the score stood even, but only because Thorby had missed most of his desserts. *Sisu* was enormously slowed, almost to planetary speeds, and Losian's sun loomed large on the screens. Thorby decided, with mildest regret, that his ability to fight would not be tested this jump.

Then the general alarm made him rear up against safety belts. Jeri had been talking; his head jerked around, he looked at displays, and his hands moved to his controls. "Get on it!" he yelped. "This one's real."

Thorby snapped out of shock and bent over his board. The analog globe was pouring data to them; the ballistic situation had built up. Good heavens, it was *close!* And matching in fast! How had anything moved in so close without being detected? Then he quit thinking and started investigating answers . . . no, not yet . . . before long though . . . could the bandit turn a little at that boost and reduce his approach? . . . try a projection at an assumed six gravities of turning . . . would a missile reach him? . . . would it still reach him if he did not—

He heardly felt Mata's gentle touch on his shoulder. But he heard Jeri snap, "Stay out, Sis! We're on it, we're on it!"

A light blinked on Thorby's board; the squawk horn sounded, "Friendly craft, friendly craft! Losian planetary patrol, identified. Return to watch-and-watch."

Thorby took a deep breath, felt a great load lift.

"*Continue your run!*" screamed Jeri.

"*Huh?*"

"*Finish your run!* That's no Losian craft; *that's a raider!* Losians can't maneuver that way! You've got it, boy, you've got it! *Nail him!*"

Thorby heard Mata's frightened gasp, but he was again at his problem. Change anything? Could he reach him? Could he still reach him in the cone of possible maneuver? *Now!* He armed his board and let the computer give the order, on projection.

He heard Jeri's voice faintly; Jeri seemed to be talking very slowly. "Missile away. I think you got him . . . but you were eager. Get off another one before their beam hits us."

Automatically Thorby complied. Time was too short to try another solution; he ordered the machine to send another missile according to projection. He then saw by his board that the target was no longer under power and decided with a curiously empty feeling that his first missile had destroyed it.

"That's all!" Jeri announced. "Now!"

"What?"

"Who had it? You or me? Three desserts."

"*I* had it," Thorby said with certainty. In another level he decided that he would never really be a Trader—to Jeri that target had been—just fraki. Or three desserts.

"Wrong. That puts me three up. I turned coward and kept control myself. Of course the bombs were disarmed and the launchers locked as soon as the Captain gave the

106

word . . . but I didn't have the nerve to risk an accident with a friendly ship."

"*Friendly* ship!"

"Of course. But for you, Assistant Junior Controlman, it was your first real one . . . as I intended."

Thorby's head floated. Mata said, "Bud, you're mean to collect. You cheated."

"Sure I cheated. But he's a blooded controlman now, just the same. And I'm going to collect, just the very same. Ice cream tonight!"

Chapter 10

THORBY DID NOT STAY an assistant junior firecontrolman; Jeri moved up to astrogation trainee; Mata took charge of the starboard room, and Thorby was officially posted as the new Starboard Junior Firecontrolman, with life and death in his forefinger. He was not sure that he liked it.

Then that arrangement tumbled almost as quickly.

Losian is a "safe" planet. Inhabited by civilized non-humans, it is a port safe from ground raids; no dirtside defensive watches were necessary. Men could leave the ship for pleasure and even women could do so. (Some of the women aboard had not left the ship, save at Gatherings of the People, since being exchanged to *Sisu* as girls.)

Losian was to Thorby his "first" foreign land, Jubbul being the only planet clear in his memory. So he was very eager to see it. But work came first. When he was confirmed as a firecontrolman, he was transferred from hydroponics into the junior vacancy among the Supercargo's clerks. It increased Thorby's status; business carried more prestige than housekeeping. Theoretically he was now qualified to check cargo; in fact a senior clerk did that while Thorby sweated, along with junior male relatives from every department. Cargo was an all-hands operation, as *Sisu* never permitted stevedores inside, even if it meant paying for featherbedding.

The Losians have never invented tariff; crated bales of verga leaves were turned over to purchaser right outside the ship. In spite of blowers the hold reeked of their spicy, narcotic fragrance and reminded Thorby of months past and light-years away when he had huddled, a fugitive in danger of being shortened, into a hole in one crate while a friendly stranger smuggled him through the Sargon's police.

It didn't seem possible. *Sisu* was home. Even as he mused, he thought in the Family's language.

He realized with sudden guilt that he had not thought about Pop very often lately. Was he forgetting Pop? No, no! He could never forget, not anything . . . Pop's tones of voice, the detached look when he was about to comment unfavorably, his creaking movements on chilly mornings, his unfailing patience no matter what—why, in all those years Pop had never been angry with him—yes, he had, once.

" *'I am not your master!'* "

Pop had been angry that once. It had scared Thorby; he hadn't understood.

Now, across long space and time, Thorby suddenly understood. Only one thing could make Pop angry: Pop had been explosively insulted at the assertion that Baslim the Cripple was master to a slave. Pop, who maintained that a wise man could not be insulted, since truth could not insult and untruth was not worthy of notice.

Yet Pop had been insulted by the truth, for certainly Pop had been his master; Pop had bought him off the block. No, that was nonsense! He hadn't been Pop's slave; he had been Pop's son . . . Pop was never his master, even the times he had given him a quick one across the behind for goofing. Pop . . . was just 'Pop.'

Thorby knew then that the one thing that Pop hated was slavery.

Thorby was not sure why he was sure, but he was. He could not recall that Pop had ever said a word about slavery, as such; all Thorby could remember Pop saying was that a man need never be other than free in his own mind.

"Hey!"

The Supercargo was looking at him. "Sir?"

"Are you moving that crate, or making a bed of it?"

Three local days later Thorby had finished showering, about to hit dirt with Fritz, when the deckmaster stuck his head in the washroom, spotted him, and said, "Captain's compliments and Clerk Thorby Baslim-Krausa will attend him."

"Aye aye, Deckmaster," Thorby answered and added something under his breath. He hurried into clothes, stuck his head into his bunkie, gave the sad word to Fritz and rushed to the Cabin, hoping that the Deckmaster had told the Captain that Thorby had been showering.

The door was open. Thorby started to report formally when the Captain looked up. "Hello, Son. Come in."

Thorby shifted gears from Ship to Family. "Yes, Father."

"I'm about to hit dirt. Want to come along?"

"Sir? I mean, 'Yes, Father!' that 'ud be swell!"

"Good. I see you're ready. Let's go." He reached in a drawer and handed Thorby some twisted bits of wire. "Here's pocket money; you may want a souvenir."

Thorby examined it. "What's this stuff worth, Father?"

"Nothing—once we're off Losian. So give me back what you have left so I can turn it in for credit. They pay us off in thorium and goods."

"Yes, but how will I know how much to pay for a thing?"

"Take their word for it. They won't cheat and won't bargain. Odd ones. Not like Lotarf . . . on Lotarf, if you buy a beer without an hour's dickering you're ahead."

Thorby felt that he understood Lotarfi better than he did Losians. There was something indecent about a purchase without a polite amount of dickering. But fraki had barbaric customs; you had to cater to them—Sisu prided herself on never having trouble with fraki.

"Come along. We can talk as we go."

As they were being lowered Thorby looked at the ship

nearest them, Free Trader *El Nido,* Garcia clan. "Father, are we going to visit with them?"

"No, I exchanged calls the first day."

"I didn't mean that. Will there be any parties?"

"Oh. Captain Garcia and I agreed to dispense with hospitality; he's anxious to jump. No reason why you shouldn't visit them though, subject to your duties." He added, "Hardly worth it; she's like *Sisu,* only not as modern."

"Thought I might look at her computer rooms."

They hit ground and stepped off. "Doubt if they'd let you. They're a superstitious lot." As they stepped clear of the hoist a baby Losian came streaking up, circled and sniffed their legs. Captain Krausa let the little thing investigate him, then said mildly, "That's enough," and gently pushed it away. Its mother whistled it back, picked it up and spanked it. Captain Krausa waved to her, called out, "Hello, friend!"

"Hello, Trader Man," she answered in Interlingua shrill and sibilant. She was two-thirds Thorby's height, on four legs with forelimbs elevated—the baby had been on all six. Both were sleek and pretty and sharp-eyed. Thorby was amused by them and only slightly put off by the double mouth arrangement—one for eating, one for breathing and talking.

Captain Krausa continued talking. "That was a nice run you made on that Losian craft."

Thorby blushed. "You knew about that, Father?"

"What kind of a captain am I if I don't? Oh, I know what's worrying you. Forget it. If I give you a target, you burn it. It's up to me to kill your circuits if we make friendly identification. If I slap the God-be-thanked switch, you can't get your computer to fire, the bombs are disarmed, the launching gear is locked, the Chief can't move the suicide switch. So even if you hear me call off the action— or you get excited and don't hear—it doesn't matter. Finish your run; it's good practice."

"Oh. I didn't know, Father."

"Didn't Jeri tell you? You must have noticed the switch; it's the big red one, under my right hand."

"Uh, I've never been in the Control Room, Father."

"Eh? I must correct that; it might belong to you someday. Remind me . . . right after we go irrational."

"I will, Father." Thorby was pleased at the prospect of entering the mysterious shrine—he was sure that half of his relatives had never visited it—but he was surprised at the comment. Could a former fraki be eligible for command? It was legal for an adopted son to succeed to the worry seat; sometimes captains had no sons of their own. But an ex-fraki?

Captain Krausa was saying, "I haven't given you the attention I should, Son . . . not the care I should give Baslim's son. But it's a big family and my time is so taken up. Are they treating you all right?"

"Why, sure, Father!"

"Mmm . . . glad to hear it. It's—well, you weren't born among the People, you know."

"I know. But everybody has treated me fine."

"Good. I've had good reports about you. You seem to learn fast, for a—you learn fast."

Thorby sourly finished the phrase in his mind. The Captain went on, "Have you been in the Power Room?"

"No, sir. Just the practice room once."

"Now is a good time, while we're grounded. It's safer and the prayers and cleansing aren't so lengthy." Krausa paused. "No, we'll wait until your status is clear—the Chief is hinting that you are material for his department. He has some silly idea that you will never have children anyway and he might regard a visit as an opportunity to snag you. Engineers!"

Thorby understood this speech, even the last word. Engineers were regarded as slightly balmy; it was commonly believed that radiations from the artificial star that gave *Sisu* her life ionized their brain tissues. True or not, engineers could get away with outrageous breeches of etiquette—"not guilty by reason of insanity" was an unspoken defense for them once they had been repeatedly exposed to the hazards of their trade. The Chief Engineer even talked back to Grandmother.

But junior engineers were not allowed to stand power room watches until they no longer expected to have children; they took care of auxiliary machinery and stood training watches in a dummy power room. The People were cautious about harmful mutations, because they were more exposed to radiation hazards than were planet dwellers. One never saw overt mutation among them; what happened to babies distorted at birth was a mystery so taboo that Thorby was not even aware of it; he simply knew that power watchstanders were old men.

Nor was he interested in progeny; he simply saw in the Captain's remarks a hint that the Chief Engineer considered that Thorby could reach the exalted status of power watchstander quickly. The idea dazzled him. The men who wrestled with the mad gods of nuclear physics held status just below astrogators . . . and, in their own opinion, higher. Their opinion was closer to fact than was the official one; even a deputy captain who attempted to pull rank on a man standing power room watches was likely to wind up counting stores while the engineer rested in sick bay, then went back to doing as he pleased. Was it possible that an ex-fraki could aspire to such heights? Perhaps someday be Chief Engineer and sass the Chief Officer with impunity? "Father," Thorby said eagerly, "the Chief Engineer thinks I can learn power room rituals?"

"Wasn't that what I said?"

"Yes, sir. Uh . . . I wonder why he thought so?"

"Are you dense? Or unusually modest? Any man who can handle firecontrol mathematics can learn nuclear engineering. But he can learn astrogation, too, which is just as important."

Engineers never handled cargo; the only work they did in port was to load tritium and deuterium, or other tasks strictly theirs. They did no housekeeping. They . . . "Father? I think I might like to be an engineer."

112

"So? Well, now that you've thought so, forget it."

"But—"

" 'But' what?"

"Nothing, sir. Yes, sir."

Krausa sighed. "Son, I have obligations toward you; I'm carrying them out as best I can." Krausa thought over what he could tell the lad. Mother had pointed out that if Baslim had wanted the boy to know the message he had carried, Baslim would have put it in Interlingua. On the other hand, since the boy now knew the Family language perhaps he had translated it himself. No, more likely he had forgotten it. "Thorby, do you know who your family is?"

Thorby was startled. "Sir? My family is *Sisu*."

"Certainly! I mean your family before that."

"You mean Pop? Baslim the Cripple?"

"No, no! He was your foster father, just as I am now. Do you know what family you were born in?"

Thorby said bleakly, "I don't think I had one."

Krausa realized that he had poked a scar, said hastily, "Now, Son, you don't have to copy all the attitudes of your messmates. Why, if it weren't for fraki, with whom would we trade? How would the People live? A man is fortunate to be born People, but there is nothing to be ashamed of in being born fraki. Every atom has its purpose."

"I'm not ashamed!"

"Take it easy!"

"Sorry sir. I'm not ashamed of my ancestors. I simply don't know who they were. Why, for all I know, they may have been People."

Krausa was startled. "Why, so they could have been," he said slowly. Most slaves were purchased on planets that respectable traders never visited, or were born on estates of their owners . . . but a tragic percentage were *People*, stolen by raiders. This lad— Had any ship of the People been lost around the necessary time? He wondered if, at the next Gathering, he might dig up identification from the Commodore's files?

But even that would not exhaust the possibilities; some chief officers were sloppy about sending in identifications at birth, some waited until a Gathering. Mother, now, never grudged the expense of a long n-space message; she wanted her children on record at once—*Sisu* was never slack.

Suppose the boy were born People and his record had never reached the Commodore? How unfair to lose his birthright!

A thought tip-toed through his brain: a slip could be corrected in more ways than one. If any Free Ship had been lost— He could not remember.

Nor could he talk about it. But what a wonderful thing to give the lad an ancestry! If he could . . .

He changed the subject. "In a way, lad, you were always of the People."

"Huh? Excuse me, Father?"

"Son, Baslim the Cripple was an honorary member of the People."

"*What?* How, Father? What ship?"

"All ships. He was elected at a Gathering. Son, a long time ago a shameful thing happened. Baslim corrected it. It put all the People in debt to him. I have said enough. Tell me, have you thought of getting married?"

Marriage was the last thing on Thorby's mind; he was blazing anxious to hear more about what Pop had done that had made him incredibly one of the People. But he recognized the warning with which an elder closed a taboo subject.

"Why, no, Father."

"Your Grandmother thinks that you have begun to notice girls seriously."

"Well, sir, Grandmother is never wrong . . . but I hadn't been aware of it."

"A man isn't complete without a wife. But I don't think you're old enough. Laugh with all the girls and cry with none—and remember our customs." Krausa was thinking that he was bound by Baslim's injunction to seek aid of the Hegemony in finding where the lad had come from. It would be awkward if Thorby married before the opportunity arose. Yet the boy had grown taller in the months he had been in *Sisu*. Adding to Krausa's fret was an uneasy feeling that his half-conceived notion of finding (or faking) an ancestry for Thorby conflicted with his unbreakable obligations to Baslim.

Then he had a cheerful idea. "Tell you what, Son! It's possible that the girl for you isn't aboard. After all, there are only a few in port side purdah—and picking a wife is a serious matter. She can gain you status or ruin you. So why not take it easy? At the Great Gathering you will meet hundreds of eligible girls. If you find one you like and who likes you, I'll discuss it with your Grandmother and if she approves, we'll dicker for her exchange. We won't be stingy either. How does that sound?"

It put the problem comfortably in the distance. "It sounds fine, Father!"

"I have said enough." Krausa thought happily that he would check the files while Thorby was meeting those "hundreds of girls"—and he need not review his obligation to Baslim until he had done so. The lad might be a born member of the People—in fact his obvious merits made fraki ancestry almost unthinkable. If so, Baslim's wishes would be carried out in the spirit more than if followed to the letter. In the meantime—forget it!

They completed the mile to the edge of the Losian community. Thorby stared at sleek Losian ships and thought uneasily that he had tried to burn one of those pretty things out of space. Then he reminded himself that Father had said it was not a firecontrolman's business to worry about what target was handed him.

When they got into city traffic he had no time to worry. Losians do not use passenger cars, nor do they favor anything as stately as a sedan chair. On foot, they scurry twice as fast as a man can run; in a hurry, they put on a vehicle which makes one think of jet propulsion. Four and sometimes six limbs are encased in sleeves which end in something like skates. A framework fits the body and carries a bulge for the power plant (what sort Thorby could not imagine). Encased in this mechanical clown suit, each becomes a guided missile, accelerating with careless abandon, showering sparks, filling the air with earsplitting noises, cornering in defiance of friction, inertia, and gravity, cutting in and out, never braking until the last minute.

Pedestrians and powered speed maniacs mix democratically, with no perceptible rules. There seems to be no age limit for driver's licenses and the smallest Losians are simply more reckless editions of their elders.

Thorby wondered if he would ever get out into space alive.

A Losian would come zipping toward Thorby on the wrong side of the street (there was no right side), squeal to a stop almost on Thorby's toes, zig aside while snatching breath off his face and heart out of his mouth—and never touch him. Thorby would jump. After a dozen escapes he tried to pattern himself after his foster father. Captain Krausa plowed stolidly ahead, apparently sure that the wild drivers would treat him as a stationary object. Thorby found it hard to live by that faith, but it seemed to work.

Thorby could not make out how the city was organized. Powered traffic and pedestrians poured through any opening and the convention of private land and public street did not seem to hold. At first they proceeded along an area which Thorby classified as a plaza, then they went up a ramp, through a building which had no clear limits—no vertical walls, no defined roof—out again and down, through an arch which skirted a hole. Thorby was lost.

Once he thought they must be going through a private home—they pushed through what must have been a dinner party. But the guests merely pulled in their feet.

Krausa stopped. "We're almost there. Son, we're visiting the fraki who bought our load. This meeting heals the trouble between us caused by buying and selling. He has offended me by offering payment; now we have to become friends again."

"We don't get paid?"

"What would your Grandmother say? We've already been paid—but now I'll give it to him free and he'll give me the thorium just because he likes my pretty blue eyes. Their customs don't allow anything as crass as selling."

"They don't trade with each other?"

"Of course they do. But the theory is that one fraki gives another anything he needs. It's sheer accident that the other happens to have money that he is anxious to press on the other as a gift—and that the two gifts balance. They are shrewd merchants, Son; we never pick up an extra credit here."

"Then why this nonsense?"

"Son, if you worry about why fraki do what they do, you'll drive yourself crazy. When you're on their planet, do it their way . . . it's good business. Now listen. We'll have a meal of friendship . . . only they can't, or they'll lose face. So there will be a screen between us. You have to be present, because the Losian's son will be there—only it's a daughter. And the fraki I'm going to see is the mother, not the father. Their males live in purdah . . . I think. But notice that when I speak through the interpreter, I'll use masculine gender."

"Why?"

"Because they know enough about our customs to know that masculine gender means the head of the house. It's logical if you look at it correctly."

Thorby wondered. Who was head of the Family? Father? Or Grandmother? Of course, when the Chief Officer issued an order, she signed it "By Order of the Captain," but that was just because . . . no. Well, anyhow—

Thorby suddenly suspected that the customs of the Family might be illogical in spots. But the Captain was speaking. "We don't actually eat with them; that's another fiction. You'll be served a green, slimy liquid. Just raise it to your lips; it would burn out your gullet. Otherwise—" Captain Krausa paused while a Losian scorcher avoided the end of his nose. "Otherwise listen so that you will know how to behave next time. Oh yes!—after I ask how old my host's

117

son is, you'll be asked how old you are. You answer 'forty.' "
"Why?"
"Because that is a respectable age, in their years, for a son who is assisting his father."

They arrived and seemed still to be in public. But they squatted down opposite two Losians while a third crouched nearby. The screen between them was the size of a kerchief; Thorby could see over it. Thorby tried to look, listen, and learn, but the traffic never let up. It shot around and cut between them, with happy, shrill racket.

Their host started by accusing Captain Krausa of having lured him into a misdeed. The interpreter was almost impossible to understand, but he showed surprising command of scurrilous Interlingua. Thorby could not believe his ears and expected that Father would either walk out, or start trouble.

But Captain Krausa listened quietly, then answered with real poetry—he accused the Losian of every crime from barratry to mopery and dopery in the spaceways.

This put the meeting on a friendly footing. The Losian made them a present of the thorium he had already paid, then offered to throw in his sons and everything he possessed.

Captain Krausa accepted and gave away *Sisu*, with all contents.

Both parties generously gave back the gifts. They ended at status quo, each to retain as a symbol of friendship what each now had: the Losian many hundredweight of verga leaf, the Trader slugs of thorium. Both agreed that the gifts were worthless but valuable for reasons of sentiment. In a burst of emotion the Losian gave away his son and Krausa made him (her) a present of Thorby. Inquiries followed and it was discovered that each was too young to leave the nest.

They got out of this dilemma by having the sons exchange names and Thorby found himself owner of a name he did not want and could not pronounce. Then they "ate."

The horrid green stuff was not only not fit to drink, but

when Thorby inhaled, he burned his nostrils and choked. The Captain gave him a reproving glance.

After that they left. No good-bys, they just walked off. Captain Krausa said meditatively while proceeding like a sleepwalker through the riot of traffic, "Nice people, for fraki. Never any sharp dealing and absolutely honest. I often wonder what one of them would do if I took him up on one of those offers. Pay up, probably."

"Not really!"

"Don't be sure. I might hand you in on that half-grown Losian."

Thorby shut up.

Business concluded, Captain Krausa helped Thorby shop and sight-see, which relieved Thorby, because he did not know what to buy, nor even how to get home. His foster father took him to a shop where Interlingua was understood. Losians manufacture all sorts of things of extreme complexity, none of which Thorby recognized. On Krausa's advice Thorby selected a small polished cube which, when shaken, showed endless Losian scenes in its depths. Thorby offered the shopkeeper his tokens; the Losian selected one and gave him change from a necklace of money. Then he made Thorby a present of shop and contents.

Thorby, speaking through Krausa, regretted that he had nothing to offer save his own services the rest of his life. They backed out of the predicament with courteous insults.

Thorby felt relieved when they reached the spaceport and he saw the homely, familiar lines of old *Sisu*.

When Thorby reached his bunkie, Jeri was there, feet up and hands back of his head. He looked up and did not smile.

"Hi, Jeri!"

"Hello, Thorby."

"Hit dirt?"

"No."

"I did. Look what I bought!" Thorby showed him the magic cube. "You shake it and every picture is different."

Jeri looked at one picture and handed it back. "Very nice."

"Jeri, what are you glum about? Something you ate?"

"No."

"Spill it."

Jeri dropped his feet to the deck, looked at Thorby. "I'm back in the computer room."

"Huh?"

"Oh, I don't lose status. It's just while I train somebody else."

Thorby felt a cold wind. "You mean I've been busted?"

"No."

"Then what *do* you mean?"

"Mata has been swapped."

Chapter 11

MATA SWAPPED? Gone forever? Little Mattie with the grave eyes and merry giggle? Thorby felt a burst of sorrow and realized to his surprise that it mattered.

"I don't believe it!"

"Don't be a fool."

"When? Where has she gone? Why didn't you tell me?"

"To *El Nido*, obviously; it's the only ship of the People in port. About an hour ago. I didn't tell you because I had no idea it was coming . . . until I was summoned to Grandmother's cabin to say good-by." Jeri frowned. "It had to come someday . . . but I thought Grandmother would let her stay as long as she kept her skill as a tracker."

"Then why, Jeri? *Why?*"

Jeri stood up, said woodenly, "Foster Ortho-Uncle, I have said enough."

Thorby pushed him back into his chair. "You can't get away with that, Jeri. I'm your 'uncle' only because they said I was. But I'm still the ex-fraki you taught to use a tracker and we both know it. Now talk man to man. Spill it!"

"You won't like it."

"I don't like it now! Mattie gone . . . Look, Jeri, there is nobody here but us. Whatever it is, tell me. I promise you, on *Sisu's* steel, that I won't make an uncle-and-nephew matter of it. Whatever you say, the Family will never know."

"Grandmother might be listening."

"If she is, I've ordered you to talk and it's my responsibility. But she won't be; it's time for her nap. So talk."

"Okay." Jeri looked at him sourly. "You asked for it. You mean to say you haven't the dimmest idea why Grandmother hustled my Sis out of the ship?"

"Huh? None . . . or I wouldn't ask."

Jeri made an impatient noise. "Thorby, I knew you were thick-witted. I didn't know you were deaf, dumb, and blind."

"Never mind the compliments! Tell me the score."

"You're the reason Mata got swapped. *You.*" Jeri looked at Thorby with disgust.

"*Me?*"

"Who else? Who pairs off at spat ball? Who sits together at story films? What new relative is always seen with a girl from his own moiety? I'll give you a hint—the name starts with 'T.' "

Thorby turned white. "Jeri, I never had the slightest idea."

"You're the only one in the ship who didn't." Jeri shrugged. "I'm not blaming you. It was her fault. She was chasing you, you stupid clown! What I can't figure out is why you didn't know. I tried to give you hints."

Thorby was as innocent of such things as a bird is of ballistics. "I don't believe it."

"It doesn't matter whether you do or don't . . . everybody else saw it. But you both could have gotten away with it, as long as you kept it open and harmless—and I was watching too closely for anything else—if Sis hadn't lost her head."

"Huh? How?"

121

"Sis did something that made Grandmother willing to part with a crack firecontrolman. She went to Grandmother and asked to be adopted across moiety line. In her simple, addled-pated way she figured that since you were adopted in the first place, it didn't really matter that she was your niece—just shift things around and she could marry you." Jeri grunted. "If you had been adopted on the other side, she could have wangled it. But she must have been clean off her head to think that Grandmother—*Grandmother!*—would agree to anything so scandalous."

"But . . . well, I'm not actually any relation to her. Not that I had any idea of marrying her."

"Oh, beat it! You make me tired."

Thorby moped around, unwilling to go back and face Jeri. He felt lost and alone and confused; the Family seemed as strange, their ways as difficult to understand, as the Losians.

He missed Mata. He had never missed her before. She had been something pleasant but routine—like three meals a day and the other comforts he had learned to expect in *Sisu*. Now he missed her.

Well, if that was what she wanted, why hadn't they let her? Not that he had thought about it . . . but as long as you had to get married some day, Mata would be as tolerable as any. He liked her.

Finally he remembered that there was one person with whom he could talk. He took his troubles to Doctor Mader.

He scratched at her door, received a hurried, "Come in!" He found her down on her knees, surrounded by possessions. She had a smudge on her nose and her neat hair was mussed. "Oh. Thorby. I'm glad you showed up. They told me you were dirtside and I was afraid I would miss you."

She spoke System English; he answered in it. "You wanted to see me?"

"To say good-by. I'm going home."

"Oh." Thorby felt again the sick twinge he had felt when Jeri had told about Mata. Suddenly he was wrenched with sorrow that Pop was gone. He pulled himself together and said, "I'm sorry. I'll miss you."

"I'll miss you, Thorby. You're the only one in this big ship that I felt at home with . . . which is odd, as your background and mine are about as far apart as possible. I'll miss our talks."

"So will I," Thorby agreed miserably. "When are you leaving?"

"*El Nido* jumps tomorrow. But I should transfer tonight; I don't dare miss jump, or I might not get home for years."

"*El Nido* is going to your planet?" A fantastic scheme began to shape in his mind.

"Oh, no! She's going to Thaf Beta VI. But a Hegemonic mail ship calls there and I can get home. It is too wonderful a chance to miss." The scheme died in Thorby's brain; it was preposterous, anyhow—he might be willing to chance a strange planet, but Mata was no fraki.

Doctor Mader went on, "The Chief Officer arranged it." She smiled wryly. "She's glad to get rid of me. I hadn't had any hope that she could put it over, in view of the difficulty in getting me aboard *Sisu;* I think your grandmother must have some bargaining point that she did not mention. In any case I'm to go . . . with the understanding that I remain in strict purdah. I shan't mind; I'll use the time on my data."

Mention of purdah reminded Thorby that Margaret would see Mata. He started with stumbling embarrassment to explain what he had come to talk about. Doctor Mader listened gravely, her fingers busy with packing. "I know, Thorby. I probably heard the sad details sooner than you did."

"Margaret, did you ever heard of anything so silly?" She hesitated. "Many things . . . much sillier."

"But there wasn't anything to it! And if that was what Mata wanted, why didn't Grandmother let her . . . instead of shipping her out among strangers. I . . . well, I wouldn't have minded. After I got used to it."

The fraki woman smiled. "That's the oddest gallant speech I ever heard, Thorby."

Thorby said, "Could you get a message to her for me?"

"Thorby, if you want to send her your undying love or something, then don't. Your Grandmother did the best thing for her great granddaughter, did it quickly with kindness and wisdom. Did it in Mata's interests against the immediate interests of *Sisu*, since Mata was a valuable fighting man. But your Grandmother measured up to the high standards expected of a Chief Officer; she considered the long-range interests of everyone and found them weightier than the loss of one firecontrolman. I admire her at last—between ourselves, I've always detested the old girl." She smiled suddenly. "And fifty years from now Mata will make the same sort of wise decisions; the sept of *Sisu* is sound."

"I'll be flogged if I understand it!"

"Because you are almost as much fraki as I am . . . and haven't had my training. Thorby, most things are right or wrong only in their backgrounds; few things are good or evil in themselves. But things that are right or wrong according to their culture, really *are* so. This exogamy rule the People live by, you probably think it's just a way to outsmart mutations—in fact that's the way it is taught in the ship's school."

"Of course. That's why I can't see—"

"Just a second. So you can't see why your Grandmother should object. But it's essential that the People marry back and forth among ships, not just because of genes—that's a side issue—but because a ship is too small to be a stable culture. Ideas and attitudes have to be cross-germinated, too, or *Sisu* and the whole culture will die. So the custom is protected by strongest possible taboo. A 'minor' break in this taboo is like a 'minor' break in the ship, disastrous unless drastic steps are taken. Now . . . do you understand that?"

"Well . . . no, I don't think so."

"I doubt if your Grandmother understands it; she just knows what's right for her family and acts with forthrightness and courage. Do you still want to send a message?"

"Uh, well, could you tell Mata that I'm sorry I didn't get to say good-by?"

"Mmm, yes. I may wait a while."

"All right."

"Feeling better yourself?"

"Uh, I guess so . . . since you say it's best for Mata." Thorby suddenly burst out, "But, Margaret, I don't know what is the matter with me! I thought I was getting the hang of things. Now it's all gone to pieces. I feel like a fraki and I doubt if I'll ever learn to be a Trader."

Her face was suddenly sad. "You were free once. It's a hard habit to get over."

"Huh?"

"You've had violent dislocations, Thorby. Your foster father—your first one, Baslim the Wise—bought you as a slave and made you his son, as free as he was. Now your second foster father, with the best of intentions, adopted you as his son, and thereby made you a slave."

"Why, Margaret!" Thorby protested. "How can you say such a thing?"

"If you aren't a slave, what are you?"

"Why, I'm a Free Trader. At least that's what Father intended, if I can ever get over my fraki habits. But I'm not a slave. The People are *free*. All of us."

"All of you . . . but not each of you."

"What do you mean?"

"The People are free. It's their proudest boast. Any of them can tell you that freedom is what makes them People and not fraki. The People are free to roam the stars, never rooted to any soil. So free that each ship is a sovereign state, asking nothing of anyone, going anywhere, fighting against any odds, asking no quarter, not even cooperating except as it suits them. Oh, the People are free; this old Galaxy has never seen such freedom. A culture of less than a hundred thousand people spread through a quarter of a billion cubic light-years and utterly free to move anywhere at any time. There has never been a culture like it and there may never be again. Free as the sky . . . more free than the stars, for the stars go where they must. Ah, yes, the People are free." She paused. "But at what price was this freedom purchased?"

Thorby blinked.

"I'll tell you. Not with poverty. The People enjoy the highest average wealth in history. The profits of your trading are fantastic. Nor has it been with cost to health or sanity. I've never seen a community with less illness. Nor have you paid in happiness or self-respect. You're a smugly happy lot, and your pride is something sinful—of course you do have a lot to be proud of. But what you *have* paid for your unparalleled freedom . . . is freedom itself. No, I'm not talking riddles. The People are free . . . at the cost of loss of individual freedom for each of you—and I don't except the Chief Officer or Captain; they are the least free of any."

Her words sounded outrageous. "How can we be both free and not free?" he protested.

"Ask Mata. Thorby, you live in a steel prison; you are allowed out perhaps a few hours every few months. You live by rules more stringent than any prison. That those rules are intended to make you all happy—and do—is beside the point; they are orders you have to obey. You sleep where you are told, you eat when you are told and what you are offered—it's unimportant that it is lavish and tasty; the point is you have no choice. You are told what to do ninety percent of the time. You are so bound by rules that much of what you say is not free speech but required ritual; you could go through a day and not utter a phrase not found in the Laws of *Sisu*. Right?"

"Yes, but—"

"Yes, with no 'buts.' Thorby, what sort of people have so little freedom? Slaves? Can you think of a better word?"

"But we can't be sold!"

"Slavery has often existed where slaves were never bought and sold, but simply inherited. As in *Sisu*. Thorby, being a slave means having someone as your master, with no hope of changing it. You slaves who call yourselves the 'People' can't even hope for manumission."

Thorby scowled. "You figure that's what's wrong with me?"

"I think your slave's collar is chafing you, in a fashion that does not trouble your shipmates—because they were born with theirs and you were once free." She looked at her belongings. "I've got to get this stuff into *El Nido*. Will you help me?"

"I'd be glad to."

"Don't expect to see Mata."

"I wasn't," Thorby fibbed. "I want to help you. I hate to see you leave."

"Truthfully, I don't hate to leave . . . but I hate to say good-by to you." She hesitated. "I want to help you, too. Thorby, an anthropologist should never interfere. But I'm leaving and you aren't really part of the culture I was studying. Could you use a hint from an old woman?"

"Why, you aren't old!"

"That's two gallant speeches. I'm a grandmother, though the Chief Officer might be startled to hear me claim that status. Thorby, I thought you would become adjusted to this jail. Now I'm not sure. Freedom is a hard habit to break. Dear, if you decide that you can't stand it, wait until the ship calls at a planet that is democratic and free and human —then hit dirt and run! But, Thorby, do this before Grandmother decides to marry you to someone, because if you wait that long—you're lost!"

Chapter 12

LOSIAN TO FINSTER, Finster to Thoth IV, Thoth IV to Woolamurra, *Sisu* went skipping around a globe of space nine hundred light-years in diameter, the center of which was legendary Terra, cradle of mankind. *Sisu* had never been to Terra; the People operate out where pickings are rich, police protection non-existent, and a man can dicker without being hampered by finicky regulations.

Ship's history alleged that the original *Sisu* had been built on Terra and that the first Captain Krausa had been born there, a (whisper it) fraki. But that was six ships ago and ship's history was true in essence, rather than fiddlin' fact. The *Sisu* whose steel now protected the blood was registered out of New Finlandia, Shiva III . . . another port she had never visited but whose fees were worth paying in order to have legal right to go about her occasions whenever, in pursuit of profit, *Sisu* went inside the globe of civilization. Shiva III was very understanding of the needs of Free Traders, not fussy about inspections, reports, and the like as long as omissions were repaired by paying penalties; many ships found her registration convenient.

On Finster Thorby learned another method of trading. The native fraki, known to science by a pseudo-Latin name and called "Those confounded slugs!" by the People, live in telepathic symbiosis with lemur-like creatures possessed of delicate, many-boned hands—"telepathy" is a conclusion; it is believed that the slow, monstrous, dominant creatures supply the brains and the lemuroids the manipulation.

The planet offers beautifully carved gem stones, raw copper, and a weed from which is derived an alkaloid used in psychotherapy. What else it could supply is a matter of conjecture; the natives have neither speech nor writing, communication is difficult.

This occasions the method of trading new to Thorby—the silent auction invented by the trading Phoenicians when the shores of Africa ran beyond the known world.

Around *Sisu* in piles were placed what the traders had to offer: heavy metals the natives needed, everlasting clocks they had learned to need, and trade goods the Family hoped to teach them to need. Then the humans went inside.

Thorby said to Senior Clerk Arly Krausa-Drotar, "We just leave that stuff lying around? If you did that on Jubbul, it would disappear as you turned your back."

"Didn't you see them rig the top gun this morning?"

"I was down in the lower hold."

"It's rigged and manned. These creatures have no morals

but they're smart. They'll be as honest as a cashier with the boss watching."

"What happens now?"

"We wait. They look over the goods. After a while . . . a day, maybe two . . . they pile stuff by our piles. We wait. Maybe they make their piles higher. Maybe they shift things around and offer us something else—and possibly we have outsmarted ourselves and missed something we would like through holding out. Or maybe we take one of our piles and split it into two, meaning we like the stuff but not the price.

"Or maybe we don't want it at any price. So we move our piles close to something they have offered that we do like. But we still don't touch their stuff; we wait.

"Eventually nobody has moved anything in quite a while. So, where the price suits us, we take in what they offer and leave our stuff. They come and take our offering away. We take in any of our own stuff where the price isn't right; they take away the stuff we turn down.

"But that doesn't end it. Now both sides know what the other one wants and what he will pay. They start making the offers; we start bidding with what we know they will accept. More deals are made. When we are through this second time, we have unloaded anything they want for stuff of theirs that we want at prices satisfactory to both. No trouble. I wonder if we do better on planets where we can talk."

"Yes, but doesn't this waste a lot of time?"

"Know anything we've got more of?"

The slow-motion auction moved without a hitch on goods having established value; deals were spottier on experimental offerings—gadgets which had seemed a good buy on Losian mostly failed to interest the Finstera. Six gross of folding knives actually intended for Woolamurra brought high prices. But the star item was not properly goods of any sort.

Grandmother Krausa, although bedfast, occasionally insisted on being carried on inspection tours; somebody always suffered. Shortly before arrival at Finster her ire had centered on nursery and bachelor quarters. In the first her eye lit on a stack of lurid picture books. She ordered them confiscated; they were "fraki trash."

The bachelors were inspected when word had gone out that she intended to hit only nursery, purdah, and galley; Grandmother saw their bunkies before they could hide their pin-up pictures.

Grandmother was shocked! Not only did pin-up pictures follow comic books, but a search was made for the magazines from which they had been clipped. The contraband was sent to auxiliary engineering, there to give up identities into elemental particles.

The Supercargo saw them there and got an idea; they joined the offerings outside the ship.

Strangely carved native jewels appeared beside the waste paper—chrysoberyl and garnet and opal and quartz.

The Supercargo blinked at the gauds and sent word to the Captain.

The booklets and magazines were redistributed, each as a separate offering. More jewels—

Finally each item was broken down into pages; each sheet was placed alone. An agreement was reached: one brightly colored sheet, one jewel. At that point bachelors who had managed to hide cherished pin-ups found patriotism and instinct for trade out-weighing possessiveness—after all they could restock at the next civilized port. The nursery was combed for more adventure comics.

For the first time in history comic books and pin-up magazines brought many times their weights in fine jewelry.

Thoth IV was followed by Woolamurra and each jump zig-zagged closer to the coming Great Gathering of the People; the ship was seized with carnival fever. Crew members were excused from work to practice on musical instruments, watches were rearranged to permit quartets to sing together, a training table was formed for athletes and they were excused from all watches save battle stations in order to train themselves into exhausted sleep. Headaches and tempers developed over plans for hospitality fit to support the exalted pride of *Sisu*.

Long messages flitted through n-space and the Chief Engineer protested the scandalous waste of power with sharp comments on the high price of tritium. But the Chief Officer cheerfully okayed the charge vouchers. As the time approached, she developed a smile that creased her wrinkles in unaccustomed directions, as if she knew something but wasn't talking. Twice Thorby caught her smiling at him and it worried him; it was better not to catch Grandmother's attention. He had had her full attention once lately and had not enjoyed it—he had been honored by eating with her, for having burned a raider.

The bogie had appeared on *Sisu's* screens during the lift from Finster—an unexpected place to be attacked since there was not much traffic there. The alarm had come only four hours out, when *Sisu* had attained barely 5% of speed-of-light and had no hope of running for it.

The matter landed in Thorby's lap; the portside computer was disabled—it had a "nervous breakdown" and the ship's electronics men had been sweating over it since jump. Thorby's nephew Jeri had returned to astrogation, the new trainee having qualified on the long jump from Losian—he was a stripling in whom Thorby had little confidence, but Thorby did not argue when Jeri decided that Kenan Drotar was ready for a watch even though he had never experienced a "real one." Jeri was anxious to go back to the control room for two reasons, status, and an unmentioned imponderable: the computer room was where Jeri had served with his missing kid sister.

So when the raider popped up, it was up to Thorby.

He felt shaky when he first started to test the problem, being acutely aware that the portside computer was out. The greatest comfort to a firecontrolman is faith in the superman abilities of the team on the other side, a feeling of "Well, even if I goof, those bulging brains will nail him," while that team is thinking the same thing. It helps to produce all-important relaxation.

This time Thorby did not have that spiritual safety net. Nor any other. The Finstera are not a spacefaring people; there was no possibility that the bogie would be identified as theirs. Nor could he be a trader; he had too many gravities in his tail. Nor a Hegemonic Guard; Finster was many light-years outside civilization. Thorby knew with sick certainty that sometime in the next hour his guesses must produce an answer; he must launch and hit—or shortly thereafter he would be a slave again and all his family with him.

It spoiled his timing, it slowed his thoughts.

But presently he forgot the portside computer, forgot the Family, forgot even the raider as such. The raider's movements became just data pouring into his board and the problem something he had been trained to do. His teammate slammed in and strapped himself into the other chair while General Quarters was still clanging, demanded to know the score. Thorby didn't hear him, nor did he hear the clanging stop. Jeri came in thereafter, having been sent down by the Captain; Thorby never saw him. Jeri motioned the youngster out of the twin seat, got into it himself, noted that the switch had Thorby's board in control, did not touch it. Without speaking he glanced over Thorby's setup and began working alternate solutions, ready to back him up by slapping the selector switch as soon as Thorby launched and then launch again, differently. Thorby never noticed.

Presently Krausa's strong bass came over the squawk line. "Starboard tracker . . . can I assist you by maneuvering?"

Thorby never heard it. Jeri glanced at him and answered, "I do not advise it, Captain."

"Very well."

The Senior Portside Firecontrolman, in gross violation of regulations, came in and watched the silent struggle, sweat greasing his face. Thorby did not know it. Nothing existed but knobs, switches, and buttons, all extensions of his nervous system. He became possessed of an overwhelming need to sneeze—repressed it without realizing it.

Thorby made infinitesimal adjustments up to the last moment, then absent-mindedly touched the button that told the computer to launch as the projected curve maximized. Two heartbeats later an atomic missile was on its way.

Jeri reached for the selector switch—stopped as he saw Thorby go into frenzied activity, telling his board to launch again on the assumption that the target had cut power. Then incoming data stopped as the ship went blind. Paralysis hit them.

Post-analysis showed that the paralyzing beam was on them seventy-one seconds. Jeri came out of it when it ceased; he saw Thorby looking dazedly at his board . . . then become violently active as he tried to work a new solution based on the last data.

Jeri put a hand on him. "The run is over, Thorby."

"Huh?"

"You got him. A sweet run. Mata would be proud of you."

Sisu was blind for a day, while repairs were made in her n-space eyes. The Captain continued to boost; there was nothing else to do. But presently she could see again and two days later she plunged into the comforting darkness of multi-space. The dinner in Thorby's honor was that night.

Grandmother made the usual speech, giving thanks that the Family was again spared, and noting that the son of *Sisu* beside her was the instrument of that happy but eminently deserved outcome. Then she lay back and gobbled her food, with her daughter-in-law hovering over her.

Thorby did not enjoy the honor. He had no clear recollection of the run; it felt as if he were being honored by mistake. He had been in semi-shock afterwards, then his imagination started working.

They were only pirates, he knew that. Pirates and slavers, they had tried to steal *Sisu*, had meant to enslave the Family. Thorby had hated slavers before he could remember—nothing so impersonal as the institution of slavery, he hated slavers in his baby bones before he knew the word.

He was sure that Pop approved of him; he knew that Pop, gentle as he was, would have shortened every slaver in the Galaxy without a tear.

Nevertheless Thorby did not feel happy. He kept thinking about a live ship—suddenly all dead, gone forever in a burst of radiance. Then he would look at his forefinger and wonder. He was caught in the old dilemma of the man with unintegrated values, who eats meat but would rather somebody else did the butchering.

When the dinner in his honor arrived he was three nights short on sleep and looked it. He pecked at his food.

Midway in the meal he became aware that Grandmother was glaring; he promptly spilled food on his dress jacket. "Welll" she snarled. "Have a nice nap?"

"Uh, I'm sorry, Grandmother. Did you speak to me?"

He caught his Mother's warning look but it was too late; Grandmother was off. "I was waiting for *you* to say something to *me!*"

"Uh ... it's a nice day."

"I had not noticed that it was unusual. It rarely rains in space."

"I mean it's a nice party. Yes, a real nice party. Thank you for giving it, Grandmother."

"That's better. Young man, it is customary, when a gentleman dines with a lady, to offer her polite conversation. This may not be the custom among fraki, but it is invariable among People."

"Yes, Grandmother. Thank you, Grandmother."

"Let's start again. It's a nice party, yes. We try to make everyone feel equal, while recognizing the merits of each. It is gratifying to have a chance—at last—to join with our Family in noting a virtue in you ... one commendable if not exceptional. Congratulations. Now it's your turn."

Thorby slowly turned purple.

She sniffed and said, "What are you doing to get ready for the Gathering?"

"Uh, I don't know, Grandmother. You see, I don't sing, or play, or dance—and the only games I know are chess and spat ball and ... well, I've never seen a Gathering. I don't know what they're like."

"Hmmph! So you haven't."

Thorby felt guilty. He said, "Grandmother . . . you must have been to lots of Gatherings. Would you tell me about them?"

That did it. She relaxed and said in hushed voice, "They don't have the Gatherings nowadays that they had when I was a girl . . ." Thorby did not have to speak again, other than sounds of awed interest. Long after the rest were waiting for Grandmother's permission to rise, she was saying, ". . . and I had my choice of a hundred ships, let me tell you. I was a pert young thing, with a tiny foot and a saucy nose, and my Grandmother got offers for me throughout the People. But I knew *Sisu* was for me and I stood up to her. Oh, I was a lively one! Dance all night and as fresh for the games next day as a—"

While it was not a merry occasion, it was not a failure.

Since Thorby had no talent he became an actor.

Aunt Athena Krausa-Fogarth, Chief of Commissary and superlative cook, had the literary disease in its acute form; she had written a play. It was the life of the first Captain Krausa, showing the sterling nobility of the Krausa line. The first Krausa had been a saint with heart of steel. Disgusted with the evil ways of fraki, he had built *Sisu* (single-handed), staffed it with his wife (named Fogarth in draft, changed to Grandmother's maiden name before the script got to her; and with their remarkable children. As the play ends they jump off into space, to spread culture and wealth through the Galaxy.

Thorby played the first Krausa. He was dumbfounded, having tried out because he was told to. Aunt Athena seemed almost as surprised; there was a catch in her voice when she announced his name. But Grandmother seemed pleased. She showed up for rehearsals and made suggestions which were happily adopted.

The star playing opposite Thorby was Loeen Garcia, late of *El Nido*. He had not become chummy with Mata's exchange; he had nothing against her but had not felt like it. But he found Loeen easy to know. She was a dark, soft beauty, with an intimate manner. When Thorby was required to ignore taboo and *kiss* her, in front of Grandmother and everybody, he blew his lines.

But he tried. Grandmother snorted in disgust. "What are you trying to do! Bite her? And don't let go as if she were radioactive. She's your wife, stupid. You've just carried her into your ship. You're alone with her, you love her. Now do it . . . no, no, no! Athena!"

Thorby looked wildly around. It did not help to catch sight of Fritz with eyes on the overhead, a beatific smile on his face.

"Athena! Come here, Daughter, and show this damp young hulk how a woman should be kissed. Kiss him yourself and then have him try again. Places, everyone."

Aunt Athena, twice Thorby's age, did not upset him so much. He complied clumsily with her instructions, then managed to kiss Loeen without falling over her feet.

It must have been a good play; it satisfied Grandmother. She looked forward to seeing it at the Gathering.

But she died on Woolamurra.

Chapter 13

WOOLAMURRA IS A lush pioneer planet barely inside the Terran Hegemony; it was *Sisu's* last stop before diving deeper for the Gathering. Rich in food and raw materials, the fraki were anxious to buy manufactured articles. *Sisu* sold out of Losian artifacts and disposed of many Finsteran jewels. But Woolamurra offered little which would bring a profit and money was tight in terms of power metal—Woolamurra had not prospected much and was anxious to keep what radioactives it had for its infant industry.

So *Sisu* accepted a little uranium and a lot of choice meats and luxury foods. *Sisu* always picked up gourmet delicacies; this time she stocked tons more than the Family could consume, but valuable for swank at the Gathering.

The balance was paid in tritium and deuterium. A hydrogen-isotopes plant is maintained there for Hegemonic ships but it will sell to others. *Sisu* had last been able to fuel at Jubbul—Losian ships use a different nuclear reaction.

Thorby was taken dirtside by his Father several times in New Melbourne, the port. The local language is System English, which Krausa understood, but the fraki spoke it with clipped haste and an odd vowel shift; Captain Krausa found it baffling. It did not sound strange to Thorby; it was as if he'd heard it before. So Krausa took him to help out.

This day they went out to complete the fuel transaction and sign a waiver required for private sales. The commercial tenders accepted by *Sisu* had to be certified by the central bank, then be taken to the fuel plant. After papers were stamped and fees paid, the Captain sat and chatted with the director. Krausa could be friendly with a fraki on terms of complete equality, never hinting at the enormous social difference between them.

While they chatted, Thorby worried. The fraki was talking about Woolamurra. "Any cobber with strong arms and enough brain to hold his ears apart can go outback and make a fortune."

"No doubt," agreed the Captain. "I've seen your beef animals. Magnificent."

Thorby agreed. Woolamurra might be short on pavement, arts, and plumbing; the planet was bursting with opportunity. Besides that, it was a pleasant, decent world, comfortably loose. It matched Doctor Mader's recipe: "—wait until your ship calls at a planet that is democratic, free, and human . . . then run!"

Life in *Sisu* had become more pleasant even though he was now conscious of the all-enveloping, personally-restricting quality of life with the Family. He was beginning to enjoy being an actor; it was fun to hold the stage. He had even learned to handle the clinch in a manner to win from Grandmother a smile; furthermore, even though it was play-acting, Loeen was a pleasant armful. She would kiss him and murmur: "My husband! My noble husband! We will roam the Galaxy together."

It gave Thorby goose bumps. He decided that Loeen was a great actress.

They became quite friendly. Loeen was curious about what a firecontrolman did, so under the eye of Great Aunt Tora, Thorby showed her the computer room. She looked prettily confused. "Just what is n-space? Length, breadth, and thickness are all you see . . . how about these other dimensions?"

"By logic. You see four dimensions . . . those three, and time. Oh, you can't *see* a year, but you can measure it."

"Yes, but how can logic—"

"Easy as can be. What is a point? A location in space. But suppose there isn't any space, not even the four ordinary dimensions. No space. Is a point conceivable?"

"Well, I'm thinking about one."

"Not without thinking about space. If you think about a point, you think about it *somewhere*. If you have a line, you can imagine a point somewhere on it. But a point is just a location and if there isn't anywhere for it to be located, it's nothing. Follow me?"

Great Aunt Tora interrupted. "Could you children continue this in the lounge? My feet hurt."

"Sorry, Great Aunt. Will you take my arm?"

Back in the lounge Thorby said, "Did you soak up that about a point needing a line to hold it?"

"Uh, I think so. Take away its location and it isn't there at all."

"Think about a line. If it isn't in a surface, does it exist?"

"Uh, that's harder."

"If you get past that, you've got it. A line is an ordered sequence of points. But where does the order come from? From being in a surface. If a line isn't held by a surface, then it could collapse into itself. It hasn't any width. You wouldn't even know it had collapsed . . . nothing to compare it with. But every point would be just as close to every other point, no 'ordered sequence.' Chaos. Still with me?"

"Maybe."

"A point needs a line. A line needs a surface. A surface has to be part of solid space, or its structure vanishes. And a solid needs hyperspace to hold it . . . and so on up. Each dimension demands one higher, or geometry ceases to exist. The universe ceases to exist." He slapped the table. "But it's here, so we know that multi-space still functions . . . even though we can't see it, any more than we can see a passing second."

"But where does it all stop?"

"It can't. Endless dimensions."

She shivered. "It scares me."

"Don't worry. Even the Chief Engineer only has to fret about the first dozen dimensions. And—look, you know we turn inside out when the ship goes irrational. Can you feel it?"

"No. And I'm not sure I believe it."

"It doesn't matter, because we aren't equipped to feel it. It can happen while eating soup and you never spill a drop, even though the soup turns inside out, too. So far as we are concerned it's just a mathematical concept, like the square root of minus one—which we tangle with when we pass speed-of-light. It's that way with all multi-dimensionality. You don't have to feel it, see it, understand it; you just have to work logical symbols about it. But it's real, if 'real' means anything. Nobody has ever seen an electron. Nor a thought. You can't see a thought, you can't measure, weigh, nor taste it—but thoughts are the most real things in the Galaxy." Thorby was quoting Baslim.

She looked at him admiringly. "You must be awfully brainy, Thorby. 'Nobody ever saw a thought.' I like that."

Thorby graciously accepted the praise.

When he went to his bunkie, he found Fritz reading in bed. Thorby was feeling the warm glow that comes from giving the word to an eager mind. "Hi, Fritz! Studying? Or wasting your youth?"

"Hi. Studying. Studying art."

Thorby glanced over. "Don't let Grandmother catch you."

"Got to have something to trade those confounded slugs next time we touch Finster." Woolamurra was "civilization"; the bachelors had replenished their art. "You look as if you had squeezed a bonus out of a Losian. What clicks?"

"Oh, just talking with Loeen. I was introducing her to n-space . . . and darn if she didn't catch on fast."

Fritz looked judicial. "Yes, she's bright." He added, "When is Grandmother posting the banns?"

"What are you talking about!"

"No banns?"

"Don't be silly."

"Mmm . . . you find her good company. Bright, too. Want to know how bright?"

"Well?"

"So bright that she taught in *El Nido*'s school. Her specialty was math. Multi-dimensional geometry, in fact."

"I don't believe it!"

"Happens I transcribed her record. But ask her."

"I shall! Why isn't she teaching math here?"

"Ask Grandmother. Thorby, my skinny and retarded brother—I think you were dropped on your head. But, sorry as you are, I love you for the fumbling grace with which you wipe drool off your chin. Want a hint from an older and wiser head?"

"Go ahead. You will anyhow."

"Thanks. Loeen is a fine girl and it might be fun to solve equations with her for life. But I hate to see a man leap into a sale before he checks the market. If you just hold off through this next jump, you'll find that the People have several young girls. Several thousand."

"I'm not looking for a wife!"

"Tut, tut! It's a man's duty. But wait for the Gathering, and we'll shop. Now shut up, I want to study art."

"Who's talking?"

Thorby did not ask Loeen what she had done in *El Nido*, but it did open his eyes to the fact that he was playing the leading role in a courtship without having known it. It scared him. Doctor Mader's words haunted his sleep "—before Grandmother decides to marry you to someone . . . if you wait that long—you're lost!"

Father and the Woolamurra official gossiped while Thorby fretted. Should he leave *Sisu*? If he wasn't willing to be a trader all his life he had to get out while still a bachelor. Of course, he could stall—look at Fritz. Not that he had anything against Loeen, even if she had made a fool of him.

But if he was going to leave—and he had doubts as to whether he could stand the custom-ridden monotonous life forever—then Woolamurra was the best chance he might have in years. No castes, no guilds, no poverty, no immigration laws—why, they even accepted mutants! Thorby had seen hexadactyls, hirsutes, albinos, lupine ears, giants, and other changes. If a man could work, Woolamurra could use him.

What should he do? Say, "Excuse me, please," leave the room—then start running? Stay lost until *Sisu* jumped? He couldn't do *that*! Not to father, not to *Sisu*; he owed them too much.

What, then? Tell Grandmother he wanted off? If she let him off, it would probably be some chilly spot between stars! Grandmother would regard ingratitude to *Sisu* as the unforgivable sin.

And besides . . . The Gathering was coming. He felt a great itch to see it. And it wouldn't be right to walk out on the play. He was not consciously rationalizing; although stage-struck, he still thought that he did not want to play the hero in a melodrama—whereas he could hardly wait.

So he avoided his dilemma by postponing it.

Captain Krausa touched his shoulder. "We're leaving."

"Oh. Sorry, Father. I was thinking."

"Keep it up, it's good exercise. Good-by, Director, and thanks. I look forward to seeing you next time we call."

"You won't find me, Captain. I'm going to line me out a station, as far as eye can reach. Land of me own. If you ever get tired of steel decks, there's room here for you. And your boy."

Captain Krausa's face did not show his revulsion. "Thanks. But we wouldn't know which end of a plow to grab. We're traders."

"Each cat his own rat."

When they were outside Thorby said, "What did he mean, Father? I've seen cats, but what is a rat?"

"A rat is a sorci, only thinner and meaner. He meant that each man has his proper place."

"Oh." They walked in silence. Thorby was wondering if he had as yet found his proper place.

Captain Krausa was wondering the same thing. There was a ship just beyond *Sisu;* its presence was a reproach. It was a mail courier, an official Hegemonic vessel, crewed by Guardsmen. Baslim's words rang accusingly in his mind: "—when opportunity presents, I ask that you deliver him to the commander of any Hegemonic military vessel."

This was not a "military" vessel. But that was a quibble; Baslim's intentions were plain and this ship would serve. Debts must be paid. Unfortunately Mother interpreted the words strictly. Oh, he knew why; she was determined to show off the boy at the Gathering. She intended to squeeze all possible status out of the fact that *Sisu* had paid the People's debt. Well, that was understandable.

But it wasn't fair to the boy!

Or was it? For his own reasons Krausa was anxious to take the lad to the Gathering. He was certain now that Thorby's ancestry must be of the People—and in the Commodore's files he expected to prove it.

On the other hand— He had agreed with Mother over Mata Kingsolver; a minx should not be allowed to back a taboo lad into a corner, better to ship her at once. But didn't Mother think he could see what she was up to now?

He wouldn't permit it! By *Sisu*, he wouldn't! The boy was too young and he would forbid it . . . at least until he proved that the boy was of the People, in which case the debt to Baslim was paid.

But that mail courier out there whispered that he was being as unwilling to acknowledge honest debt as he was accusing Mother of being.

But it was for the lad's own good!

What is justice?

Well, there was one fair way. Take the lad and have a showdown with Mother. Tell the lad *all* of Baslim's message. Tell him that he could take passage in the courier to the central worlds, tell him how to go about finding his family. But tell him, too, that he, the Krausa, believed that Thorby was of the People and that the possibility could and should be checked first. Yes, and tell him bluntly that Mother was trying to tie him down with a wife. Mother would scream and quote the Laws—but this was not in the Chief Officer's jurisdiction; Baslim had laid the injunction on *him.* And besides, it was right; the boy himself should choose.

Spine stiffened but quaking, Captain Krausa strode back to face his Mother.

As the hoist delivered them up the Deck Master was waiting. "Chief Officer's respects and she wishes to see the Captain, sir."

"That's a coincidence," Krausa said grimly. "Come, Son. We'll both see her."

"Yes, Father."

They went around the passageway, reached the Chief Officer's cabin. Krausa's wife was outside. "Hello, my dear. The Decker said that Mother had sent for me."

"I sent for you."

"He got the message garbled. Whatever it is, make it quick, please. I am anxious to see Mother anyhow."

"He did not get it garbled; the Chief Officer did send for you."

"Eh?"

"Captain, your Mother is dead."

Krausa listened with blank face, then it sank in and he slapped the door aside, ran to his Mother's bed, threw himself down, clutched the tiny, wasted form laid out in state, and began to weep racking, terrible sounds, the grief of a man steeled against emotion, who cannot handle it when he breaks.

Thorby watched with awed distress, then went to his bunkie and thought. He tried to figure out why he felt so badly. He had not loved Grandmother—he hadn't even *liked* her.

Then why did he feel so lost?

It was almost like when Pop died. He loved Pop—but not her.

He found that he was not alone; the entire ship was in shock. There was not one who could remember, or imagine, *Sisu* without her. She *was* Sisu. Like the undying fire that moved the ship, Grandmother had been an unfailing force, dynamic, indispensable, basic. Now suddenly she was gone.

She had taken her nap as usual, grumbling because Woolamurra's day fitted their schedule so poorly—typical fraki inefficiency. But she had gone to sleep with iron discipline that had adapted itself to a hundred time schedules.

When her daughter-in-law went to wake her, she could not be waked.

Her bedside scratch pad held many notes: Speak to Son about this. Tell Tora to do that. Jack up the C.E. about temperature control. Go over banquet menus with Athena. Rhoda Krausa tore out the page, put it away for reference, straightened her, then ordered the Deck Master to notify her husband.

The Captain was not at dinner. Grandmother's couch had been removed; the Chief Officer sat where it had been. In the Captain's absence the Chief Officer signalled the Chief Engineer; he offered the prayer for the dead, she gave the responses. Then they ate in silence. No funeral would be held until Gathering.

The Chief Officer stood up presently. "The Captain wishes to announce," she said quietly, "that he thanks those who attempted to call on him. He will be available tomorrow." She paused. " 'The atoms come out of space and to space they return. The spirit of *Sisu* goes on.' "

Thorby suddenly no longer felt lost.

Chapter 14

THE GREAT GATHERING was even more than Thorby had imagined. Mile after mile of ships, more than eight hundred bulky Free Traders arranged in concentric ranks around a circus four miles across . . . *Sisu* in the innermost circle—which seemed to please Thorby's Mother—then more ships than Thorby knew existed: *Kraken, Deimos, James B. Quinn, Firefly, Bon Marché, Dom Pedro, Cee Squared, Omega, El Nido*—Thorby resolved to see how Mata was doing—*Saint Christopher, Vega, Vega Prime, Galactic Banker, Romany Lass* . . . Thorby made note to get a berthing chart . . . *Saturn, Chiang, Country Store, Joseph Smith, Aloha* . . .

There were too many. If he visited ten ships a day, he might see most of them. But there was too much to do and see; Thorby gave up the notion.

Inside the circle was a great temporary stadium, larger than the New Amphitheatre at Jubbulpore. Here elections would be held, funerals and weddings, athletic contests, entertainments, concerts—Thorby recalled that *Spirit of Sisu* would be performed there and trembled with stage fright.

Between stadium and ships was a midway—booths, rides, games, exhibits educational and entertaining, one-man pitches, dance halls that never closed, displays of engineering gadgets, fortunetellers, gambling for prizes and cash, open-air bars, soft drink counters offering anything from berry juices of the Pleiades worlds to a brown brew certified to be the ancient, authentic Terran *Coca-Cola* as licensed for bottling on Hekate.

When he saw this maelstrom Thorby felt that he had wandered into Joy Street—bigger, brighter, and seven times busier than Joy Street with the fleet in. This was the fraki's chance to turn a fairly honest credit while making suckers of the shrewdest businessmen in the Galaxy; this was the day, with the lid off and the Trader without his guards up —they'd sell you your own hat if you laid it on the counter.

Fritz took Thorby dirtside to keep him out of trouble, although Fritz's sophistication was hardly complete, since he had seen just one Great Gathering. The Chief Officer lectured the young people before granting hit-dirt, reminding them that *Sisu* had a reputation for proper behavior, and then issued each a hundred credits with a warning that it must last throughout the Gathering.

Fritz advised Thorby to cache most of it. "When we go broke, we can sweet-talk Father out of pocket money. But it's not smart to take it all."

Thorby agreed. He was not surprised when he felt the touch of a pickpocket; he grabbed a wrist to find out what he had landed.

First he recovered his wallet. Then he looked at the thief. He was a dirty-faced young fraki who reminded Thorby poignantly of Ziggie, except that this kid had two hands. "Better luck next time," he consoled him. "You don't have the touch yet."

The kid seemed about to cry. Thorby started to turn him loose, then said, "Fritz, check your wallet."

Fritz did so, it was gone. "Well, I'll be—"

"Hand it over, kid."

"I didn't take it! You let me go!"

"Cough up . . . before I unscrew your skull."

The kid surrendered Fritz's wallet; Thorby turned him loose. Fritz said, "Why did you do that? I was trying to spot a cop."

"That's why."

"Huh? Talk sense."

"I tried to learn that profession once. It's not easy."

"You? A poor joke, Thorby."

"Remember me? The ex-fraki, the beggar's boy? That clumsy attempt to equalize the wealth made me homesick. Fritz, where I come from, a pickpocket has status. I was merely a beggar."

"Don't let Mother hear that."

"I shan't. But I am what I am and I know what I was and I don't intend to forget. I never learned the pickpocket art, but I was a good beggar, I was taught by the best. My Pop. Baslim the Cripple. I'm not ashamed of him and all the Laws of *Sisu* can't make me."

"I did not intend to make you ashamed," Fritz said quietly.

They walked on, savoring the crowd and the fun. Presently Thorby said, "Shall we try that wheel? I've spotted the gimmick."

Fritz shook his head. "Look at those so-called prizes."

"Okay. I was interested in how it was rigged."

"Thorby—"

"Yeah? Why the solemn phiz?"

"You know who Baslim the Cripple really was?"

Thorby considered it. "He was my Pop. If he had wanted me to know anything else, he would have told me."

"Mmm . . . I suppose so."

"But you know?"

"Some."

"Uh, I am curious about one thing. What was the debt that made Grandmother willing to adopt me?"

"Uh, 'I have said enough.' "

"You know best."

"Oh, confound it, the rest of the People know! It's bound to come up at this Gathering."

"Don't let me talk you into anything, Fritz."

"Well . . . look, Baslim wasn't always a beggar."

"So I long since figured out."

"What he was is not for me to say. A lot of People kept his secret for years; nobody has told me that it is all right to talk. But one fact is no secret among the People . . . and you're one of the People. A long time ago, Baslim saved a whole Family. The People have never forgotten it. The *Hansea*, it was . . . the *New Hansea* is sitting right over there. The one with the shield painted on her. I can't tell you more, because a taboo was placed on it—the thing was so shameful that we never talk about it. I have said enough. But you could go over to the *New Hansea* and ask to look through her old logs. If you identified yourself—who you are in relation to Baslim—they couldn't refuse. Though the Chief Officer might go to her cabin afterwards and have weeping hysterics."

"Hmm . . . I don't want to know badly enough to make a lady cry. Fritz? Let's try this ride." So they did—and after speeds in excess of light and accelerations up to one hundred gravities, Thorby found a roller coaster too exciting. He almost lost his lunch.

A Great Gathering, although a time of fun and renewed friendships, has its serious purposes. In addition to funerals, memorial services for lost ships, weddings, and much transferring of young females, there is also business affecting the whole People and, most important, the paramount matter of buying ships.

Hekate has the finest shipyards in the explored Galaxy. Men and women have children; ships spawn, too. *Sisu* was gravid with people, fat with profit in uranium and thorium; it was time that the Family split up. At least a third of the families had the same need to trade wealth for living room; fraki shipbrokers were rubbing their hands, mentally figuring commissions. Starships do not sell like cold drinks; shipbrokers and salesmen often live on dreams. But perhaps a hundred ships would be sold in a few weeks.

Some would be new ships from the yards of Galactic Transport, Ltd., daughter corporation of civilization-wide Galactic Enterprises, or built by Space Engineers Corporation, or Hekate Ships, or Propulsion, Inc., or Hascomb & Sons—all giants in the trade. But there was cake for everyone. The broker who did not speak for a builder might have an exclusive on a second-hand ship, or a line to a rumor of a hint that the owners of a suitable ship might listen if the price was right—a man could make a fortune if he kept his eyes open and his ear to the ground. It was a time to by-pass mails and invest in expensive n-space messages; the feast would soon be over.

A family in need of space had two choices: either buy another ship, split and become two families, or a ship could join with another in purchasing a third, to be staffed from each. Twinning gave much status. It was proof that the family which managed it were master traders, able to give their kids a start in the world without help. But in practice the choice usually dwindled to one: join with another ship and split the expense, and even then it was often necessary to pledge all three ships against a mortgage on the new one.

It had been thirty years since *Sisu* had split up. She had had three decades of prosperity; she should have been able to twin. But ten years ago at the last Great Gathering Grandmother had caused *Sisu* to guarantee along with parent ships the mortgage against a ship newly born. The new ship gave a banquet honoring *Sisu*, then jumped off into dark and never came back. Space is vast. Remember her name at Gathering.

The result was that *Sisu* paid off one-third of forty percent of the cost of the lost ship; the blow hurt. The parent ships would reimburse *Sisu*—debts are always paid—but they had left the last Gathering lean from having spawned; coughing up each its own liability had left them skin and bones. You don't dun a sick man; you wait.

Grandmother had not been stupid. The parent ships, *Caesar Augustus* and *Dupont*, were related to *Sisu;* one takes care of one's own. Besides, it was good business; a trader unwilling to lend credit will discover that he has none. As it was, *Sisu* could write a draft on any Free Trader anywhere and be certain that it would be honored.

But it left *Sisu* with less cash than otherwise at a time when the Family should split.

Captain Krausa hit dirt the first day and went to the Commodore's Flag, *Norbert Wiener*. His wife stayed aboard but was not idle; since her succession to Chief Officer, she hardly slept. Today she worked at her desk, stopping for face-to-face talks with other chief officers via the phone exchange set up by city services for the Gathering. When her lunch was fetched, she motioned to put it down; it was still untouched when her husband returned. He came in and sat down wearily. She was reading a slide rule and checked her answer on a calculator before she spoke. "Based on a Hascomb F-two ship, the mortgage would run just over fifty percent."

"Rhoda, you know *Sisu* can't finance a ship unassisted."

"Don't be hasty, dear. Both *Gus* and *Dupont* would co-sign . . . in their case, it's the same as cash."

"If their credit will stretch."

"And *New Hansea* would jump at it—under the circum-stances—and—"

"Rhoda! You were young, two Gatherings ago, but you are aware that the debt lies equally on all . . . not just *Hansea*. That was unanimous."

"I was old enough to be your wife, Fjalar. Don't read the Laws to me. But *New Hansea* would jump at the chance . . . under a secrecy taboo binding till the end of time. Nevertheless the carrying charges would eat too much. Did you get to see a *Galactic Lambda?*"

"I don't need to; I've seen the specs. No legs."

"You men! I wouldn't call eighty gravities 'no legs.' "

"You would if you had to sit in the worry seat. *Lambda* class were designed for slow freight inside the Hegemonic sphere; that's all they're good for."

"You're too conservative, Fjalar."

"And I'll continue to be where safety of a ship is con-cerned."

"No doubt. And I'll have to find solutions that fit your prejudices. However, *Lambda* class is just a possibility. There is also you-know-which. She'll go cheap."

He frowned. "An unlucky ship."

"It will take powerful cleansing to get those bad thoughts out. But think of the price."

"It's more than bad thoughts in you-know-which-ship. I

never heard of a chief officer suiciding before. Or a captain going crazy. I'm surprised they got here."

"So am I. But she's here and she'll be up for sale. And any ship can be cleansed."

"I wonder."

"Don't be superstitious, dear. It's a matter of enough care with the rituals, which is my worry. However, you can forget the you-know-which-one. I think we'll split with another ship."

"I thought you were set on doing it alone?"

"I've merely been exploring our strength. But there are things more important than setting up a new ship single-handed."

"There certainly are! Power, a good weapons system, working capital, blooded officers in key spots—why, we can't man two ships. Take firecontrolmen alone. If—"

"Stop fretting. We could handle those. Fjalar, how would you like to be Deputy Commodore?"

He braked at full power. "Rhoda! Are you feverish?"

"No."

"There are dozens of skippers more likely to be tapped. I'll never be Commodore—and what's more, I don't want it."

"I may settle for Reserve Deputy, since Commodore Denbo intends to resign after the new deputy is elected. Never mind; you will be Commodore at the next Gathering."

"Preposterous!"

"Why are men so impractical? Fjalar, all you think about is your control room and business. If I hadn't kept pushing, you would never have reached deputy captain."

"Have you ever gone hungry?"

"I'm not complaining, dear. It was a great day for me when I was adopted by *Sisu*. But listen. We have favors coming from many sources, not just *Gus* and *Dupont*. Whatever ship we join with will help. I intend to leave the matter open until after election—and I've had tentative offers all morning, strong ships, well connected. And finally, there's *New Hansea*."

"What about *New Hansea?*"

"Timed properly, with the Hanseatics proposing your name, you'll be elected by acclamation."

"Rhoda!"

"You won't have to touch it. And neither will Thorby. You two will simply appear in public and be your charming, male, non-political selves. I'll handle it. By the way, it's too late to pull Loeen out of the play but I'm going to break that up fast. Your Mother did not see the whole picture. I want my sons married—but it is essential that Thorby *not* be married, nor paired off, until *after* the election. Now . . . did you go to the flagship?"

"Certainly."

"What ship was he born in? It could be important."

Krausa gave a sigh. "Thorby was not born of the People."

"What? Nonsense! You mean that identification is not certain. Mmm . . . which missing ships are possibilities?"

"I said he was not of the People! There is a not a ship missing, nor a child missing from a ship, which can be matched with his case. He would have to be much older, or much younger, than he is."

She shook her head. "I don't believe it."

"You mean you don't want to!"

"I *don't* believe it. He's People. You can tell it in his walk, his manner, his good mind, everything about him. Hmm . . . I'll look at the files myself."

"Go ahead. Since you don't believe *me.*"

"Now, Fjalar, I didn't say—"

"Oh, yes, you did. If I told you it was raining dirtside, and you didn't want rain, you—"

"Please, dear! You know it never rains this time of year on Hekate. I was just—"

"*Sky around us!*"

"There's no need to lose your temper. It doesn't become a captain."

"It doesn't become a captain to have his word doubted in his own ship, either!"

"I'm sorry, Fjalar." She went on quietly, "It won't hurt

152

to look. If I widened the search, or looked through unfiled material—you know how clerks are with deadfile data. Mmm . . . it would help if I knew who Thorby's parents were—before election. While I shan't permit him to marry before then, I might line up important support if it was assumed that immediately after, a wedding could be expec—"

"Rhoda."

"What, dear? The entire *Vega* group could be swayed, *if* a presumption could be established about Thorby's birth . . . *if* an eligible daughter of theirs—"

"Rhoda!"

"I was talking, dear."

"For a moment, I'll talk. The Captain. Wife, he's fraki blood. Furthermore, Baslim knew it . . . and laid a strict injunction on me to help him find his family. I had hoped—yes, and believed—that the files would show that Baslim was mistaken." He frowned and chewed his lip. "A Hegemonic cruiser is due here in two weeks. That ought to give you time to assure yourself that I can search files as well as any clerk."

"What do you mean?"

"Is there doubt? Debts are always paid . . . and there is one more payment due."

She stared. "Husband, are you out of your mind?"

"I don't like it any better than you do. He's not only a fine boy; he's the most brilliant tracker we've ever had."

"Trackers!" she said bitterly. "Who cares about that? Fjalar, if you think that I will permit one of my sons to be turned over to *fraki*—" She choked up.

"He *is* fraki."

"He is *not*. He is *Sisu*, just as I am. I was adopted, so was he. We are both *Sisu*, we will always be."

"Have it your way. I hope he will always be *Sisu* in his heart. But the last payment must be made."

"That debt was paid in full, long ago!"

"The ledger doesn't show it."

"Nonsense! Baslim wanted the boy returned to his fam-

153

ily. Some fraki family—if fraki have families. So we gave him a family—our own, clan and sept. Is that not better payment than some flea-bitten fraki litter? Or do you think so little of *Sisu?*"

She glared up at him, and the Krausa thought bitterly that there must be something to the belief that the pure blood of the People produced better brains. In dickering with fraki he never lost his temper. But Mother—and now Rhoda—could always put him in the wrong.

At least Mother, hard as she had been, had never asked the impossible. But Rhoda . . . well, Wife was new to the job. He said tensely, "Chief Officer, this injunction was laid on me personally, not on *Sisu.* I have no choice."

"So? Very well, Captain—we'll speak of it later. And now, with all respect to you, sir, I have work to do."

Thorby had a wonderful time at the Gathering but not as much fun as he expected; repeatedly Mother required him to help entertain chief officers of other ships. Often a visitor brought a daughter or granddaughter along and Thorby had to keep the girl busy while the elders talked. He did his best and even acquired facility in the half-insulting small talk of his age group. He learned something that he called dancing which would have done credit to any man with two left feet and knees that bent backwards. He could now put his arm around a girl when music called for it without chills and fever.

Mother's visitors quizzed him about Pop. He tried to be polite but it annoyed him that everyone knew more about Pop than he did—except the things that were important.

But it did seem that duty could be shared. Thorby realized that he was junior son, but Fritz was unmarried, too. He suggested that if Fritz were to volunteer, the favor could be returned later.

Fritz gave a raucous laugh. "What can you offer that can repay me for dirtside time at Gathering?"

"Well . . ."

"Precisely. Seriously, old knucklehead, Mother wouldn't

listen, even if I were insane enough to offer. She says you, she means you." Fritz yawned. "Man, am I dead! Little red-head off the *Saint Louis* wanted to dance all night. Get out and let me sleep before the banquet."

"Can you spare a dress jacket?"

"Do your own laundry. And cut the noise."

But on this morning one month after grounding Thorby was hitting dirt with Father, with no chance that Mother would change their minds; she was out of the ship. It was the Day of Remembrance. Services did not start until noon but Mother left early for something to do with the election tomorrow.

Thorby's mind was filled with other matters. The services would end with a memorial to Pop. Father had told him that he would coach him in what to do, but it worried him, and his nerves were not soothed by the fact that *Spirit of Sisu* would be staged that evening.

His nerves over the play had increased when he discovered that Fritz had a copy and was studying it. Fritz had said gruffly, "Sure, I'm learning your part! Father thought it would be a good idea in case you fainted or broke your leg. I'm not trying to steal your glory; it's intended to let you relax—if you can relax with thousands staring while you smooch Loeen."

"Well, could you?"

Fritz looked thoughtful. "I could try. Loeen looks cuddly. Maybe I should break your leg myself."

"Bare hands?"

"Don't tempt me. Thorby, this is just precaution, like having two trackers. But nothing less than a broken leg can excuse you from strutting your stuff."

Thorby and his Father left *Sisu* two hours before the services. Captain Krausa said, "We might as well enjoy ourselves. Remembrance is a happy occasion if you think of it the right way—but those seats are hard and it's going to be a long day."

"Uh, Father . . . just what is it I'll have to do when it comes time for Pop—for Baslim?"

"Nothing much. You sit up front during the sermon and give responses in the Prayer for the Dead. You know how, don't you?"

"I'm not sure."

"I'll write it out for you. As for the rest . . . well, you'll see me do the same for my Mother—your Grandmother. You watch and when it comes your turn, you do the same."

"All right, Father."

"Now let's relax."

To Thorby's surprise Captain Krausa took a slideway outside the Gathering, then whistled down a ground car. It seemed faster than those Thorby had seen on Jubbul and almost as frantic as the Losians. They reached the rail station with nothing more than an exchange of compliments between their driver and another, but the ride was so exciting that Thorby saw little of the City of Artemis.

He was again surprised when Father bought tickets. "Where are we going?"

"A ride in the country." The Captain glanced at his watch. "Plenty of time."

The monorail gave a fine sensation of speed. "How fast are we going, Father?"

"Two hundred kilometers an hour, at a guess." Krausa had to raise his voice.

"It seems faster."

"Fast enough to break your neck. That's as fast as a speed can be."

They rode for half an hour. The countryside was torn up by steel mills and factories for the great yards, but it was new and different; Thorby stared and decided that the Sargon's reserve was a puny enterprise compared with this. The station where they got off lay outside a long, high wall; Thorby could see space ships beyond it. "Where are we?"

"Military field. I have to see a man—and today there is just time." They walked toward a gate. Krausa stopped, looked around; they were alone. "Thorby—"

"Yes, Father?"

156

"Do you remember the message from Baslim you delivered to me?"

"Sir?"

"Can you repeat it?"

"Huh? Why, I don't know, Father. It's been a long time."

"Try it. Start in: 'To Captain Fjalar Krausa, master of Starship *Sisu*, from Baslim the Cripple: Greetings, old friend!—'"

" ' "Greetings, old friend," ' " Thorby repeated. " 'Greetings to your family, clan, and sib, and'—why, I understand it!"

"Of course," the Krausa said gently, "this is the Day of Remembrance. Go on."

Thorby went on. Tears started down his cheeks as he heard Pop's voice coming from his own throat: " '—and my humblest respects to your revered mother. I am speaking to you through the mouth of my adopted son. He does not understand Suomic'—oh, but I *do!*"

"Go on."

When Thorby reached: " 'I am already dead—' " he broke down. Krausa blew his nose vigorously, told him to proceed. Thorby managed to get to the end, though his voice was shaking. Then Krausa let him cry a moment before telling him sternly to wipe his face and brace up. "Son . . . you heard the middle part? You understood it?"

"Yes . . . uh, yes. I guess so."

"Then you know what I have to do."

"You mean . . . I have to leave *Sisu?*"

"What did Baslim say? 'When opportunity presents—' This is the first opportunity I've had . . . and I've had to squeeze to get it. It's almost certainly the last. Baslim didn't make me a gift of you, Son—just a loan. And now I must pay back the loan. You see that, don't you?"

"Uh . . . I guess so."

"Then let's get on with it." Krausa reached inside his jacket, pulled out a sheaf of bills and shoved them at Thorby. "Put this in your pocket. I would have made it more, but it was all I could draw without attracting your Mother's suspicions. Perhaps I can send you more before you jump."

Thorby held it without looking at it, although it was more money than he had ever touched before. "Father . . . you mean I've *already left Sisu?*"

Krausa had turned. He stopped. "Better so, Son. Good-bys are not comfort; only remembrance is a comfort. Besides, it has to be this way."

Thorby swallowed. "Yes, sir."

"Let's go."

They walked quickly toward the guarded gate. They were almost there when Thorby stopped. "Father . . . I don't want to go!"

Krausa looked at him without expression. "You don't have to."

"I thought you said I did have to?"

"No. The injunction laid on me was to deliver you and to pass on the message Baslim sent to me. But there my duty ends, my debt is paid. I won't order you to leave the Family. The rest was Baslim's idea . . . conceived, I am sure, with the best of intentions for your welfare. But whether or not you are obligated to carry out his wishes is something between you and Baslim. I can't decide it for you. Whatever debt you may or may not owe Baslim, it is separate from the debt the People owed to him."

Krausa waited while Thorby stood mute, trying to think. What had Pop expected of him? What had he told him to do? *"Can I depend on you? You won't goof off and forget it?"* Yes, but *what*, Pop? *"Don't burn any offerings . . . just deliver a message, and then one thing more: do whatever this man suggests."* Yes, Pop, but the man won't *tell* me!

Krausa said urgently, "We haven't much time. I have to get back. But, Son, whatever you decide, it's final. If you don't leave *Sisu* today, you won't get a second chance. I'm sure of that."

"It's the very last thing that I want from you, son . . . can I depend on you?" Pop said urgently, inside his head.

Thorby sighed. "I guess I have to, Father."

"I think so, too. Now let's hurry."

The gate pass office could not be hurried, especially as Captain Krausa, although identifying himself and son by ship's papers, declined to state his business with the commander of Guard Cruiser *Hydra* other than to say that it was "urgent and official."

But eventually they were escorted by a smart, armed fraki to the cruiser's hoist and turned over to another. They were handed along inside the ship and reached an office marked "Ship's Secretary—Enter Without Knocking." Thorby concluded that *Sisu* was smaller than he had thought and he had never seen so much polished metal in his life. He was rapidly regretting his decision.

The Ship's Secretary was a polite, scrubbed young man with the lace orbits of a lieutenant. He was also very firm. "I'm sorry, Captain, but you will have to tell me your business . . . if you expect to see the Commanding Officer."

Captain Krausa said nothing and sat tight.

The nice young man colored, drummed on his desk. He got up. "Excuse me a moment."

He came back and said tonelessly, "The Commanding Officer can give you five minutes." He led them into a larger office and left them. An older man was there, seated at a paper-heaped desk. He had his blouse off and showed no insignia of rank. He got up, put out his hand, and said, "Captain Krausa? Of Free Trader . . . *Seezoo*, is it? I'm Colonel Brisby, commanding."

"Glad to be aboard, Skipper."

"Glad to have you. How's business?" He glanced at Thorby. "One of your officers?"

"Yes and no."

"Eh?"

"Colonel? May I ask in what class you graduated?"

"What? Oh-Eight. Why do you ask?"

"I think you can answer that. This lad is Thorby Baslim, adopted son of Colonel Richard Baslim. The Colonel asked me to deliver him to you."

159

Chapter 15

"WHAT?"

"The name means something to you?"

"Of course it does." He stared at Thorby. "There's no resemblance."

" 'Adopted' I said. The Colonel adopted him on Jubbul."

Colonel Brisby closed the door. Then he said to Krausa, "Colonel Baslim is dead. Or 'missing and presumed dead,' these past two years."

"I know. The boy has been with me. I can report some details of the Colonel's death, if they are not known."

"You were one of his couriers?"

"Yes."

"You can prove it?"

"X three oh seven nine code FT."

"That can be checked. We'll assume it is for the moment. By what means do you identify . . . Thorby Baslim?"

Thorby did not follow the conversation. There was a buzzing in his ears, as if the tracker was being fed too much power, and the room was swelling and then growing smaller. He did figure out that this officer knew Pop, which was good . . . but what was this about Pop being a colonel? Pop was Baslim the Cripple, licensed mendicant under the mercy of . . . under the mercy . . .

Colonel Brisby told him sharply to sit down, which he was glad to do. Then the Colonel speeded up the air blower. He turned to Captain Krausa. "All right, I'm sold. I don't know what regulation I'm authorized to do it under . . . we are required to give assistance to 'X' Corps people, but this is not quite that. But I can't let Colonel Baslim down."

" 'Distressed citizen,' " suggested Krausa.

"Eh? I don't see how that can be stretched to fit a person on a planet under the Hegemony, who is obviously not distressed—other than a little white around the gills, I mean. But I'll do it."

"Thank you, Skipper." Krausa glanced at his watch. "May I go? In fact I must."

"Just a second. You're simply leaving him with me?"

"I'm afraid that's the way it must be."

Brisby shrugged. "As you say. But stay for lunch. I want to find out more about Colonel Baslim."

"I'm sorry, I can't. You can reach me at the Gathering, if you need to."

"I will. Well, coffee at least." The ship commander reached for a button.

"Skipper," Krausa said with distress, looking again at his watch, "I must leave *now*. Today is our Remembrance . . . and my Mother's funeral is in fifty minutes."

"What? Why didn't you say so? Goodness, man! You'll never make it."

"I'm very much afraid so . . . but I *had* to do this."

"We'll fix that." The Colonel snatched open the door. "Eddie! An air car for Captain Krausa. Speed run. Take him off the top and put him down where he says. Crash!"

"Aye aye, Skipper!"

Brisby turned back, raised his eyebrows, then stepped into the outer office. Krausa was facing Thorby, his mouth working painfully. "Come here, Son."

"Yes, Father."

"I have to go now. Maybe you can manage to be at a Gathering . . . some day."

"I'll try, Father!"

"If not . . . well, the blood stays in the steel, the steel stays in the blood. You're still *Sisu.*"

" 'The steel stays in the blood.' "

"Good business, Son. Be a good boy."

"Good . . . business! Oh, Father!"

"Stop it! You'll have me doing it. Listen, I'll take your responses this afternoon. You must not show up."

"Yes, sir."

"Your Mother loves you . . . and so do I."

Brisby tapped on the open door. "Your car is waiting, Captain."

"Coming, Skipper." Krausa kissed Thorby on both cheeks and turned suddenly away, so that all Thorby saw was his broad back.

Colonel Brisby returned presently, sat down, looked at Thorby and said, "I don't know quite what to do with you. But we'll manage." He touched a switch. "Have someone dig up the berthing master-at-arms, Eddie." He turned to Thorby. "We'll make out, if you're not too fussy. You traders live pretty luxuriously, I understand."

"Sir?"

"Yes?"

"Baslim was a colonel? Of your service?"

"Well . . . yes."

Thorby had now had a few minutes to think—and old memories had been stirred mightily. He said hesitantly, "I have a message for you—I think."

"From Colonel Baslim?"

"Yes, sir. I'm supposed to be in a light trance. But I think I can start it." Carefully, Thorby recited a few code groups. "Is this for you?"

Colonel Brisby again hastily closed the door. Then he said earnestly, "Don't *ever* use that code unless you are certain everyone in earshot is cleared for it and the room has been debugged."

"I'm sorry, sir."

"No harm done. But anything in that code is hot. I just hope that it hasn't cooled off in two years." He touched the talker switch again. "Eddie, cancel the master-at-arms. Get me the psych officer. If he's out of the ship, have him chased down." He looked at Thorby. "I still don't know what to do with you. I ought to lock you in the safe."

The long message was squeezed out of Thorby in the presence only of Colonel Brisby, his Executive Officer Vice Colonel "Stinky" Stancke, and the ship's psychologist Medical-Captain Isadore Krishnamurti. The session went slowly; Dr. Kris did not often use hypnotherapy. Thorby was so tense that he resisted, and the Exec had a blasphemous time with recording equipment. But at last the psychologist straightened up and wiped his face. "That's all, I think," he said wearily. "But what is it?"

"Forget you heard it, Doc," advised Brisby. "Better yet, cut your throat."

"Gee, thanks, Boss."

Stancke said, "Pappy, let's run him through again. I've got this mad scientist's dream working better. His accent may have garbled it."

"Nonsense. The kid speaks pure Terran."

"Okay, so it's my ears. I've been exposed to bad influences—been aboard too long."

"If," Brisby answered calmly, "that is a slur on your commanding officer's pure speech, I consider the source. Stinkpot, is it true that you Riffs write down anything you want understood?"

"Only with Araleshi . . . sir. Nothing personal, you asked. Well, how about it? I've got the noise filtered out."

"Doc?"

"Hmm . . . The subject is fatigued. Is this your only opportunity?"

"Eh? He'll be with us quite a while. All right, wake him."

Shortly Thorby was handed over to the berthing P.O. Several liters of coffee, a tray of sandwiches, and one skipped meal later the Colonel and his second in command had recorded in clear the thousands of words of old Baslim the Beggar's final report. Stancke sat back and whistled. "You can relax, Pappy. This stuff didn't cool off—a half-life of a century, on a guess."

Brisby answered soberly, "Yes, and a lot of good boys will die before it does."

"You ain't foolin'. What gets me is that trader kid—running around the Galaxy with all that 'burn-before-reading' between his ears. Shall I slide down and poison him?"

"What, and have to fill out all those copies?"

"Well, maybe Kris can wipe it out of his tender gray matter without resorting to a trans-orbital."

"Anybody touches that kid and Colonel Baslim will rise up out of his grave and strangle him, is my guess. Did you know Baslim, Stinky?"

"One course under him in psychological weapons, my last year at the Academy. Just before he went 'X' Corps. Most brilliant mind I've ever met—except yours, of course, Pappy, sir, boss."

"Don't strain yourself. No doubt he was a brilliant teacher —he would be tops at anything. But you should have known him before he was on limited duty. I was privileged to serve under him. Now that I have a ship of my own I just ask myself: 'What would Baslim do?' He was the best commanding officer a ship ever had. It was during his second crack at colonel—he had been up to wing marshal and put in for reduction to have a ship again, to get away from a desk."

Stancke shook his head. "I can't wait for a nice cushy desk, where I can write recommendations nobody will read."

"You aren't Baslim. If it wasn't hard, he didn't like it."

"I'm no hero. I'm more the salt of the earth. Pappy, were you with him in the rescue of the *Hansea*?"

"You think I would fail to wear the ribbon? No, thank goodness; I had been transferred. That was a hand-weapons job. Messy."

"Maybe you would have had the sense not to volunteer."

"Stinky, even you would volunteer, fat and lazy as you are—if Baslim asked for volunteers."

"I'm not lazy, I'm efficient. But riddle me this: what was a C.O. doing leading a landing party?"

"The Old Man followed regulations only when he agreed with them. He wanted a crack at slavers with his own hands —he hated slavers with a cold passion. So he comes back a hero and what can the Department do? Wait until he gets out of the hospital and court-martial him? Stinky, even top brass can be sensible when they have their noses rubbed in it. So they cited him for above-and-beyond under unique circumstances and put him on limited duty. But from here on, when 'unique circumstances' arise, every commanding officer knows that he can't thumb through the book for an alibi. It'll be up to him to continue the example."

"Not me," Stancke said firmly.

"You. When you're a C.O. and comes time to do something unpleasant, there you'll be, trying to get your tummy in and your chest out, with your chubby little face set in hero lines. You won't be able to help it. The Baslim conditioned-reflex will hit you."

Around dawn they got to bed. Brisby intended to sleep late but long habit took him to his desk only minutes late. He was not surprised to find his professedly-lazy Exec already at work.

His Paymaster-Lieutenant was waiting. The fiscal officer was holding a message form; Brisby recognized it. The night before, after hours of dividing Baslim's report into phrases, then recoding it to be sent by split routes, he had realized that there was one more chore before he could sleep: arrange for identification search on Colonel Baslim's adopted son. Brisby had no confidence that a waif picked up on Jubbul could be traced in the vital records of the Hegemony —but if the Old Man sent for a bucket of space, that was what he wanted and no excuses. Toward Baslim, dead or not, Colonel Brisby maintained the attitudes of a junior officer. So he had written a despatch and left word with the duty officer to have Thorby finger-printed and the prints coded at reveille. Then he could sleep.

Brisby looked at the message. "Hasn't this gone out?" he demanded.

"The photo lab is coding the prints now, Skipper. But the Comm Office brought it to me for a charge, since it is for service outside the ship."

"Well, assign it. Do I have to be bothered with every routine matter?"

The Paymaster decided that the Old Man had been missing sleep again. "Bad news, Skipper."

"Okay, spill it."

"I don't know of a charge to cover it. I doubt if there is an appropriation to fit even if we could figure out a likely-sounding charge."

"I don't care what charge. Pick one and get that message moving. Use that general one. Oh-oh-something."

" 'Unpredictable Overhead, Administrative.' It won't work, Skipper. Making an identity search on a civilian cannot be construed as ship's overhead. Oh, I can put that charge number on and you'll get an answer. But—"

"That's what I want. An answer."

"Yes, sir. But eventually it reaches the General Accounting Office and the wheels go around and a card pops out with a red tag. Then my pay is checked until I pay it back. That's why they make us blokes study law as well as accounting."

"You're breaking my heart. Okay, Pay, if you're too sissy to sign it, tell me what charge number that overhead thing is; I'll write it in and sign my name and rank. Okay?"

"Yes, sir. But, Skipper—"

"Pay, I've had a hard night."

"Yes, sir. I'm required by law to advise you. You don't have to take it, of course."

"Of course," Brisby agreed grimly.

"Skipper, have you any notion how expensive an identification search can be?"

"It can't be much. I can't see why you are making such an aching issue of it. I want a clerk to get off his fundament and look in the files. I doubt if they'll bill us. Routine courtesy."

"I wish I thought so, sir. But you've made this an unlimited search. Since you haven't named a planet, first it will go to Tycho City, live files and dead. Or do you want to limit it to live files?"

Brisby thought. If Colonel Baslim had believed that this young man had come from inside civilization, then it was likely that the kid's family thought he was dead. "No."

"Too bad. Dead files are three times as big as the live.

So they search at Tycho. It takes a while, even with machines—over twenty billion entries. Suppose you get a null result. A coded inquiry goes to vital bureaus on all planets, since Great Archives are never up to date and some planetary governments don't send in records anyhow. Now the cost mounts, especially if you use n-space routing; exact coding on a fingerprint set is a fair-sized book. Of course if you take one planet at a time and use mail—"

"No."

"Well . . . Skipper, why not put a limit on it? A thousand credits, or whatever you can afford if—I mean 'when'— they check your pay."

"A thousand credits? Ridiculous!"

"If I'm wrong, the limitation won't matter. If I'm right— and I am, a thousand credits could just be a starter—then your neck isn't out too far."

Brisby scowled. "Pay, you aren't working for me to tell me I can't do things."

"Yes, sir."

"You're here to tell me how I *can* do what I'm going to do anyhow. So start digging through your books and find out how. Legally. And free."

"Aye aye, sir."

Brisby did not go right to work. He was fuming—some day they would get the service so fouled up in red tape they'd never get a ship off the ground. He bet that the Old Man had gone into the Exotic Corps with a feeling of relief—"X" Corps agents didn't have red tape; one of 'em finds it necessary to spend money, he just did so, ten credits or ten million. That was how to operate—pick your men, then trust them. No regular reports, no forms, no nothing— just do what needs to be done.

Whereupon he picked up the ship's quarterly fuel and engineering report. He put it down, reached for a message form, wrote a follow-up on Baslim's report, informing Exotic Bureau that the unclassified courier who had delivered report was still in jurisdiction of signer and in signer's opinion additional data could be had if signer were authorized to discuss report with courier at discretion.

He decided not to turn it over to the code and cipher group; he opened his safe and set about coding it. He had just finished when the Paymaster knocked. Brisby looked up. "So you found the paragraph."

"Perhaps, Skipper. I've been talking with the Executive Officer."

"Shoot."

"I see we have subject person aboard."

"Now don't tell me I need a charge for that!"

"Not at all, Skipper. I'll absorb his ration in the rush. You keep him aboard forever and I won't notice. Things don't get awkward until they get on the books. But how long do you expect to keep him? It must be more than a day or two, or you wouldn't want an identity search."

The Commanding Officer frowned. "It may be quite a while. First I've got to find out who he is, where he's from. Then, if we're going that way, I intend to give him an unlogged lift. If we aren't—well, I'll pass him along to a ship that is. Too complicated to explain, Pay—but necessary."

"Okay. Then why not enlist him?"

"Huh?"

"It would clear up everything."

Brisby frowned. "I see. I could take him along legally . . . and arrange a transfer. And it would give you a charge number. But . . . well, suppose Shiva III is the spot—and his enlistment is not up. Can't just tell him to desert. Besides I don't know that he wants to enlist."

"You can ask him. How old is he?"

"I doubt if he knows. He's a waif."

"So much the better. You ship him. Then when you find out where he has to go, you discover an error in his age . . . and correct it. It turns out that he reaches his majority in time to be paid off on his home planet."

Brisby blinked. "Pay, are all paymasters dishonest?"

"Only the good ones. You don't like it, sir?"

"I love it. Okay, I'll check. And I'll hold up that despatch. We'll send it later."

The Paymaster looked innocent. "Oh, no, sir, we won't ever send it."

"How's that?"

"It won't be necessary. We enlist him to fill vacancy in complement. We send in records to BuPersonnel. They make the routine check, name and home planet—Hekate, I suppose, since we got him here. By then we're long gone. They don't find him registered here. Now they turn it over to Bu-Security, who sends us a priority telling us not to permit subject personnel to serve in sensitive capacity. But that's all, because it's possible that this poor innocent citizen never got registered. But they can't take chances, so they start the very search you want, first Tycho, then everywhere else, security priority. So they identify him and unless he's wanted for murder it's a routine muddle. Or they can't identify him and have to make up their minds whether to register him, or give him twenty-four hours to get out of the Galaxy—seven to two they decide to forget it—except that someone aboard is told to watch him and report suspicious behavior. But the real beauty of it is that the job carries a BuSecurity cost charge."

"Pay, do you think that Security has agents in this vessel I don't know about?"

"Skipper, what do you think?"

"Mmm . . . I don't know—but if I were Chief of Security I would have! Confound it, if I lift a civilian from here to the Rim, that'll be reported too—no matter what I log."

"Shouldn't be surprised, sir."

"Get out of here! I'll see if the lad will buy it." He flipped a switch. "Eddie!" Instead of sending for Thorby, Brisby directed the Surgeon to examine him, since it was pointless to pressure him to enlist without determining whether or not he could. Medical-Major Stein, accompanied by Medical-Captain Krishnamurti, reported to Brisby before lunch.

"Well?"

"No physical objection, Skipper. I'll let the Psych Officer speak for himself."

"All right. By the way, how old is he?"

"He doesn't know."

"Yes, yes," Brisby agreed impatiently, "but how old do you think he is?"

Dr. Stein shrugged. "What's his genetic picture? What environment? Any age-factor mutations? High or low gravity planet? Planetary metabolic index? He could be as young as ten standard years, as old as thirty, on physical appearance. I can assign a fictional adjusted age, on the assumption of no significant mutations and Terra-equivalent environment—an unjustified assumption until they build babies with data plates—an adjusted age of not less than fourteen standard years, not more than twenty-two."

"Would an adjusted age of eighteen fit?"

"That's what I said."

"Okay, make it just under that—minority enlistment."

"There's a tattoo on him," Dr. Krishnamurti offered, "which might give a clue. A slave mark."

"The deuce you say!" Colonel Brisby reflected that his follow-up despatch to "X" Corps was justified. "Dated?"

"Just a manumission—a Sargonese date which fits his story. The mark is a factor's mark. No date."

"Too bad. Well, now that he is clear with Medical, I'll send for him."

"Colonel."

"Eh? Yes, Kris?"

"I cannot recommend enlistment."

"Huh? He's as sane as you are."

"Surely. But he is a poor risk."

"Why?"

"I interviewed subject under light trance this morning. Colonel, did you ever keep a dog?"

"No. Not many where I come from."

"Very useful laboratory animals, they parallel many human characteristics. Take a puppy, abuse him, kick him, mistreat him—he'll revert to feral carnivore. Take his litter

170

brother, pet him, talk to him, let him sleep with you, but train him—he's a happy, well-behaved house pet. Take another from that same litter, pet him on even days and kick him on odd days. You'll have him so confused that he'll be ruined for either role; he can't survive as a wild animal and he doesn't understand what is expected of a pet. Pretty soon he won't eat, he won't sleep, he can't control his functions; he just cowers and shivers."

"Hmm . . . do you psychologists do such things often?"

"I never have. But it's in the literature . . . and this lad's case parallels it. He's undergone a series of traumatic experiences in his formative years, the latest of which was yesterday. He's confused and depressed. Like that dog, he may snarl and bite at any time. He ought not to be exposed to new pressures; he should be cared for where he can be given psychotherapy."

"Phooey!"

The psychological officer shrugged. Colonel Brisby added, "I apologize, Doctor. But I know something about this case, with all respect to your training. This lad has been in good environment the past couple of years." Brisby recalled the farewell he had unwillingly witnessed. "And before that, he was in the hands of Colonel Richard Baslim. Heard of him?"

"I know his reputation."

"If there is any fact I would stake my ship on, it is that Colonel Baslim would *never* ruin a boy. Okay, so the kid has had a rough time. But he has also been succored by one of the toughest, sanest, most humane men ever to wear our uniform. You bet on your dogs; I'll back Colonel Richard Baslim. Now . . . are you advising me not to enlist him?"

The psychologist hesitated. Brisby said, "Well?"

Major Stein interrupted. "Take it easy, Kris; I'm overriding you."

Brisby said, "I want a straight answer, then *I'll* decide."

Dr. Krishnamurti said slowly, "Suppose I record my opinions but state that there are no certain grounds for refusing enlistment?"

"Why?"

"Obviously you want to enlist this boy. But if he gets into trouble—well, my endorsement could get him a medical discharge instead of a sentence. He's had enough bad breaks."

Colonel Brisby clapped him on the shoulder. "Good boy, Kris! That's all, gentlemen."

Thorby spent an unhappy night. The master-at-arms billeted him in senior P.O.s quarters and he was well treated, but embarrassingly aware of the polite way in which those around him did not stare at his gaudy *Sisu* dress uniform. Up till then he had been proud of the way *Sisu's* dress stood out; now he was learning painfully that clothing has its proper background. That night he was conscious of snores around him . . . strangers . . . fraki—and he yearned to be back among People, where he was known, understood, recognized.

He tossed on a harder bed than he was used to and wondered who would get his own?

He found himself wondering whether anyone had ever claimed the hole he still thought of as "home." Would they repair the door? Would they keep it clean and decent the way Pop liked? *What would they do with Pop's leg?*

Asleep, he dreamt of Pop and of *Sisu*, all mixed up. At last, with Grandmother shortened and a raider bearing down, Pop whispered, *"No more bad dreams, Thorby. Never again, son. Just happy dreams."*

He slept peacefully then—and awoke in this forbidding place with gabbling fraki all around him. Breakfast was substantial but not up to Aunt Athena's high standards; however he was not hungry.

After breakfast he was quietly tasting his misery when he was required to undress and submit to indignities. It was his first experience with medical men's offhand behavior with human flesh—he loathed the poking and prodding.

172

When the Commanding Officer sent for him Thorby was not even cheered by seeing the man who knew Pop. This room was where he had had to say a last "good-business" to Father; the thoughts lingering there were not good.

He listened listlessly while Brisby explained. He woke up a little when he understood that he was being offered status—not much, he gathered. But status. The fraki had status among themselves. It had never occurred to him that fraki status could matter even to fraki.

"You don't have to," Colonel Brisby concluded, "but it will make simpler the thing Colonel Baslim wanted me to do—find your family, I mean. You would like that, wouldn't you?"

Thorby almost said that he knew where his Family was. But he knew what the Colonel meant: his own sib, whose existence he had never quite been able to imagine. Did he really have blood relatives somewhere?

"I suppose so," he answered slowly. "I don't know."

"Mmm . . ." Brisby wondered what it was like to have no frame to your picture. "Colonel Baslim was anxious to have me locate your family. I can handle it easier if you are officially one of us. Well? It's Guardsman third class . . . thirty credits a month, all you can eat and not enough sleep. And glory. A meager amount."

Thorby looked up. "This is the same Fam—service my Pop—Colonel Baslim, you call him—was in? He really was?"

"Yes. Senior to what you will be. But the same service. I think you started to say 'family.' We like to think of the Service as one enormous family. Colonel Baslim was one of the more distinguished members of it."

"Then I want to be adopted."

"Enlisted."

"Whatever the word is."

Chapter 16

FRAKI WEREN'T BAD when you got to know them.

They had their secret language, even though they thought they talked Interlingua. Thorby added a few dozen verbs and a few hundred nouns as he heard them; after that he tripped over an occasional idiom. He learned that his light-years as a trader were respected, even though the People were considered odd. He didn't argue; fraki couldn't know better.

H.G.C. *Hydra* lifted from Hekate, bound for the Rim worlds. Just before jump a money order arrived accompanied by a supercargo's form which showed the draft to be one eighty-third of *Sisu*'s appreciation from Jubbulpore to Hekate —as if, thought Thorby, he were a girl being swapped. It was an uncomfortably large sum and Thorby could find no entry charging him interest against a capital share of the ship—which he felt should be there for proper accounting; it wasn't as if he had been born in the ship. Life among the People had made the beggar boy conscious of money in a sense that alms never could—books must balance and debts must be paid.

He wondered what Pop would think of all that money. He felt easier when he learned that he could deposit it with the Paymaster.

With the draft was a warm note, wishing him good business wherever he went and signed: "Love, Mother." It made Thorby feel better and much worse.

A package of belongings arrived with a note from Fritz: "Dear Brother, Nobody briefed me about recent mysterious happenings, but things were crisp around the old ship for a few days. If such were not unthinkable, I would say there had been a difference of opinion at highest level. Me, I have no opinions, except that I miss your idle chatter and blank expressions. Have fun and be sure to count your change.

"*Fritz*

"P.S. The play was an artistic success—and Loeen *is* cuddly."

Thorby stored his *Sisu* belongings; he was trying to be a Guardsman and they made him uncomfortable. He discovered that the Guard was not the closed corporation the People were; it required no magic to make a Guardsman if a man had what it took, because nobody cared where a man came from or what he had been. The *Hydra* drew its company from many planets; there were machines in BuPersonnel to ensure this. Thorby's shipmates were tall and short, bird-boned and rugged, smooth and hairy, mutated and superficially unmutated. Thorby hit close to norm and his Free Trader background was merely an acceptable eccentricity; it made him a spaceman of sorts even though a recruit.

In fact, the only hurdle was that he was a raw recruit. "Guardsman 3/c" he might be but a boot he would remain until he proved himself, most especially since he had not had boot training.

But he was no more handicapped than any recruit in a military outfit having proud *esprit de corps*. He was assigned a bunk, a mess, a working station, and a petty officer to tell him what to do. His work was compartment cleaning, his battle station was runner for the Weapons Officer in case phones should fail—it meant that he was available to fetch coffee.

Otherwise he was left in peace. He was free to join a bull session as long as he let his seniors sound off, he was invited into card games when a player was needed, he was not shut out of gossip, and he was privileged to lend jumpers and socks to seniors who happened to be short. Thorby had had experience at being junior; it was not difficult.

The *Hydra* was heading out for patrol duty; the mess talk centered around "hunting" prospects. The *Hydra* had fast "legs," three hundred gravities; she sought action with outlaws where a merchantman such as the *Sisu* would avoid it if possible. Despite her large complement and heavy weapons, the *Hydra* was mostly power plant and fuel tanks.

Thorby's table was headed by his petty officer, Ordnance-man 2/c Peebie, down as "Decibel." Thorby was eating one day with his ears tuned down, while he debated visiting the library after dinner or attending the stereo show in the messroom, when he heard his nickname: "Isn't that right, Trader?"

Thorby was proud of the nickname. He did not like it in Peebie's mouth but Peebie was a self-appointed wit— he would greet Thorby with the nickname, inquire solicitously, "How's business?" and make gestures of counting money. So far, Thorby had ignored it.

"Isn't what right?"

"Why'n't y'keep y'r ears open? Can't you hear anything but rustle and clink? I was telling 'em what I told the Weapons Officer: the way to rack up more kills is to go after 'em, not pretend to be a trader, too scared to fight and too fat to run."

Thorby felt a simmer. "Who," he said, "told you that traders were scared to fight?"

"Quit pushin' that stuff! Whoever heard of a trader burning a bandit?"

Peebie may have been sincere; kills made by traders received no publicity. But Thorby's burn increased. "I have."

Thorby meant that he had heard of traders' burning raiders; Peebie took it as a boast. "Oh, you did, did you? Listen to that, men—our peddler is a hero. He's burned a bandit all by his own little self! Tell us about it. Did you set fire to his hair? Or drop potassium in his beer?"

"I used," Thorby stated, "a Mark XIX one-stage target-seeker, made by Bethlehem-Antares and armed with a 20 megaton plutonium warhead. I launched a timed shot on closing to beaming range on a collision-curve prediction."

There was silence. Finally Peebie said coldly, "Where did you read that?"

"It's what the tape showed after the engagement. I was

senior starboard firecontrolman. The portside computer was out—so I know it was my shot that burned him."

"Now he's a weapons officer! Peddler, don't peddle it here."

Thorby shrugged. "I used to be. A weapons control officer, rather. I never learned much about ordnance."

"Modest, isn't he? Talk is cheap, Trader."

"You should know, Decibel."

Peebie was halted by his nickname; Thorby did not rate such familiarity. Another voice cut in, saying sweetly, "Sure, Decibel, talk is cheap. Now you tell about the big kills you've made. Go ahead." The speaker was non-rated but was a clerk in the executive office and immune to Peebie's displeasure.

Peebie glowered. "Enough of this prattle," he growled. "Baslim, I'll see you at oh eight hundred in combat control —we'll find out how much you know about firecontrol."

Thorby was not anxious to be tested; he knew nothing about the Hydra's equipment. But an order is an order; he was facing Peebie's smirk at the appointed time.

The smirk did not last. Hydra's instruments bore no resemblance to those in the Sisu, but the principles were the same and the senior gunnery sergeant (cybernetics) seemed to find nothing unlikely in an ex-trader knowing how to shoot. He was always looking for talent; people to handle ballistic trackers for the preposterous problems of combat at sub-light-speed were as scarce among Guardsmen as among the People.

He questioned Thorby about the computer he had handled. Presently he nodded. "I've never seen anything but schematics on a Dusseldorf tandem rig; that approach is obsolete. But if you can get a hit with that junk, we can use you." The sergeant turned to Peebie. "Thanks, Decibel. I'll mention it to the Weapons Officer. Stick around, Baslim."

Peebie looked astonished. "He's got work to do, Sarge."

Sergeant Luter shrugged. "Tell your leading P.O. that I need Baslim here."

Thorby had been shocked to hear Sisu's beautiful computers called "junk." But shortly he knew what Luter meant; the massive brain that fought for the *Hydra* was a genius among computers. Thorby would never control it alone—but soon he was an acting ordnanceman 3/c (cybernetics) and relatively safe from Peebie's wit. He began to feel like a Guardsman—very junior but an accepted shipmate.

Hydra was cruising above speed-of-light toward the Rim world Ultima Thule, where she would refuel and start prowling for outlaws. No query had reached the ship concerning Thorby's identity. He was contented with his status in Pop's old outfit; it made him proud to feel that Pop would be proud of him. He did miss *Sisu*, but a ship with no women was simpler to live in; compared with *Sisu* the *Hydra* had no restrictive regulations.

But Colonel Brisby did not let Thorby forget why he had been enlisted. Commanding officers are many linkages away from a recruit; a non-rated man might not lay eyes on his skipper except at inspections. But Brisby sent for Thorby repeatedly.

Brisby received authorization from the Exotic Corps to discuss Colonel Baslim's report with Baslim's courier, bearing in mind the critical classification of the subject. So Brisby called Thorby in.

Thorby was first warned of the necessity of keeping his mouth shut. Brisby told him that the punishment for blabbing would be as heavy as a court-martial could hand out. "But that's not the point. We have to be sure that the question never arises. Otherwise we can't discuss it."

Thorby hesitated. "How can I know that I'll keep my mouth shut when I don't know what it is?"

Brisby looked annoyed. "I can order you to."

"Yes, sir. And I'll say, 'Aye aye, sir.' But does that make you certain that I wouldn't risk a court-martial?"

"But— This is ridiculous! I want to talk about Colonel Baslim's work. But you're to keep your yap shut, you understand me? If you don't, I'll tear you to pieces with my bare hands. No young punk is going to quibble with me where the Old Man's work is concerned!"

Thorby looked relieved. "Why didn't you say it was that, Skipper? I wouldn't blab about anything of Pop's—why, that was the first thing he taught me."

"Oh." Brisby grinned. "I should have known. Okay."

"I suppose," Thorby added thoughtfully, "that it's all right to talk to *you*."

Brisby looked startled. "I hadn't realized that this cuts two ways. But it does. I can show you a despatch from his corps, telling me to discuss his report with you. Would that convince you?"

Brisby found himself showing a "Most Secret" despatch to his most junior, acting petty officer, to convince said junior that his C.O. was entitled to talk with him. At the time it seemed reasonable; it was not until later that the Colonel wondered.

Thorby read the translated despatch and nodded. "Anything you want, Skipper. I'm sure Pop would agree."

"Okay. You know what he was doing?"

"Well . . . yes and no. I saw some of it. I know what sort of things he was interested in having me notice and remember. I used to carry messages for him and it was always very secret. But I never knew why." Thorby frowned. "They said he was a spy."

"Intelligence agent sounds better."

Thorby shrugged. "If he was spying, he'd call it that. Pop never minced words."

"No, he never minced words," Brisby agreed, wincing as he recalled being scorched right through his uniform by a dressing-down. "Let me explain. Mmm . . . know any Terran history?"

"Uh, not much."

"It's a miniature history of the race. Long before space travel, when we hadn't even filled up Terra, there used to be dirtside frontiers. Every time new territory was found, you always got three phenomena: traders ranging out ahead and taking their chances, outlaws preying on the honest men—and a traffic in slaves. It happens the same way today, when we're pushing through space instead of across

179

oceans and prairies. Frontier traders are adventurers taking great risks for great profits. Outlaws, whether hill bands or sea pirates or the raiders in space, crop up in any area not under police protection. Both are temporary. But slavery is another matter—the most vicious habit humans fall into and the hardest to break. It starts up in every new land and it's terribly hard to root out. After a culture falls ill of it, it gets rooted in the economic system and laws, in men's habits and attitudes. You abolish it; you drive it underground—there it lurks, ready to spring up again, in the minds of people who think it is their 'natural' right to own other people. You can't reason with them; you can kill them but you can't change their minds."

Brisby sighed. "Baslim, the Guard is just the policeman and the mailman; we haven't had a major war in two centuries. What we do work at is the impossible job of maintaining order on the frontier, a globe three thousand light-years in circumference—no one can understand how big that is; the mind can't swallow it.

"Nor can human beings police it. It gets bigger every year. Dirtside police eventually close the gaps. But with us, the longer we try the more there is. So to most of us it's a job, an honest job, but one that can never be finished.

"But to Colonel Richard Baslim it was a passion. Especially he hated the slave trade, the thought of it could make him sick at his stomach—I've seen. He lost his leg and an eye—I suppose you know—while rescuing a shipload of people from a slaving compound.

"That would satisfy most officers—go home and retire. Not old Spit-and-Polish! He taught a few years, then he went to the one corps that might take him, chewed up as he was, and presented a plan.

"The Nine Worlds are the backbone of the slave trade. The Sargony was colonized a long time ago, and they never accepted Hegemony after they broke off as colonies. The Nine Worlds don't qualify on human rights and don't want to qualify. So we can't travel there and they can't visit our worlds.

"Colonel Baslim decided that the traffic could be rendered uneconomic if we knew how it worked in the Sargony. He reasoned that slavers had to have ships, had to have bases, had to have markets, that it was not just a vice but a business. So he decided to go there and study it.

"This was preposterous—one. man against a nine-planet empire . . . but the Exotic Corps deals in preposterous notions. Even they would probably not have made him an agent if he had not had a scheme to get his reports out. An agent couldn't travel back and forth, nor could he use the mails—there aren't any between us and them—and he certainly couldn't set up an n-space communicator; that would be as conspicuous as a brass band.

"But Baslim had an idea. The *only* people who visit both the Nine Worlds and our own are Free Traders. But they avoid politics like poison, as you know better than I, and they go to great lengths not to offend local customs. However Colonel Baslim had a personal 'in' to them.

"I suppose you know that those people he rescued were Free Traders. He told 'X' Corps that he could report back through his friends. So they let him try. It's my guess that no one knew that he intended to pose as a beggar—I doubt if he planned it; he was always great at improvising. But he got in and for years he observed and got his reports out.

"That's the background and now I want to squeeze every possible fact out of you. You can tell us about methods— the report I forwarded never said a word about methods. Another agent might be able to use his methods."

Thorby said soberly, "I'll tell you anything I can. I don't know much."

"You know more than you think you do. Would you let the psych officer put you under again and see if we can work total recall?"

"Anything is okay if it'll help Pop's work."

"It should. Another thing—" Brisby crossed his cabin, held up a sheet on which was the silhouette of a spaceship. "What ship is this?"

Thorby's eyes widened. "A Sargonese cruiser."

Brisby snatched up another one. "This?"

"Uh, it looks like a slaver that called at Jubbulpore twice a year."

"Neither one," Brisby said savagely, "is anything of the sort. These are recognition patterns out of my files—of ships built by our biggest shipbuilder. If you saw them in Jubbulpore, they were either copies, or bought from us!"

Thorby considered it. "They build ships there."

"So I've been told. But Colonel Baslim reported ships' serial numbers—how he got them I couldn't guess; maybe you can. He claims that the slave trade is getting help from our own worlds!" Brisby looked unbearably disgusted.

Thorby reported regularly to the Cabin, sometimes to see Brisby, sometimes to be interviewed under hypnosis by Dr. Krishnamurti. Brisby always mentioned the search for Thorby's identity and told him not to be discouraged; such a search took a long time. Repeated mention changed Thorby's attitude about it from something impossible to something which was going to be true soon; he began thinking about his family, wondering who he was?—it was going to be nice to know, to be like other people.

Brisby was reassuring himself; he had been notified to keep Thorby off sensitive work the very day the ship jumped from Hekate when he had hoped that Thorby would be identified at once. He kept the news to himself, holding fast to his conviction that Colonel Baslim was never wrong and that the matter would be cleared up.

When Thorby was shifted to Combat Control, Brisby worried when the order passed across his desk—that was a "security" area, never open to visitors—then he told himself that a man with no special training couldn't learn anything there that could really affect security and that he was already using the lad in much more sensitive work. Brisby felt that he was learning things of importance—that the Old Man, for example, had used the cover personality of a one-legged beggar to hide two-legged activities . . . but had actually been a beggar; he and the boy had lived only on alms. Brisby admired such artistic perfection—it should be an example to other agents.

But the Old Man always had been a shining example. So Brisby left Thorby in combat control. He omitted to make permanent Thorby's acting promotion in order that the record of change in rating need not be forwarded to BuPersonnel. But he became anxious to receive the despatch that would tell him who Thorby was.

His executive was with him when it came in. It was in code, but Brisby recognized Thorby's serial number; he had written it many times in reports to "X" Corps. "Look at this, Stinky! This tells us who our foundling is. Grab the machine; the safe is open."

Ten minutes later they had processed it; it read:

—"NULL RESULT FULL IDENTSEARCH BASLIM THORBY GDS-MN THIRD. AUTH & DRT TRANSFER ANY RECEIVING STATION RETRANSFER HEKATE INVESTIGATION DISPOSITION—CHFBUPERS."

"Stinky, ain't that a mess?"

Stancke shrugged. "It's how the dice roll, boss."

"I feel as if I had let the Old Man down. He was sure the kid was a citizen."

"I misdoubt there are millions of citizens who would have a bad time proving who they are. Colonel Baslim may have been right—and still it can't be proved."

"I hate to transfer him. I feel responsible."

"Not your fault."

"You never served under Colonel Baslim. He was easy to please . . . all he wanted was one-hundred-percent perfection. And this doesn't feel like it."

"Quit blaming yourself. You have to accept the record."

"Might as well get it over with. Eddie! I want to see Ordnanceman Baslim."

Thorby noticed that the Skipper looked grim—but then he often did. "Acting Ordnanceman Third Class Baslim reporting, sir."

"Thorby . . ."

"Yes, sir?" Thorby was startled. The Skipper sometimes

used his first name because that was what he answered to under hypnosis—but this was not such a time.

"The identification report on you came."

"Huh?" Thorby was startled out of military manners. He felt a surge of joy—he was going to know who he was!

"They can't identify you." Brisby waited, then said sharply, "Did you understand?"

Thorby swallowed. "Yes, sir. They don't know who I am. I'm not . . . anybody."

"Nonsense! You're still yourself."

"Yes, sir. Is that all, sir? May I go?"

"Just a moment. I have to transfer you back to Hekate." He added hastily, seeing Thorby's expression, "Don't worry. They'll probably let you serve out your enlistment if you want to. In any case, they can't do anything to you; you haven't done anything wrong."

"Yes, sir," Thorby repeated dully.

Nothing and nobody— He had a blinding image of an old, old nightmare . . . standing on the block, hearing an auctioneer chant his description, while cold eyes stared at him. But he pulled himself together and was merely quiet the rest of the day. It was not until the compartment was dark that he bit his pillow and whispered brokenly, "Pop . . . oh, *Pop!*"

The Guards uniform covered Thorby's legs, but in the showers the tattoo on his left thigh could be noticed. When this happened, Thorby explained without embarrassment what it signified. Responses varied from curiosity, through half-disbelief, to awed surprise that here was a man who had been through it—capture, sale, servitude, and miraculously, free again. Most civilians did not realize that slavery still existed; Guardsmen knew better.

No one was nasty about it.

But the day after the null report on identification Thorby encountered "Decibel" Peebie in the showers. Thorby did not speak; they had not spoken much since Thorby had moved out from under Peebie, even though they sat at the same table. But now Peebie spoke. "Hi, Trader!"

"Hi." Thorby started to bathe.

"What's on your leg? Dirt?"

"Where?"

"On your thigh. Hold still. Let's see."

"Keep your hands to yourself!"

"Don't be touchy. Turn around to the light. What is it?"

"It's a slaver's mark," Thorby explained curtly.

"No foolin'? So you're a slave?"

"I used to be."

"They put chains on you? Make you kiss your master's foot?"

"Don't be silly!"

"Look who's talking! You know what, Trader boy? I heard about that mark—and I think you had it tattooed yourself. To make big talk. Like that one about how you blasted a bandit ship."

Thorby cut his shower short and got out.

At dinner Thorby was helping himself from a bowl of mashed potatoes. He heard Peebie call out something but his ears filtered out "Decibel's" endless noise.

Peebie repeated it. "Hey, Slave! Pass the potatoes! You know who I mean! Dig the dirt out of your ears!"

Thorby passed him the potatoes, bowl and all, in a flat trajectory, open face of the bowl plus potatoes making perfect contact with the open face of Decibel.

The charge against Thorby was "Assaulting a Superior Officer, the Ship then being in Space in a Condition of Combat Readiness." Peebie appeared as complaining witness.

Colonel Brisby stared over the mast desk and his jaw muscles worked. He listened to Peebie's account: "I asked him to pass the potatoes . . . and he hit me in the face with them."

"That was all?"

"Well, sir, maybe I didn't say please. But that's no reason—"

"Never mind the conclusions. The fight go any farther?"

"No, sir. They separated us."

"Very well. Baslim, what have you to say for yourself?"

"Nothing, sir."

"Is that what happened?"

"Yes, sir."

Brisby stopped to think, while his jaw muscles twitched. He felt angry, an emotion he did not permit himself at mast —he felt let down. Still, there must be more to it.

Instead of passing sentence he said, "Step aside. Colonel Stancke—"

"Yes, sir?"

"There were other men present. I want to hear from them."

"I have them standing by, sir."

"Very well."

Thorby was convicted—three days bread & water, solitary, sentence suspended, thirty days probation; acting rank stricken.

Decibel Peebie was convicted (court trial waived when Brisby pointed out how the book could be thrown at him) of "Inciting to Riot, specification: using derogatory language with reference to another Guardsman's Race, Religion, Birthplace, or Condition previous to entering Service, the Ship then being etc."—sentence three days B & W, sol., suspended, reduction one grade, ninety days probation in ref. B & W, sol., only.

The Colonel and Vice Colonel went back to Brisby's office. Brisby was looking glum; mast upset him at best. Stancke said, "Too bad you had to clip the Baslim kid. I think he was justified."

"Of course he was. But 'Inciting to riot' is no excuse for riot. Nothing is."

"Sure, you had to. But I don't like that Peebie character. I'm going to make a careful study of his efficiency marks."

"Do that. But, confound it, Stinky—I have a feeling I started the fight myself."

"Huh?"

"Two days ago I had to tell Baslim that we hadn't been

186

able to identify him. He walked out in a state of shock. I should have listened to my psych officer. The lad has scars that make him irresponsible under the right—I mean the 'wrong'—stimulus. I'm glad it was mashed potatoes and not a knife."

"Oh, come now, boss! Mashed potatoes are hardly a deadly weapon."

"You weren't here when he got the bad news. Not knowing who he is hurts him."

Stancke's pudgy face pouted in thought. "Boss? How old was this kid when he was captured?"

"Eh? Kris thinks he was about four."

"Skipper, that backwoods place where you were born: at what age were you fingerprinted, blood-typed, retina-photographed and so forth?"

"Why, when I started school."

"Me, too. I'll bet they wait that long most places."

Brisby blinked. "That's why they wouldn't have anything on him!"

"Maybe. But on Riff they take identity on a baby before he leaves the delivery room."

"My people, too. But—"

"Sure, sure! It's common practice. But *how*?"

Brisby looked blank, then banged the desk. "*Footprints!* And we didn't send them in." He slapped the talkie. "Eddie! Get Baslim here on the double!"

Thorby was glumly removing the chevron he had worn by courtesy for so short a time. He was scared by the peremptory order; it boded ill. But he hurried. Colonel Brisby glared at him. "Baslim, take off your shoes!"

"Sir?"

"Take off your shoes!"

Brisby's despatch questioning failure to identify and supplying BuPers with footprints was answered in forty-eight hours. It reached the *Hydra* as she made her final approach to Ultima Thule. Colonel Brisby decoded it when the ship had been secured dirtside.

It read: "—GUARDSMAN THORBY BASLIM IDENTIFIED MISS-

187

ING PERSON THOR BRADLEY RUDBEK TERRA NOT HEKATE TRANSFER RUDBEK FASTEST MILORCOM TERRA DISCHARGE ARRIVAL NEXTKIN NOTIFIED REPEAT FASTEST CHFBUPERS."

Brisby was chuckling. "Colonel Baslim is *never* wrong. Dead or alive, he's never wrong!"

"Boss . . ."

"Huh?"

"Read it again. Notice who he is."

Brisby reread the despatch. Then he said in a hushed voice, "Why do things like this always happen to *Hydra?*" He strode over and snatched the door. "Eddie!"

Thorby was on beautiful Ultima Thule for two hours and twenty-seven minutes; what he saw of the famous scenery after coming three hundred light-years was the field between the *Hydra* and Guard Mail Courier *Ariel*. Three weeks later he was on Terra. He felt dizzy.

Chapter 17

LOVELY TERRA, Mother of Worlds! What poet, whether or not he has been privileged to visit her, has not tried to express the homesick longing of men for mankind's birthplace . . . her cool green hills, cloud-graced skies, restless oceans, her warm maternal charm.

Thorby's first sight of legendary Earth was by view screen of G.M.C. *Ariel*. Guard Captain N'Gangi, skipper of the mail ship, stepped up the gain and pointed out arrow-sharp shadows of the Egyptian Pyramids. Thorby didn't realize the historical significance and was looking in the wrong place. But he enjoyed seeing a planet from space; he had never been thus privileged before.

Thorby had a dull time in the *Ariel*. The mail ship, all legs and tiny payload, carried a crew of three engineers and three astrogators, all of whom were usually on watch or asleep. He started off badly because Captain N'Gangi had been annoyed by a "hold for passenger" despatch from the *Hydra*—mail ships don't like to hold; the mail must go through.

But Thorby behaved himself, served the precooked meals, and spent his time plowing through the library (a drawer under the skipper's bunk); by the time they approached Sol the commanding officer was over his pique . . . to have the feeling brought back by orders to land at Galactic Enterprises' field instead of Guard Base. But N'Gangi shook hands as he gave Thorby his discharge and the paymaster's draft.

Instead of scrambling down a rope ladder (mail couriers have no hoists), Thorby found that a lift came up to get him. It leveled off opposite the hatch and offered easy exit. A man in spaceport uniform of Galactic Enterprises met him. "Mr. Rudbek?"

"That's me—I guess."

"This way, Mr. Rudbek, if you please."

The elevator took them below ground and into a beautiful lounge. Thorby, mussed and none too clean from weeks in a crowded steel box, was uneasy. He looked around.

Eight or ten people were there, two of whom were a gray-haired, self-assured man and a young woman. Each was dressed in more than a year's pay for a Guardsman. Thorby did not realize this in the case of the man but his Trader's eye spotted it in the female; it took money to look that demurely provocative.

In his opinion the effect was damaged by her high-fashion hairdo, a rising structure of green blending to gold. He blinked at the cut of her clothes; he had seen fine ladies in Jubbulpore where the climate favored clothing only for decoration, but the choice in skin display seemed different here. Thorby realized uneasily that he was again going to have to get used to new customs.

The important-looking man met him as he got out of the lift. "Thor! Welcome home, lad!" He grabbed Thorby's hand. "I'm John Weemsby. Many is the time I've bounced you on my knee. Call me Uncle Jack. And this is your cousin Leda."

The girl with green hair placed hands on Thorby's shoulders and kissed him. He did not return it; he was much too startled. She said, "It's wonderful to have you home, Thor."

"Uh, thanks."

"And now you must greet your grandparents," Weemsby announced. "Professor Bradley . . . and your Grandmother Bradley."

Bradley was older than Weemsby, slight and erect, a paunch, neatly trimmed beard; he was dressed like Weemsby in daytime formal jacket, padded tights and short cape, but not as richly. The woman had a sweet face and alert blue eyes; her clothing did not resemble that of Leda but seemed to suit her. She pecked Thorby on the cheek and said gently, "It's like having my son come home."

The elderly man shook hands vigorously. "It's a miracle, son! You look just like our boy—your father. Doesn't he, dear?"

"He does!"

There was chitchat which Thorby answered as well as he could. He was confused and terribly self-conscious; it was more embarrassing to meet these strangers who claimed him as their blood than it had been to be adopted into *Sisu*. These old people—they were his grandparents? Thorby couldn't believe it even though he supposed they were.

To his relief the man—Weemsby?—who claimed to be his Uncle Jack said with polite authority, "We had better go. I'll bet this boy is tired. So I'll take him home. Eh?"

The Bradleys murmured agreement; the party moved toward the exit. Others in the room, all men none of whom had been introduced, went with them. In the corridor they stepped on a glideway which picked up speed until walls were whizzing past. It slowed as they neared the end—miles away, Thorby judged—and was stationary for them to step off.

This place was public; the ceiling was high and the walls were lost in crowds; Thorby recognized the flavor of a transport station. The silent men with them moved into blocking positions and their party proceeded in a direct line regardless of others. Several persons tried to break through and one man managed it. He shoved a microphone at Thorby and said rapidly, "Mr. Rudbek, what is your opinion of the—"

A guard grabbed him. Mr. Weemsby said quickly, "Later, later! Call my office; you'll get the story."

Lenses were trained on them, but from high up and far away. They moved into another passageway, a gate closed behind them. Its glideway deposited them at an elevator which took them to a small enclosed airport. A craft was waiting and beyond it a smaller one, both sleek, smooth, flattened ellipsoids. Weemsby stopped. "You'll be all right?" he asked Mrs. Bradley.

"Oh, surely," answered Professor Bradley.

"The car was satisfactory?"

"Excellent. A nice hop—and, I'm sure, a good one back."

"Then we'll say good-by. I'll call you—when he's had a chance to get oriented. You understand?"

"Oh, surely. We'll be waiting." Thorby got a peck from his grandmother, a clap on the shoulder from his grandfather. Then he embarked with Weemsby and Leda in the larger car. Its skipper saluted Mr. Weemsby, then saluted Thorby—Thorby managed to return it.

Mr. Weemsby paused in the central passage. "Why don't you kids go forward and enjoy the hop? I've got calls waiting."

"Certainly, Daddy."

"You'll excuse me, Thor? Business goes on—it's back to the mines for Uncle Jack."

"Of course . . . Uncle Jack."

Leda led him forward and they sat down in a transparent bubble on the forward surface. The car rose straight up until they were several thousand feet high. It made a traffic-circle sweep over a desert plain, then headed north toward mountains.

"Comfy?" asked Leda.

"Quite. Uh, except that I'm dirty and mussed."

"There's a shower abaft the lounge. But we'll be home shortly—so why not enjoy the trip?"

"All right." Thorby did not want to miss any of fabulous Terra. It looked, he decided, like Hekate—no, more like Woolamurra, except that he had never seen so many buildings. The mountains—

He looked again. "What's that white stuff? Alum?"

Leda looked. "Why, that's snow. Those are the Sangre de Cristos."

" 'Snow,' " Thorby repeated. "That's frozen water."

"You haven't seen snow before?"

"I've heard of it. It's not what I expected."

"It *is* frozen water—and yet it isn't exactly; it's more feathery." She reminded herself of Daddy's warning; she must not show surprise at anything.

"You know," she offered, "I think I'll teach you to ski."

Many miles and some minutes were used explaining what skiing was and why people did it. Thorby filed it away as something he might try, more likely not. Leda said that a broken leg was "all that could happen." This is fun? Besides, she had mentioned how cold it could be. In Thorby's mind cold was linked with hunger, beatings, and fear. "Maybe I could learn," he said dubiously, "but I doubt it."

"Oh, sure you can!" She changed the subject. "Forgive my curiosity, Thor, but there is a faint accent in your speech."

"I didn't know I had an accent—"

"I didn't mean to be rude."

"You weren't. I suppose I picked it up in Jubbulpore. That's where I lived longest."

" 'Jubbulpore' . . . let me think. That's—"

"Capital of the Nine Worlds."

"Oh, yes! One of our colonies, isn't it?"

Thorby wondered what the Sargon would think of that. "Uh, not exactly. It is a sovereign empire now—their tradition is that they were never anything else. They don't like to admit that they derive from Terra."

"What an odd point of view."

A steward came forward with drinks and dainty nibbling foods. Thor accepted a frosted tumbler and sipped cautiously. Leda continued, "What were you doing there, Thor? Going to school?"

Thorby thought of Pop's patient teaching, decided that was not what she meant. "I was begging."

"What?"

"I was a beggar."

"Excuse me?"

"A beggar. A licensed mendicant. A person who asks for alms."

"That's what I thought you said," she answered. "I know what a beggar is; I've read books. But—excuse me, Thor; I'm just a home girl—I was startled."

She was not a "home girl"; she was a sophisticated woman adjusted to her environment. Since her mother's death she had been her father's hostess and could converse with people from other planets with aplomb, handling small talk of a large dinner party with gracious efficiency in three languages. Leda could ride, dance, sing, swim, ski, supervise a household, do arithmetic slowly, read and write if necessary, and make the proper responses. She was an intelligent, pretty, well-intentioned woman, culturally equivalent to a superior female head-hunter—able, adjusted and skilled.

But this strange lost-found cousin was a new bird to her. She said hesitantly, "Excuse my ignorance, but we don't have anything like that on Earth. I have trouble visualizing it. Was it terribly unpleasant?"

Thorby's mind flew back; he was squatting in lotus seat in the great Plaza with Pop sprawled beside him, talking. "It was the happiest time of my life," he said simply.

"Oh." It was all she could manage.

But Daddy had left them so that she could get to work. Asking a man about himself never failed. "How does one get started, Thor? I wouldn't know where to begin."

"I was taught. You see, I was up for sale and—" He thought of trying to explain Pop, decided to let it wait. "—an old beggar bought me."

" 'Bought' you?"

"I was a slave."

Leda felt as if she had stepped off into water over her head. Had he said "cannibal," "vampire," or "warlock" she could have been no more shocked. She came up, mentally gasping. "Thor—if I have been rude, I'm sorry—but we all are curious about the time—goodness! it's been over fifteen years—that you have been missing. But if you don't want to answer, just say so. You were a nice little boy and I was fond of you—please don't slap me down if I ask the wrong question."

"You don't believe me?"

"How could I? There haven't been slaves for centuries."

Thorby wished that he had never had to leave the *Hydra*, and gave up. He had learned in the Guard that the slave trade was something many fraki in the inner worlds simply hadn't heard of. "You knew me when I was little?"

"Oh, yes!"

"Why can't I remember you? I can't remember anything back before I was a—I can't remember Terra."

She smiled. "I'm three years older than you. When I saw you last, I was six—so I remember—and you were three, so you've forgotten."

"Oh." Thorby decided that here was a chance to find out his own age. "How old are you now?"

She smiled wryly. "Now I'm the same age you are—and I'll stay that age until I'm married. Turn about, Thorby—when you ask the wrong question, I shan't be offended. You don't ask a lady her age on Terra; you assume that she is younger than she is."

"So?" Thorby pondered this curious custom. Among People a female claimed the highest age she could, for status.

"So. For example, your mother was a lovely lady but I never knew her age. Perhaps she was twenty-five when I knew her, perhaps forty."

"You knew my parents?"

"Oh, yes! Uncle Creighton was a darling with a boomy voice. He used to give me handfuls of dollars to buy candy sticks and balloons with my own sweaty little hand." She frowned. "But I can't remember his face. Isn't that silly? Never mind, Thor; tell me anything you want to. I'd be happy to hear anything you don't mind telling."

"I don't mind," Thorby answered, "but, while I must have been captured, I don't remember it. As far as I remember, I never had parents; I was a slave, several places and masters—until I reached Jubbulpore. Then I was sold again and it was the luckiest thing that ever happened to me."

Leda lost her company smile. She said in a still voice, "You *really* mean it. Or do you?"

Thorby suffered the ancient annoyance of the returned traveler. "If you think that slavery has been abolished . . . well, it's a big galaxy. Shall I roll up my trouser leg and show you?"

"Show me what, Thor?"

"My slave's mark. The tattoo a factor uses to identify merchandise." He rolled up his left trouser. "See? The date is my manumission—it's Sargonese, a sort of Sanskrit; I don't suppose you can read it."

She stared, round-eyed. "How horrible! How perfectly horrible!"

He covered it. "Depends on your master. But it's not good."

"But why doesn't somebody *do* something?"

He shrugged. "It's a long way off."

"But—" She stopped as her father came out.

"Hi, kids. Enjoying the hop, Thor?"

"Yes, sir. The scenery is wonderful."

"The Rockies aren't a patch on the Himalayas. But our Tetons are pretty wonderful . . . and there they are. We'll be home soon." He pointed. "See? There's Rudbek."

"That city is named Rudbek?"

"It used to be Johnson's Hole, or some such, when it was a village. But I wasn't speaking of Rudbek City; I meant our home—your home—'Rudbek.' You can see the tower above the lake . . . with the Grand Tetons behind it. Most magnificent setting in the world. You're Rudbek of Rudbek at Rudbek . . . 'Rudbek Cubed,' your father called it . . . but he married into the name and wasn't impressed by it. I like it; it has a rolling thunder, and it's good to have a Rudbek back in residence."

Thorby wallowed in his bath, from needle shower, through hot pool whose sides and bottom massaged him with a thousand fingers, to lukewarm swimming plunge that turned cooler while he was in it. He was cautious in the last, having never learned to swim.

And he had never had a valet. He had noticed that Rudbek had dozens of people in it—not many for its enormous size, but he began to realize that most of them were servants. This impressed him not as much as it might have; he knew how many, many slaves staffed any rich household on Jubbul; he did not know that a living servant on Terra was the peak of ostentatious waste, greater than sedan chairs on Jubbul, much greater than the lavish hospitality at the Gatherings. He simply knew that valets made him nervous and now he had a squad of three. Thorby refused to let anyone bathe him; he gave in to being shaved because the available razor was a classic straight-edge and his own would not work on Rudbek's power supply. Otherwise he merely accepted advice about unfamiliar clothing.

The clothing waiting for him in wardrobe loads did not fit perfectly; the chief valet snipped and rewelded, muttering apologies. He had Thorby attired, ruffled jabot to tights, when a footman appeared. "Mr. Weemsby sends greetings to Rudbek and asks that he come to the great hall."

Thorby memorized the route as he followed.

Uncle Jack, in midnight and scarlet, was waiting with Leda, who was wearing . . . Thorby was at loss; colors kept changing and some it was hardly there. But she looked well. Her hair was now iridescent. He spotted among her jewels a bauble from Finster and wondered if it had shipped in *Sisu*—why, it was possible that he had listed it himself!

Uncle Jack said jovially, "There you are, lad! Refreshed? We won't wear you out, just a family dinner."

The dinner included twelve people and started with a reception in the great hall, drinks, appetizers, passed by soft-footed servants, music, while others were presented. "Rudbek of Rudbek, Lady Wilkes—your Aunt Jennifer, lad, come from New Zealand to welcome you"—"Rudbek of Rudbek, Judge Bruder and Mrs. Bruder—Judge is Chief Counsel," and so on. Thorby memorized names, linked them with faces, thinking that it was like the Family—except that relationship titles were not precise definitions; he had trouble estimating status. He did not know which of eighty-odd relations "cousin" meant with respect to Leda, though he supposed that she must be a first cross-cousin, since Uncle Jack had a surname not Rudbek; so he thought of her as taboo —which would have dismayed her.

He did realize that he must be in the sept of a wealthy family. But what his status was nobody mentioned, nor could he figure out status of others. Two of the youngest women dropped him curtseys. He thought the first had stumbled and tried to help her. But when the second did it, he answered by pressing his palms together.

The older women seemed to expect him to treat them with respect. Judge Bruder he could not classify. He hadn't been introduced as a relative—yet this was a family dinner. He fixed Thorby with an appraising eye and barked, "Glad to have you back, young man! There should be a Rudbek at Rudbek. Your holiday has caused trouble—hasn't it, John?"

"More than a bit," agreed Uncle Jack, "but we'll get straightened out. No hurry. Give the lad a chance to find himself."

"Surely, surely. Thumb in the dike."

Thorby wondered what a dike was, but Leda came up and placed her hand on his elbow. She steered him to the banquet hall; others followed. Thorby sat at one end of a long table with Uncle Jack at the other; Aunt Jennifer was on Thorby's right and Leda on his left. Aunt Jennifer started asking questions and supplying answers. He admitted that he had just left the Guard, she had trouble understanding that he had not been an officer; he let it ride and mentioned nothing about Jubbulpore—Leda had made him wary of the subject. It did not matter; he asked a question about New Zealand and received a guidebook lecture.

Then Leda turned from Judge Bruder and spoke to Thorby; Aunt Jennifer turned to the man on her right.

The tableware was in part strange, especially chop tongs and skewers. But spoons were spoons and forks were forks; by keeping his eye on Leda he got by. Food was served formally, but he had seen Grandmother so served; table manners were not great trouble to a man coached by Fritz's sharp-tongued kindness.

Not until the end was he stumped. The Butler-in-Chief presented him with an enormous goblet, splashed wetness in it and waited. Leda said softly, "Taste it, nod, and put it down." He did so; as the butler moved away, she whispered, "Don't drink it, it's bottled lightning. By the way, I told Daddy, 'No toasts.'"

At last the meal was over. Leda again cued him. "Stand up." He did and everyone followed.

The "family dinner" was just a beginning. Uncle Jack was in evidence only at dinners, and not always then. He excused his absences with, "Someone has to keep the fires burning. Business won't wait." As a trader Thorby understood that Business was Business, but he looked forward to a long talk with Uncle Jack, instead of so much social life. Leda was helpful but not informative. "Daddy is awfully busy. Different companies and things. It's too complicated for me. Let's hurry; the others are waiting."

Others were always waiting. Dancing, skiing—Thorby loved the flying sensation but considered it a chancy way to travel, particularly when he fetched up in a snow bank, having barely missed a tree—card parties, dinners with young people at which he took one end of the table and Leda the other, more dancing, hops to Yellowstone to feed the bears, midnight suppers, garden parties. Although Rudbek estate lay in the lap of the Tetons with snow around it, the house had an enormous tropical garden under a dome so pellucid that Thorby did not realize it was there until Leda had him touch it. Leda's friends were fun and Thorby gradually became sophisticated in small talk. The young men called him "Thor" instead of "Rudbek" and called Leda "Slugger." They treated him with familiar respect, and showed interest in the fact that he had been in the Guard and had visited many worlds, but they did not press personal questions. Thorby volunteered little, having learned his lesson.

But he began to tire of fun. A Gathering was wonderful but a working man expects to work.

The matter came to a head. A dozen of them were skiing and Thorby was alone on the practice slope. A man glided down and snowplowed to a stop. People hopped in and out at the estate's field day and night; this newcomer was Joel de la Croix.

"Hi, Thor."

"Hi, Joe."

"I've been wanting to speak to you. I've an idea I would like to discuss, after you take over. Can I arrange to see you, without being baffled by forty-'leven secretaries?"

"When I take over?"

"Or later, at your convenience. I want to talk to the boss; after all, you're the heir. I don't want to discuss it with Weemsby . . . even if he would see me." Joe looked anxious. "All I want is ten minutes. Say five if I don't interest you at once. 'Rudbek's promise.' Eh?"

Thorby tried to translate. Take over? Heir? He answered carefully, "I don't want to make any promises now, Joel."

De la Croix shrugged. "Okay. But think about it. I can prove it's a moneymaker."

"I'll think about it," Thorby agreed. He started looking for Leda. He got her alone and told her what Joe had said.

She frowned slightly. "It probably wouldn't hurt, since you aren't promising anything. Joel is a brilliant engineer. But better ask Daddy."

"That's not what I meant. What did he mean: 'take over'?"

"Why, you will, eventually."

"Take over *what?*"

"Everything. After all, you're Rudbek of Rudbek."

"What do you mean by 'everything'?"

"Why, why—" She swept an arm at mountain and lake, at Rudbek City beyond. "All of it, Rudbek. Lots of things. Things personally yours, like your sheep station in Australia and the house in Majorca. And business things. Rudbek Associates is many things—here and other planets. I couldn't begin to describe them. But they're yours, or maybe 'ours' for the whole family is in it. But you are the Rudbek of Rudbek. As Joe said, the heir."

Thorby looked at her, while his lips grew dry. He licked them and said, "Why wasn't I told?"

She looked distressed. "Thor dear! We've let you take your time. Daddy didn't want to worry you."

"Well," he said, "I'm worried now. I had better talk to Uncle Jack."

John Weemsby was at dinner but so were many guests. As they were leaving Weemsby motioned Thorby aside. "Leda tells me you're fretting."

"Not exactly. I want to know some things."

"You shall—I was hoping that you would tire of your vacation. Let's go to my study."

They went there; Weemsby dismissed his second-shift secretary and said, "Now what do you want to know?"

"I want to know," Thorby said slowly, "what it means to be 'Rudbek of Rudbek.' "

Weemsby spread his hands. "Everything . . . and nothing. You are titular head of the business, now that your father is dead . . . if he is."

"Is there any doubt?"

"I suppose not. Yet you turned up."

"Supposing he is dead, what am I? Leda seems to think I own just about everything. What did she mean?"

Weemsby smiled. "You know girls. No head for business. The ownership of our enterprises is spread around—most of it is in our employees. But, if your parents are dead, you come into stock in Rudbek Associates, which in turn has an interest in—sometimes a controlling interest—in other things. I couldn't describe it now. I'll have the legal staff do it—I'm a practical man, too busy making decisions to worry about who owns every share. But that reminds me . . . you haven't had a chance to spend much money, but you might want to." Weemsby opened a drawer, took out a pad. "There's a megabuck. Let me know if you run short."

Thorby thumbed through it. Terran currency did not bother him: a hundred dollars to the credit—which he thought of as five loaves of bread, a trick the Supercargo taught him—a thousand credits to the supercredit, a thousand supercredits to the megabuck. So simple that the People translated other currencies into it, for accounting.

But each sheet was ten thousand credits . . . and there were a hundred sheets. "Did I . . . inherit this?"

"Oh, that's just spending money—checks, really. You convert them at dispensers in stores or banks. You know how?"

"No."

"Don't get a thumbprint on the sensitized area until you insert it in the dispenser. Have Leda show you—if that girl could make money the way she spends it, neither you nor I would have to work. But," Weemsby added, "since we do, let's do a little." He took out a folder and spread papers. "Although this isn't hard. Just sign at the bottom of each, put your thumbprint by it, and I'll call Beth in to notarize. Here, we can open each one to the last page. I had better hold 'em—the consarned things curl up."

Weemsby held one for Thorby's signature. Thorby hesitated, then instead of signing, reached for the document. Weemsby held on. "What's the trouble?"

"If I'm going to sign, I ought to read it." He was thinking of something Grandmother used to be downright boring about.

Weemsby shrugged. "They are routine matters that Judge Bruder prepared for you." Weemsby placed the document on the others, tied the stack, and closed the folder. "These papers tell me to do what I have to do anway. Somebody has to do the chores."

"Why do I have to sign?"

"This is a safety measure."

"I don't understand."

Weemsby sighed. "The fact is, you don't understand business. No one expects you to; you haven't had any chance to learn. But that's why I have to keep slaving away; business won't wait." He hesitated. "Here's the simplest way to put it. When your father and mother went on a second honeymoon, they had to appoint someone to act while they were gone. I was the natural choice, since I was their business manager and your grandfather's before that—he died before they went away. So I was stuck with it while they went jaunting. Oh, I'm not complaining; it's not a favor one would refuse a member of the family. Unfortunately they did not come back, so I was left holding the baby.

"But now *you* are back and we must make sure everything is orderly. First it is necessary for your parents to be declared legally dead—that must be done before you can inherit. That will take a while. So here I am, *your* business manager, too—manager for all the family—and I don't have anything from you telling me to act. These papers do that."

Thorby scratched his cheek. "If I haven't inherited yet, why do you need anything from me?"

Weemsby smiled. "I asked that myself. Judge Bruder thinks it is best to tie down all possibilities. Now since you are of legal age—"

" 'Legal age'?" Thorby had never heard the term; among the People, a man was old enough for whatever he could do.

Weemsby explained. "So, since the day you passed your eighteenth birthday, you have been of legal age, which simplifies things—it means you don't have to become a ward of a court. We have your parents' authorization; now we add yours—and then it doesn't matter how long it takes the courts to decide that your parents are dead, or to settle their wills. Judge Bruder and I and the others who have to do the work can carry on without interruption. A time gap is avoided . . . one that might cost the business many megabucks. Now do you understand?"

"I think so."

"Good. Let's get it done." Weemsby started to open the folder.

Grandmother always said to read before signing—then think it over. "Uncle Jack, I want to read them."

"You wouldn't understand them."

"Probably not." Thorby picked up the folder. "But I've got to learn."

Weemsby reached for the folder. "It isn't necessary."

Thorby felt a surge of obstinacy. "Didn't you say Judge Bruder prepared these for me?"

"Yes."

"Then I want to take them to my apartment and try to understand them. If I'm 'Rudbek of Rudbek' I ought to know what I'm doing."

Weemsby hesitated, then shrugged. "Go ahead. You'll find that I'm simply trying to do for you what I have always been doing."

"But I still ought to understand what I'm doing."

"Very well! Good night."

Thorby read till he fell asleep. The language was baffling but the papers did seem to be what Uncle Jack said they were—instructions to John Weemsby to continue the routine business of a complex setup. He fell asleep full of terms like "full power of attorney," "all manner of business," "receive and pay monies," "revocable only by mutual consent," "waiver of personal appearance," "full faith and credence," and "voting proxy in all stockholding and/or directorial meetings, special or annual."

As he dozed off it occurred to him that he had not asked to see the authorizations given by his parents.

Sometime during the night he seemed to hear Grandmother's impatient voice: "—*then think it over! If you don't understand it, and the laws under which it will be executed, then don't sign it!—no matter how much profit may appear to be in store. Too lazy and too eager can ruin a trader."*

He stirred restlessly.

Chapter 18

HARDLY ANYONE came down for breakfast in Rudbek. But breakfast in bed was not in Thorby's training; he ate alone in the garden, luxuriating in hot mountain sunshine and lush tropical flowers while enjoying the snowy wonderland around him. Snow fascinated him—he had never dreamed that anything could be so beautiful.

But the following morning Weemsby came into the garden only moments after Thorby sat down. A chair was placed under Weemsby; a servant quickly laid a place. He said, "Just coffee. Good morning, Thor."

"Good morning, Uncle Jack."

"Well, did you get your studying done?"

"Sir? Oh, yes. That is, I fell asleep reading."

Weemsby smiled. "Lawyerese is soporific. Did you satisfy yourself that I had told you correctly what they contained?"

"Uh, I think so."

"Good." Weemsby put down his coffee and said to a servant, "Hand me a house phone. Thor, you irritated me last night."

"I'm sorry, sir."

"But I realize you were right. You should read what you sign—I wish I had time to! I have to accept the word of my staff in routine matters or I would never have time for policy . . . and I assumed that you would do the same with me. But caution is commendable." He spoke into the phone. "Carter, fetch those papers from Rudbek's apartment. The garden."

Thorby wondered if Carter could find the stuff—there

was a safe in his study but he had not learned to use it, so he had hidden the papers behind books. He started to mention it but Uncle Jack was talking.

"Here is something you will want to see . . . an inventory of real property you own—or will own, when the wills are settled. These holdings are unconnected with the business."

Thorby looked through it with amazement. Did he really own an island named Pitcairn at fifteen something south and a hundred and thirty west—whatever that meant? A domehouse on Mars? A shooting lodge in Yukon—where was "Yukon" and why shoot there? You ought to be in free space to risk shooting. And what were all these other things?

He looked for one item. "Uncle Jack? How about Rudbek?"

"Eh? You're sitting on it."

"Yes . . . but do I own it? Leda said I did."

"Well, yes. But it's entailed—that means your great-great-grandfather decided that it should never be sold . . . so that there would always be a Rudbek at Rudbek."

"Oh."

"I thought you might enjoy looking over your properties. I've ordered a car set aside for you. Is that one we hopped here in satisfactory?"

"What? Goodness, yes!" Thorby blinked.

"Good. It was your mother's and I've been too sentimental to dispose of it. But it has had all latest improvements added. You might persuade Leda to hop with you; she is familiar with most of that list. Take some young friends along and make a picnic of it, as long as you like. We can find a congenial chaperone."

Thorby put the list down. "I probably will, Uncle Jack . . . presently. But I ought to get to work."

"Eh?"

"How long does it take to learn to be a lawyer here?"

Weemsby's face cleared. "I see. Lawyers' quaint notions of language can shock a man. It takes four or five years."

"It does?"

"The thing for you is two or three years at Harvard or some other good school of business."

"I need that?"

"Definitely."

"Unh . . . you know more about it than I do—"

"I should! By now."

"—but couldn't I learn something about the business before I go to school? I haven't any idea what it is."

"Plenty of time."

"But I want to learn *now*."

Weemsby started to cloud, then smiled and shrugged. "Thor, you have your mother's stubbornness. All right, I'll order a suite for you at the main office in Rudbek City— and staff it with people to help you. But I warn you, it won't be fun. Nobody owns a business; the business owns him. You're a slave to it."

"Well . . . I ought to try."

"Commendable spirit." The phone by Weemsby's cup blinked; he picked it up, frowned, said, "Hold on." He turned to Thorby. "That idiot can't find those papers."

"I meant to tell you. I hid them—I didn't want to leave them out."

"I see. Where are they?"

"Uh, I'll have to dig them out."

Weemsby said in the phone, "Forget it." He tossed the phone to a servant and said to Thorby, "Then fetch them, if you don't mind."

Thorby did mind. So far he had had four bites; it annoyed him to be told to run an errand while eating. Besides . . . was he "Rudbek of Rudbek"? or still messenger for the weapons officer? "I'll be going up after breakfast."

Uncle Jack looked vexed. But he answered, "I beg your pardon. If you can't tear yourself away, would you please tell *me* where to find them? I have a hard day ahead and I would like to dispose of this triviality and go to work. *If* you don't mind."

Thorby wiped his mouth. "I would rather not," he said slowly, "sign them now."

"What? You told me that you had satisfied yourself."

"No, sir, I told you that I had read them. But I don't understand them. Uncle Jack, where are the papers that my parents signed?"

"Eh?" Weemsby looked at him sharply. "Why?"

"I want to see them."

Weemsby considered. "They must be in the vault at Rudbek City."

"All right. I'll go there."

Weemsby suddenly stood up. "If you will excuse me, I'll go to work," he snapped. "Young man, some day you will realize what I have done for you! In the meantime, since you choose to be uncooperative, I still must get on with my duties."

He left abruptly. Thorby felt hurt—he didn't want to be uncooperative . . . but if they had waited for years, why couldn't they wait a little longer and give him a chance?

He recovered the papers, then phoned Leda. She answered, with vision switched off. "Thor dear, what are you doing up in the middle of the night?"

He explained that he wanted to go to the family's business offices. "I thought maybe you could direct me."

"You say Daddy said to?"

"He's going to assign me an office."

"I won't just direct you; I'll take you. But give a girl a chance to get a face on and swallow orange juice."

He discovered that Rudbek was connected with their offices in Rudbek City by high-speed sliding tunnel. They arrived in a private foyer guarded by an elderly receptionist. She looked up. "Hello, Miss Leda! How nice to see you!"

"You, too, Aggie. Will you tell Daddy we're here?"

"Of course." She looked at Thorby.

"Oh," said Leda. "I forgot. This is Rudbek of Rudbek."

Aggie jumped to her feet. "Oh, dear me! I didn't *know*—I'm sorry, sir!"

Things happened quickly. In minutes Thorby found himself with an office of quiet magnificence, with a quietly magnificent secretary who addressed him by his double-barreled title but expected him to call her "Dolores." There seemed to be unlimited genies ready to spring out of walls at a touch of her finger.

Leda stuck with him until he was installed, then said, "I'll run along, since you insist on being a dull old businessman." She looked at Dolores. "Or will it be dull? Perhaps I should stay." But she left.

Thorby was intoxicated with being immensely wealthy and powerful. Top executives called him "Rudbek," junior executives called him "Rudbek of Rudbek," and those still more junior crowded their words with "sirs"—he could judge status by how he was addressed.

While he was not yet active in business—he saw Weemsby rarely and Judge Bruder almost never—anything he wanted appeared quickly. A word to Dolores and a respectful young man popped in to explain legal matters; another word and an operator appeared to show moving stereocolor of business interests anywhere, even on other planets. He spent days looking at such pictures, yet still did not see them all.

His office became so swamped with books, spools, charts, brochures, presentations, file jackets, and figures, that Dolores had the office next door refitted as a library. There were figures on figures, describing in fiscal analog enterprises too vast to comprehend otherwise. There were so many figures, so intricately related, that his head ached. He began to have misgivings about the vocation of tycoon. It wasn't all just being treated with respect, going through doors first and always getting what you asked for. What was the point if you were so snowed under that you could not enjoy it? Being a Guardsman was easier.

Still, it was nice to be important. Most of his life he had been nobody, and at best he had been very junior.

If only Pop could see him now!—surrounded by lavish furnishings, a barber to trim his hair while he worked (Pop used to cut it under a bowl), a secretary to anticipate his wishes, and dozens of people eager to help. But Pop's face in this dream was wearing Pop's reproving expression; Thorby wondered what he had done wrong, and dug harder into the mess of figures.

Eventually a pattern began to emerge. The business was Rudbek & Associates, Ltd. So far as Thorby could tell this firm did nothing. It was chartered as a private investment trust and just owned things. Most of what Thorby would own, when his parents' wills were proved, was stock in this company. Nor would he own it all; he felt almost poverty-stricken when he discovered that mother and father together held only eighteen percent of many thousand shares.

Then he found out about "voting" and "non-voting"; the shares coming to him were eighteen-fortieths of the voting shares; the remainder was split between relatives and non-relatives.

Rudbek & Assocs. owned stock in other companies—and here it got complicated. Galactic Enterprises, Galactic Acceptance Corporation, Galactic Transport, Interstellar Metals, Three Planets Fiscal (which operated on twenty-seven planets), Havermeyer Laboratories (which ran barge lines and bakeries as well as research stations)—the list looked endless. These corporations, trusts, cartels, and banking houses seemed as tangled as spaghetti. Thorby learned that he owned (through his parents) an interest in a company called "Honace Bros., Pty." through a chain of six companies —18% of 31% of 43% of 19% of 44% of 27%, a share so microscopic that he lost track. But his parents owned directly seven per cent of Honace Brothers—with the result that his indirect interest of one-twentieth of one per cent controlled it utterly but paid little return, whereas seven per cent owned directly did not control—but paid one hundred and forty times as much.

It began to dawn on him that control and ownership were only slightly related; he had always thought of "ownership" and "control" as being the same thing; you owned a thing, a begging bowl, or a uniform jacket—of course you controlled it!

The converging, diverging, and crossing of corporations and companies confused and disgusted him. It was as complex as a firecontrol computer without a computer's cool logic. He tried to draw a chart and could not make it work. The ownership of each entity was tangled in common stocks, preferred stocks, bonds, senior and junior issues, securities with odd names and unknown functions; sometimes one company owned a piece of another directly and another piece through a third, or two companies might each own a little of the other, or sometimes a company owned part of itself in a tail-swallowing fashion. It didn't make sense.

This wasn't "business"—what the People did was *business* . . . buy, sell, make a profit. But this was a silly game with wild rules.

Something else fretted him. He had not known that Rudbek built spaceships. Galactic Enterprises controlled Galactic Transport, which built ships in one of its many divisions. When he realized it he felt a glow of pride, then discovered gnawing uneasiness—something Colonel Brisby had said . . . something Pop had proved: that the "largest" or it might have been "one of the largest" builders of starships was mixed up in the slave trade.

He told himself he was being silly—this beautiful office was about as far from the dirty business of slave traffic as anything could be. But as he was dropping to sleep one night he came wide awake with the black, ironic thought that one of those slave ships in whose stinking holds he had ridden might have been, at that very time, the property of the scabby, frightened slave he was then.

It was a nightmare notion; he pushed it away. But it took the fun out of what he was doing.

One afternoon he sat studying a long memorandum from the legal department—a summary, so it said, of Rudbek & Assocs.' interests—and found that he had dragged to a halt. It seemed as if the writer had gone out of his way to confuse things. It would have been as intelligible in ancient Chinese—more so; Sargonese included many Mandarin words.

He sent Dolores out and sat with his head in his hands. Why, oh, why hadn't he been left in the Guard? He had been happy there; he had understood the world he was in.

Then he straightened up and did something he had been putting off; he returned a vuecall from his grandparents. He had been expected to visit them long since, but he had felt compelled to try to learn his job first.

Indeed he was welcome! "Hurry, son—we'll be waiting." It was a wonderful hop across prairie and the mighty Mississippi (small from that height) and over city-pocked farm land to the sleepy college town of Valley View, where sidewalks were stationary and time itself seemed slowed. His grandparents' home, imposing for Valley View, was homey after the awesome halls of Rudbek.

But the visit was not relaxing. There were guests at dinner, the president of the college and department heads, and many more after dinner—some called him "Rudbek of Rudbek," others addressed him uncertainly as "Mr. Rudbek," and still others, smug with misinformation as to how the nabob was addressed by familiars, simply as "Rudbek." His grandmother twittered around, happy as only a proud hostess can be, and his grandfather stood straight and addressed him loudly as "Son."

Thorby did his best to be a credit to them. He soon realized that it was not what he said but the fact of talking to Rudbek that counted.

The following night, which his grandmother reluctantly kept private, he got a chance to talk. He wanted advice.

First information was exchanged. Thorby learned that his father, on marrying the only child of his grandfather Rudbek, had taken his wife's family name. "It's understandable," Grandfather Bradley told him. "Rudbek has to have a Rudbek. Martha was heir but Creighton had to preside—board meetings and conferences and at the dinner table for that matter. I had hoped that my son would pursue the muse of history, as I have. But when this came along, what could I do but be happy for him?"

His parents and Thorby himself had been lost as a consequence of his father's earnest attempt to be in the fullest sense Rudbek of Rudbek—he had been trying to inspect as much of the commercial empire as possible. "Your father was always conscientious and when your Grandfather Rudbek died before your father completed his apprenticeship, so to speak, Creighton left John Weemsby in charge— John is, I suppose you know, the second husband of your other grandmother's youngest sister Aria—and Leda, of course, is Aria's daughter by her first marriage."

"No, I hadn't known." Thorby translated the relationships into *Sisu* terms . . . and reached the startling conclusion that Leda was in the other moiety!—if they had such things here, which they didn't. And Uncle Jack—well, he wasn't "uncle"—but how would you say it in English?

"John had been a business secretary and factotum to your other grandfather and he was the perfect choice, of course; he knew the inner workings better than anyone, except your grandfather himself. After we got over the shock of our tragic loss we realized that the world must go on and that John could handle it as well as if he had been Rudbek himself."

"He's been simply wonderful!" grandmother chirped.

"Yes, he has. I must admit that your grandmother and I became used to a comfortable scale of living after Creighton married. College salaries are never what they should be; Creighton and Martha were very generous. Your grandmother and I might have found it difficult after we realized that our son was gone, never to come back, had not John told us not to worry. He saw to it that our benefit continued just as before."

"And increased it," Grandmother Bradley added emphatically.

"Well, yes. All the family—we think of ourselves as part of Rudbek family even though we bear a proud name of our own—all of the family have been pleased with John's stewardship."

Thorby was interested in something other than "Uncle Jack's" virtues. "You told me that we left Akka, jumping for Far-Star, and never made it? That's a long, long way from Jubbul."

"I suppose it is. The College has only a small Galactovue and I must admit that it is hard to realize that what appears to be an inch or so is actually many light-years."

"About a hundred and seventy light-years, in this case."

"Let me see, how much would that be in miles?"

"You don't measure it that way, any more than you measure that couchomat you're on in microns."

"Come now, young man, don't be pedantic."

"I wasn't being, Grandfather. I was thinking that it was a long way from where I was captured to where I was last sold. I hadn't known it."

"I heard you use that term 'sold' once before. You must realize that it is not correct. After all, the serfdom practiced in the Sargony is not chattel slavery. It derives from the ancient Hindu gild or 'caste' system—a stabilized social order with mutal obligations, up and down. You must not call it 'slavery.'"

"I don't know any other word to translate the Sargonese term."

"I could think of several, though I don't know Sargonese . . . it's not a useful tongue in scholarship. But, my dear Thor, you aren't a student of human histories and culture. Grant me a little authority in my own field."

"Well . . ." Thorby felt baffled. "I don't know System English perfectly and there's a lot of history I don't know—there's an awful lot of history."

"So there is. As I am the first to admit."

"But I can't translate any better—I was sold and I was a slave!"

"Now, Son."

"Don't contradict your grandfather, dear, that's a good boy."

Thorby shut up. He had already mentioned his years as a beggar—and discovered that his grandmother was horrified, had felt that he had disgraced himself, though she did not quite say so. And he had already found that while his grandfather knew much about many things, he was just as certain of his knowledge when Thorby's eyes had reported things differently. Thorby concluded glumly that it was part of being senior and nothing could be done about it. He listened while Grandfather Bradley discoursed on the history of the Nine Worlds. It didn't agree with what the Sargonese believed but wasn't too far from what Pop had taught him—other than about slavery. He was glad when the talk drifted back to the Rudbek organization. He admitted his difficulties.

"You can't build Rome in a day, Thor."

"It looks as if I never would learn! I've been thinking about going back into the Guard."

His grandfather frowned. "That would not be wise."

"Why not, sir?"

"If you don't have talent for business, there are other honorable professions."

"Meaning the Guard isn't?"

"Mmm . . . your grandmother and I are philosophical pacifists. It cannot be denied that there is never a moral justification for taking human life."

"Never," agreed grandmother firmly.

Thorby wondered what Pop would think? Shucks, he knew!—Pop cut 'em down like grass to rescue a load of slaves. "What do you do when a raider jumps you?"

"A what?"

"A pirate. You've got a pirate on your tail and closing fast."

"Why, you run, I suppose. It's not moral to stay and do battle. Thor, nothing is ever gained by violence."

"But you *can't* run; he has more legs. It's you or him."

"You mean 'he.' Then you surrender; that defeats his purpose . . . as the immortal Gandhi proved."

Thorby took a deep breath. "Grandfather, I'm sorry but it *doesn't* defeat his purpose. You have to fight. Raiders take slaves. The proudest thing I ever did was to burn one."

"Eh? 'Burn one'?"

"Hit him with a target-seeker. Blast him out of the sky."

214

Grandmother gasped. At last his grandfather said stiffly, "Thor, I'm afraid you've been exposed to bad influences. Not your fault, perhaps. But you have many misconceptions, both in fact and in evaluation. Now be logical. If you 'burned him' as you say, how do you *know* he intended—again, as you say—to 'take slaves'? What could he do with them? Nothing."

Thorby kept silent. It made a difference which side of the Plaza you saw a thing from . . . and if you didn't have status, you weren't listened to. That was a universal rule.

Grandfather Bradley continued, "So we'll say no more about it. On this other matter I'll give you the advice I would give your departed father: if you feel that you have no head for trade, you don't have to enter it. But to run away and join the Guard, like some childish romantic—no, Son! But you needn't make up your mind for years. John is a very able regent; you don't have a decision facing you." He stood up. "I know, for I've discussed this with John, and he's willing, in all humility, to carry the burden a little farther . . . or much farther, if need be. And now we had all better seek our pillows. Morning comes early."

Thor left the next morning, with polite assurances that the house was his—which made him suspect that it was. He went to Rudbek City, having reached a decision during a restless night. He wanted to sleep with a live ship around him. He wanted to be back in Pop's outfit; being a billionaire boss wasn't his style.

He had to do something first; dig out those papers that father and mother had signed, compare them with the ones prepared for him—since father must have known what was needed—sign them, so that Uncle Jack could get on with the work after he was gone. Grandfather was right about that; John Weemsby knew how to do the job and he didn't. He should be grateful to Uncle Jack. He would thank him before he left. Then off Terra and out to where people talked his language!

He buzzed Uncle Jack's office as soon as he reached his

215

own, was told that he was out of town. He decided that he could write a note and make it sound better—oh yes! Must say good-by to Leda. So he buzzed the legal department and told him to dig his parents' authorizations out of the vault and send them to his office.

Instead of papers, Judge Bruder arrived. "Rudbek, what's this about your ordering certain papers from the vault?"

Thorby explained. "I want to see them."

"No one but officers of the company can order papers from the vault."

"What am I?"

"I'm afraid you are a young man with confused notions. In time, you will have authority. But at the moment you are a visitor, learning something about your parents' affairs."

Thorby swallowed it; it was true, no matter how it tasted. "I've been meaning to ask you about that. What's the progress in the court action to have my parents declared dead?"

"Are you trying to bury them?"

"Of course not. But it has to be done, or so Uncle Jack says. So where are we?"

Bruder sniffed. "Nowhere. Through your doing."

"What do you mean?"

"Young man, do you think that the officers of this company will initiate a process which would throw affairs of the firm into incredible confusion unless you take necessary steps to guard against it? Why, it may take *years* to settle the wills—during which, business would come to a stop . . . simply because you neglected to sign a few simple instruments which I prepared weeks ago."

"You mean nothing will be done until I sign?"

"That is correct."

"I don't understand. Suppose I were dead—or had never been born. Does business stop every time a Rudbek dies?"

"Mmm . . . well, no. A court authorizes matters to proceed. But you *are* here and we must take that into consideration. Now see here, I'm at the very end of my patience. You seem to think, simply because you've read a few balance sheets, that you understand business. You don't. For example your belief that you can order instruments turned over to you that were given to John Weemsby personally and are not even company property. If you were to attempt to take charge of the firm at this time—if we proceeded with your notion to have your parents declared dead—I can see that we would have all sorts of confusion while you were finding your balance. We can't afford it. The company can't afford it. Rudbek can't afford it. So I want those papers signed today and no more shilly-shallying. You understand?"

Thorby lowered his head. "I won't."

"What do you mean, 'You won't'?"

"I won't sign anything until I know what I'm doing. If I can't even see the papers my parents signed, then I certainly won't."

"We'll see about that!"

"I'm going to sit tight until I find out what's going on around here!"

Chapter 19

THORBY DISCOVERED that finding out was difficult. Things went on much as before but were not the same. He had vaguely suspected that the help he was being given in learning the business had sometimes been too much not well enough organized; he felt smothered in unrelated figures, verbose and obscure "summaries," "analyses" that did not analyze. But he had known so little that it took time to become even a suspicion.

The suspicion became certainty from the day he defied Judge Bruder. Dolores seemed eager as ever and people still hopped when he spoke but the lavish flow of information trickled toward a stop. He was stalled with convincing excuses but could never quite find out what he wanted to know. A "survey is being prepared" or the man who "has charge of that is out of the city" or "those are vault files and none of the delegated officers are in today." Neither Judge Bruder nor Uncle Jack was ever available and their assistants were politely unhelpful. Nor was he able to corner Uncle Jack at the estate. Leda told him that "Daddy often has to go away on trips."

Things began to be confused in his own office. Despite the library Dolores had set up she could not seem to find, or even recall, papers that he had marked for retention. Finally he lost his temper and bawled her out.

She took it quietly. "I'm sorry, sir. I'm trying very hard."

Thorby apologized. He knew a slow-down when he saw one; he had checked enough stevedores to know. But this poor creature could not help herself; he was lashing out at the wrong person. He added placatingly, "I really am sorry. Take the day off."

"Oh, I couldn't, sir."

"Who says so? Go home."

"I'd rather not, sir."

"Well . . . suit yourself. But go lie down in the ladies' lounge or something. That's an order. I'll see you tomorrow."

She looked worried and left. Thorby sat at his chaste, bare, unpowered executive desk and thought.

It was what he needed: to be left alone without a flood of facts and figures. He started digesting what he had soaked up. Presently he started listing the results.

Item: Judge Bruder and Uncle Jack had put him in Coventry for refusing to sign the proxies.

Item: He might be "Rudbek of Rudbek"—but Uncle Jack would continue to run things until Thorby's parents were legally dead.

Item: Judge Bruder had told him bluntly that no steps would be taken about the above until he admitted his incompetence and signed proxies.

Item: He did not know what his parents had signed. He had tried to force a showdown—and had failed.

Item: "Ownership" and "control" were very different. Uncle Jack controlled everything that Thorby owned; Uncle

Jack owned merely a nominal one share to qualify him as acting chairman of the board. (Leda owned a chunk as she was a Rudbek while Uncle Jack wasn't—but Uncle Jack probably controlled her stock too; Leda paid no attention to business.)

Conclusions:—

What conclusions? Was Uncle Jack doing something crooked and didn't dare let him find out? Well, it didn't look like it. Uncle Jack had salary and bonuses so large that only a miser would want more money simply as money. His parents' accounts seemed in order—they showed a huge balance; the megabuck Uncle Jack had handed him hardly made a dent. The only other withdrawals were for Grandfather and Grandmother Bradley, plus a few sums around the family or charge to the estates—nothing important, another couple of megabucks.

Conclusion: Uncle Jack was boss, liked being boss, and meant to go on being boss if possible.

"Status" . . . Uncle Jack had high status and was fighting to keep it. Thorby felt that he understood him at last. Uncle Jack put up with the overwork he complained about because he *liked* being boss—just as captains and chief officers worked themselves silly, even though every member of a Free Trader family owned the same share. Uncle Jack was "chief officer" and didn't intend to surrender his supreme status to someone a third of his age who (let's face it!) wasn't competent for the work the status required.

In this moment of insight Thorby felt that he ought to sign those proxies for Uncle Jack, who had earned the job whereas Thorby had merely inherited it. Uncle Jack must have been terribly disappointed when he had turned up alive; it must have seemed an utterly unfair twist of fate.

Well, let him have it! Settle things and join the Guard.

But Thorby was not ready to back down to Judge Bruder. He had been pushed around—and his strongest reflex was resistance to any authority he had not consented to; it had been burned into his soul with whips. He did not know this—he just knew that he was going to be stubborn. He decided that Pop would want him to be.

Thought of Pop reminded him of something. Was Rudbek connected, even indirectly, with the slave trade? He realized now why Pop wanted him to hang on—he could not quit until he knew . . . nor until he had put a stop to it if the unspeakable condition did exist. But how could he find out? He was Rudbek of Rudbek . . . but they had him tied with a thousand threads, like the fellow in that story Pop had told . . . "Gulliver and his Starship," that was it.

Well, let's see, Pop had reported to "X" Corps that there was a tie-up among some big spaceship outfit, the Sargon's government, and the raider-slavetraders. Raiders had to have ships. Ships . . . there was a book he had read last week, Galactic Transport's history of every ship they had built, from #0001 to the latest. He went into his library. Hmm . . . tall red book, not a tape.

Confounded thing was missing . . . like a lot of things lately. But he had almost renshawed the book, being interested in ships. He started making notes.

Most of them were in service inside the Hegemony, some in Rudbek interests, some in others. Some of his ships had been sold to the People, a pleasing thought. But some had wound up registered to owners he could not place . . . and yet he thought he knew the names, at least, of all outfits engaged in legitimate interstellar trade under the Hegemony —and he certainly would recognize any Free Trader clan.

No way to be sure of anything from his desk, even if he had the book. Maybe there was *no* way, from Terra . . . maybe even Judge Bruder and Uncle Jack would not know if something fishy were going on.

He got up and switched on the Galactovue he had had installed. It showed only the explored fraction of the Galaxy —even so, the scale was fantastically small.

He began operating controls. First he lighted in green the Nine Worlds. Then he added, in yellow, pestholes avoided by the People. He lighted up the two planets between which he and his parents had been captured, then did the same for every missing ship of the People concerning which he happened to know the span of the uncompleted jump.

The result was a constellation of colored lights, fairly close together as star distances go and in the same sector as the Nine Worlds. Thorby looked at it and whistled. Pop had known what he was talking about—yet it would be hard to spot unless displayed like this.

He began thinking about cruising ranges and fueling stations maintained by Galactic Transport out that way . . . then added in orange the banking offices of Galactic Acceptance Corporation in the "neighborhood."

Then he studied it.

It was not certain proof—yet what other outfit maintained such activities facing that sector?

He intended to find out.

Chapter 20

THORBY FOUND that Leda had ordered dinner in the garden. They were alone, and falling snow turned the artificial sky into an opalescent bowl. Candles, flowers, a string trio, and Leda herself made the scene delightful but Thorby failed to enjoy it, even though he liked Leda and considered the garden the best part of Rudbek Hall. The meal was almost over when Leda said, "A dollar for your thoughts."

Thorby looked guilty. "Uh, nothing."

"It must be a worrisome nothing."

"Well . . . yes."

"Want to tell Leda?"

Thorby blinked. Weemsby's daughter was the last one he could talk to. His gloom was caused by wonder as to what he could do if he became convinced that Rudbek was mixed up in slavery. "I guess I'm not cut out to be a businessman."

"Why, Daddy says you have a surprising head for figures."

Thorby snorted. "Then why doesn't he—" He stopped.

"Why doesn't he what?"

"Uh . . ." Doggone it, a man had to talk to somebody
. . . someone who sympathized—or bawled him out if
necessary. Like Pop. Like Fritz. Yeah, like Colonel Brisby.
He was surrounded by people, yet utterly alone—except
that Leda seemed to want to be friendly. "Leda, how much
of what I say to you do you tell your father?"

To his amazement she blushed. "What made you say
that, Thor?"

"Well, you are pretty close to him. Aren't you?"

She stood up suddenly. "If you've finished, let's walk."

Thorby stood up. They strolled paths, watched the storm,
listened to its soft noises against the dome. She guided them
to a spot away from the house and shielded by bushes
and there sat down on a boulder. "This is a good spot—for
private conversation."

"It is?"

"When the garden was wired, I made sure that there
was somewhere I could be kissed without Daddy's snoopers
listening in."

Thorby stared. "You mean that?"

"Surely you realize you are monitored almost everywhere
but the ski slopes?"

"I didn't. And I don't like it."

"Who does? But it is a routine precaution with anything
as big as Rudbek; you mustn't blame Daddy. I just spent
some credits to make sure the garden wasn't as well wired
as he thought. So if you have anything to say you don't
want Daddy to hear, you can talk now. He'll never know.
That's a cross-my-heart promise."

Thorby hesitated, then checked the area. He decided that
if a microphone were hidden nearby it must be disguised
as a flower . . . which was possible. "Maybe I ought to save
it for the ski slope."

"Relax, dear. If you trust me at all, trust me that this
place is safe."

"Uh, all right." He found himself blurting out his frustrations . . . his conclusion that Uncle Jack was intentionally thwarting him unless he would turn over his potential power. Leda listened gravely. "That's it. Now—am I crazy?"

She said, "Thor, you know that Daddy has been throwing me at you?"

"Huh?"

"I don't see how you could miss it. Unless you are utterly—but then, perhaps you are. Just take it as true. It's one of those obvious marriages that everyone is enthusiastic about . . . except maybe the two most concerned."

Thorby forgot his worries in the face of this amazing statement. "You mean . . . well, uh, that you—" He trailed off.

"Heavens, dear! If I intended to go through with it, would I have told you anything? Oh, I admit I promised, before you arrived, to consider it. But you never warmed to the idea—and I'm too proud to be willing under those circumstances even if the preservation of Rudbek depended on it. Now what's this about Daddy not letting you see the proxies that Martha and Creighton gave him?"

"They won't let me see them; I won't sign until they do."

"But you'll sign if they do?"

"Uh . . . maybe I will, eventually. But I want to see what arrangements my parents made."

"I can't see why Daddy opposes such a reasonable request. Unless . . ." She frowned.

"Unless what?"

"What about your shares? Have those been turned over to you?"

"What shares?"

"Why, *yours*. You know what shares I hold. They were given to me when I was born, by Rudbek—your grandfather, I mean. My uncle. You probably got twice as many, since you were expected to become the Rudbek someday."

"I haven't any shares."

She nodded grimly. "That's one reason Daddy and the Judge don't want you to see those papers. Our personal shares don't depend on anyone; they're ours to do as we please with, since we are both legal age. Your parents voted yours, just as Daddy still votes mine—but any proxy they assigned concerning your shares can't be any good now. You can pound the desk and they'll have to cough up, or shoot you." She frowned. "Not that they would shoot. Thor, Daddy is a good sort, most ways."

"I never said he wasn't."

"I don't love him but I'm fond of him. But when it comes down to it, I'm a Rudbek and he's not. That's silly, isn't it? Because we Rudbeks aren't anything special; we're just shrewd peasants. But I've got a worry, too. You remember Joel de la Croix?"

"He's the one that wanted an interview with me?"

"That's right. Joey doesn't work here any more."

"I don't understand."

"He was a rising star in the engineering department of Galactic—didn't you know? The office says he left to accept other employment; Joey says he was fired for going over their heads to speak to you." She frowned. "I didn't know what to believe. Now I believe Joey. Well, Thor, are you going to take it lying down? Or prove that you are Rudbek of Rudbek?"

Thorby chewed his lip. "I'd like to go back into the Guard and forget the whole mess. I used to wonder what it was like to be rich. Now I *am* and it turns out to be mostly headaches."

"So you'd walk out on it?" Her voice was faintly scornful.

"I didn't say *that*. I'm going to stay and find out what goes on. Only I don't know how to start. You think I should pound Uncle Jack's desk and demand my shares?"

"Unnh . . . not without a lawyer at your side."

"There are too many lawyers in this now!"

"That's why you need one. It will take a sharp one to win a scrap with Judge Bruder."

"How do I find one?"

"Goodness, I don't use lawyers. But I can find out. Now let's stroll and chat—in case anybody is interested."

Thorby spent a glum morning studying corporation law. Just past lunch Leda called. "Thor, how about taking me skiing? The storm is over and the snow is just right." She looked at him eagerly.

"Well—"

"Oh, come on!"

He went. They said nothing until they were far from the house. Then Leda said, "The man you need is James J. Garsch, New Washington."

"I thought that must be why you called. Do you want to ski? I'd like to go back and call him."

"Oh, my!" she shook her head sadly. "Thor, I may have to marry you just to mother you. You go back to the house and call a lawyer outside Rudbek—one whose reputation is sky-high. What happens?"

"What?"

"You might wake up in a quiet place with big muscular nurses around you. I've had a sleepless night and I'm convinced they mean business. So I had to make up my mind. I was willing for Daddy to run things forever . . . but if he fights dirty, I'm on your side."

"Thanks, Leda."

" 'Thanks' he says! Thor, this is for Rudbek. Now to business. You can't grab your hat and go to New Washington to retain a lawyer. If I know Judge Bruder, he has planned what to do if you try. But you can go look at some of your estate . . . starting with your house in New Washington."

"That's smart, Leda."

"I'm so smart I dazzle myself. If you want it to look good, you'll invite me along—Daddy has told me that I ought to show you around."

"Why, sure, Leda. If it won't be too much trouble."

"I'll simply force myself. We'll actually do some sightseeing, in the Department of North America, at least. The only thing that bothers me is how to get away from the guards."

"Guards?"

"Nobody high up in Rudbek ever travels without body-guards. Why, you'd be run ragged by reporters and crack-pots."

"I think," Thorby said slowly, "that you must be mistaken in my case. I went to see my grandparents. There weren't any guards."

"They specialize in being unobtrusive. I'll bet there were always at least two in your grandmother's house while you were there. See that solitary skier? Long odds he's not skiing for fun. So we have to find a way to get them off your neck while you look up Counselor Garsch. Don't worry, I'll think of something."

Thorby was immensely interested in the great capital but still more interested in getting on with his purpose. Leda did not let him hurry. "First we sightsee. We naturally would."

The house, simple compared with Rudbek—twenty rooms, only two of them large—was as ready as if he had stepped out the day before. Two of the servants he recognized as having been at Rudbek. A ground car, with driver and footman in Rudbek livery, was waiting. The driver seemed to know where to take them; they rode around in the semi-tropic winter sunshine and Leda pointed out planetary embassies and consulates. When they passed the immense pile which is headquarters of the Hegemonic Guard, Thorby had the driver slow down while he rubbernecked. Leda said, "That's your alma mater, isn't it?" Then she whispered, "Take a good look. The building opposite its main door is where you are going."

They got out at the Replica Lincoln Memorial, walked up the steps and felt the same hushed awe that millions have felt when looking at that brooding giant figure. Thorby had a sudden feeling that the statue looked like Pop—not that it did, but still it *did*. His eyes filled with tears.

Leda whispered, "This place always gets me—it's like a haunted church. You know who he was? He founded America. Ancient history is awesome."

"He did something else."

"What?"

"He freed slaves."

"Oh." She looked up with sober eyes. "That means something special to you . . . doesn't it?"

"Very special." He considered telling Leda his strongest reason for pushing the fight, since they were alone and this was a place that wouldn't be bugged. But he couldn't. He felt that Pop would not mind—but he had promised Colonel Brisby.

He puzzled over inscriptions on the walls, in letters and spelling used before English became System English. Leda tugged his sleeve and whispered, "Come on. I can never stay here long or I start crying." They tiptoed away.

Leda decided that she just had to see the show at the Milky Way. So they got out and she told the driver to pick them up in three hours and ten minutes, then Thorby paid outrageous scalpers' prices for a double booth and immediate occupancy.

"There!" she sighed as they started inside. "That's half of it. The footman will drop off as they round the corner, but we're rid of the driver for a while; there isn't a place to park around here. But the footman will be right behind us, if he wants to keep his job. He's buying a ticket this minute. Or maybe he's already inside. Don't look."

They started up the escalator. "This gives us a few seconds; he won't get on until we curve out of sight. Now listen. The people holding these seats will leave as soon as we show the tickets—only I'm going to hang onto one, pay him to stay. Let's hope it's a man because our nursemaid is going to spot that booth in minutes . . . seconds, if he was able to get our booth number down below. You keep going. When he finds our booth he'll see me in it with a man. He won't see the man's face in the dark but he'll be certain of me because of this outlandish, night-glow outfit I'm wearing. So he'll be happy. You zip out any exit but the main lobby; the driver will probably wait there. Try to be in the outer lobby a few minutes before the time I told them to have the car. If you don't make it, hire a flea-cab and go home. I'll complain aloud that you didn't like the show and went home."

Thorby decided that the "X" Corps had missed a bet in Leda. "Won't they report that they lost track of me?"

"They'll be so relieved they'll never breathe it. Here we are—keep moving. See you!"

Thorby went out a side exit, got lost, got straightened out by a cop, at last found the building across from Guard SHQ. The building directory showed that Garsch had offices on the 34th terrace; a few minutes later he faced a receptionist whose mouth was permanently pursed in "No."

She informed him frostily that the Counselor never saw anyone except by appointment. Did he care to make an inquiry appointment with one of the Counselor's associates? "Name, please!"

Thorby glanced around, the room was crowded. She slapped a switch. "Speak up!" she snapped. "I've turned on the privacy curtain."

"Please tell Mr. Garsch that Rudbek of Rudbek would like to see him."

Thorby thought that she was about to tell him not to tell fibs. Then she got up hastily and left.

She came back and said quietly, "The Counselor can give you five minutes. This way, sir."

James J. Garsch's private office was in sharp contrast with building and suite; he himself looked like an unmade bed. He wore trousers, not tights, and his belly bulged over his belt. He had not shaved that day; his grizzled beard matched the fringe around his scalp. He did not stand up. "Rudbek?"

"Yes, sir. Mr. James J. Garsch?"

"The same. Identification? Seems to me I saw your face in the news but I don't recollect."

Thorby handed over his ID folder. Garsch glanced at the public ID, studied the rare and more difficult-to-counterfeit ID of Rudbek & Assocs.

He handed it back. "Siddown. What can I do for you?"

"I need advice . . . and help."

at's what I sell. But Bruder has lawyers running out ears. What can *I* do for you?"

, is this confidential?"

rivileged, son. The word is 'privileged.' You don't ask wyer that; he's either honest or he ain't. Me, I'm mid-llin' honest. You take your chances."

"Well . . . it's a long story."

"Then make it short. You talk. I listen."

"You'll represent me?"

"You talk, I listen," Garsch repeated. "Maybe I'll go to sleep. I ain't feeling my best today. I never do."

"All right." Thorby launched into it. Garsch listened with eyes closed, fingers laced over his bulge.

"That's all," concluded Thorby, "except that I'm anxious to get straightened out so that I can go back into the Guard."

Garsch for the first time showed interest. "Rudbek of Rudbek? In the Guard? Let's not be silly, son."

"But I'm not really 'Rudbek of Rudbek.' I'm an enlisted Guardsman who got pitched into it by circumstances beyond my control."

"I knew that part of your story; the throb writers ate it up. But we all got circumstances we can't control. Point is, a man doesn't quit his job. Not when it's *his*."

"It's not mine," Thorby answered stubbornly.

"Let's not fiddle. First, we get your parents declared dead. Second, we demand their wills and proxies. If they make a fuss, we get a court order . . . and even the mighty Rudbek folds up under a simple subpoena-or-be-locked-up-for-contempt." He bit a fingernail. "Might be some time before the estate is settled and you are qualified. Court might appoint you to act, or the wills may say who, or the court might appoint somebody else. But it won't be those two, if what you say is correct. Even one of Bruder's pocket judges wouldn't dare; it would be too raw and he'd know he'd be reversed."

"But what can I do if they won't even start the action to have my parents declared dead?"

"Who told you you had to wait on them? You'r
interested party; they might not even qualify as *a*
curiae. If I recall the gossip, they're hired hands, qu
with one nominal share each. You're the number-one
terested party, so you start the action. Other relati
First cousins, maybe?"

"No first cousins. I don't know what other heirs there
may be. There's my grandparents Bradley."

"Didn't know they were alive. Will they fight you?"

Thorby started to say no, changed his mind. "I don't
know."

"Cross it when we come to it. Other heirs . . . well, we
won't know till we get a squint at the wills—and that probably won't happen until a court forces them. Any objection
to hypnotic evidence? Truth drugs? Lie detectors?"

"No. Why?"

"You're the best witness that they are dead, not just
long time missing."

"But if a person is missing long enough?"

"Depends. Any term of years is just a guide to the court,
not a rule of law. Time was when seven years would do it—
but that's no longer true. Things are roomier now."

"How do we start?"

"Got any money? Or have they got you hogtied on that?
I come high. I usually charge for each exhale and inhale."

"Well, I've got a megabuck . . . and a few thousand more.
About eight."

"Hmm . . . Haven't said I'd take this case. Has it occurred to you that your life may be in danger?"

"Huh! No, it hasn't."

"Son, people do odd things for money, but they'll do
still more drastic things for power over money. Anybody
sittin' close to a billion credits is in danger; it's like keeping
a pet rattlesnake. If I were you and started feeling ill,
I'd pick my own doctor. I'd be cautious about going through
doors and standing close to open windows." He thought.
"Rudbek is not a good place for you now; don't tempt them.

Matter of fact, you ought not to be here. Belong to the Diplomatic Club?"

"No, sir."

"You do now. People 'ud be surprised if you didn't. I'm often there, around six. Got a room there, sort of private. Twenty eleven."

" 'Twenty eleven.' "

"I still haven't said I'd take it. Got any idea what I'd have to do if I lose this case?"

"Eh? No, sir."

"What was the place you mentioned? Jubbulpore? That's where I'd have to move." Suddenly he grinned. "But I've been spoiling for a fight. Rudbek, eh? Bruder. You mentioned a megabuck?"

Thorby got out his book of checking certificates, passed them over. Garsch riffled through it, shoved it into a drawer. "We won't convert this now; they're almost certainly noting your withdrawals. Anyhow, it's going to cost you more. G'bye. Say in a couple of days."

Thorby left, feeling bucked up. He had never met a more mercenary, predatory old man—he reminded Thorby of the old, scarred freedmen professionals who swaggerred around the New Amphitheater.

As he came outdoors he saw Guard Headquarters. He looked again—then ducked through murderous traffic and ran up its steps.

Chapter 21

THORBY FOUND a circle of receptionist booths around the great foyer. He pushed through crowds pouring out and went into one. A contralto voice said, "Punch your name. State department and office into the microphone. Wait until the light appears, then state your business. You are reminded that working hours are over and only emergencies are now handled."

Thorby punched, "Thorby Baslim," into the machine, then said, "Exotic Corps."

He waited. The tape repeated, "Punch your name. State the department and office into—" It suddenly cut off. A man's voice said, "Repeat that."

"Exotic Corps."

"Business?"

"Better check my name in your files."

At last another female voice chanted, "Follow the light immediately over your head. Do not lose it."

He followed it up escalators, down slideways, and into an unmarked door, where a man not in uniform led him through two more. He faced another man in civilian clothes who stood up and said, "Rudbek of Rudbek. I am Wing Marshal Smith."

"Thorby Baslim, please, sir. Not 'Rudbek.'"

"Names aren't important but identities are. Mine isn't 'Smith,' but it will do. I suppose you have identification?"

Thorby produced his ID again. "You probably have my fingerprints."

"They'll be here in a moment. Do you mind supplying them again?"

While Thorby had his prints taken, a print file card popped out onto the Marshal's desk. He put both sets into a comparator, seemed to pay no attention but until it flashed green he spoke only politenesses.

Then he said, "All right, Thorby Baslim . . . Rudbek. What can I do for you?"

"Maybe it's what I can do for you?"

"So?"

"I came here for two reasons," Thorby stated. "The first is, I think I can add something to Colonel Baslim's final report. You know who I mean?"

"I knew him and admired him very much. Go on."

"The second is—I'd like to go back into the Guard and go 'X' Corps." Thorby couldn't recall when he had decided this, but he had—not just Pop's outfit, Pop's own corps. Pop's work.

"Smith" raised his brows. "So? Rudbek of Rudbek?"

"I'm getting that fixed." Thorby sketched rapidly how he must settle his parents' estate, arrange for handling of their affairs. "Then I'm free. I know it's presumptuous of an acting ordnanceman third class—no, I was busted from that; I had a fight—for a boot Guardsman to talk about 'X' Corps, but I think I've got things you could use. I know the People . . . the Free Traders, I mean. I speak several languages. I know how to behave in the Nine Worlds. I've been around a bit, not much and I'm no astrogator . . . but I've traveled a little. Besides that, I've seen how Pop— Colonel Baslim—worked. Maybe I could do some of it."

"You have to love this work to do it. Lots of times it's nasty . . . things a man wouldn't do, for his own self-respect, if he didn't think it was necessary."

"But I do! Uh, I was a slave. You knew that? Maybe it would help if a man knew how a slave feels."

"Perhaps. Though it might make you too emotional. Besides, slave traffic isn't all we are interested in. A man comes here, we don't promise him certain work. He does what he's told. We use him. We usually use him up. Our casualty rate is high."

"I'll do what I'm told. I just happen to be interested in the slave traffic. Why, most people here don't seem to know it exists."

"Most of what we deal in the public wouldn't believe. Can you expect the people you see around you to take seriously unbelievable stories about far-away places? You must remember that less than one percent of the race ever leaves its various planets of birth."

"Uh, I suppose so. Anyhow they don't believe it."

"That's not our worst handicap. The Terran Hegemony is no empire; it is simply leadership in a loose confederation of planets. The difference between what the Guard *could* do and what it is *allowed* to do is very frustrating. If you have come here thinking that you will see slavery abolished in your lifetime, disabuse your mind. Our most optimistic target date is two centuries away—and by that time slavery will have broken out in planets not even discovered today. Not a problem to be solved once and for all. A continuing process."

"All I want to know is, can I help?"

"I don't know. Not because you describe yourself as a junior enlisted man . . . we're all pretty much the same rank in this place. The Exotic Corps is an idea, not an organization chart. I'm not worried about what Thorby Baslim can do; he can do something, even if it's only translating. But Rudbek of Rudbek . . . mmm, I wonder."

"But I told you I was getting rid of that!"

"Well—let's wait until you have. By your own statement you are not presenting yourself for enrollment today. What about the other reason? Something to add to Colonel Baslim's report?"

Thorby hesitated. "Sir, Colonel Brisby, my C.O., told me that P—Colonel Baslim had proved a connection between the slave trade and some big starshipbuilding outfit."

"He told you that?"

"Yes, sir. You could look it up in Colonel Baslim's report."

"I don't need to. Go on."

"Well . . . is it Rudbek he was talking about? Galactic Transport, that is?"

"Smith" considered it. "Why ask me if your company is mixed up in slave trade? You tell us."

Thorby frowned. "Is there a Galactovue around here?"

"Down the hall."

"May I use it?"

"Why not?" The Wing Marshal led him through a private corridor into a conference room dominated by a star-flecked stereo display. It was much the biggest Thorby had ever seen.

He had to ask questions; it had complicated controls. Then he got to work. His face puckering with strain, Thorby painted in colored lights amid fairy stars the solid picture he had built in the Galactovue in his office. He did not explain and the officer watched in silence. Thorby stepped back at last. "That's all I know now."

234

"You missed a few." The Wing Marshal added some lights in yellow, some in red, then working slowly, added half a dozen missing ships. "But that's quite a feat to do from memory and a remarkable concatenation of ideas. I see you included yourself—maybe it does help to have a personal interest." He stepped back. "Well, Baslim, you asked a question. Are you ready to answer it?"

"I think Galactic Transport is in it up to here! Not everybody, but enough key people. Supplying ships. And repairs and fuel. Financing, maybe."

"Mmm . . ."

"Is all this physically possible otherwise?"

"You know what they would say if you accused them of slave trading—"

"Not the trade itself. At least I don't think so."

"Connected with it. First they would say that they had never heard of any slave trade, or that it was just a wild rumor. Then they would say that, in any case, they just sell ships—and is a hardware dealer who sells a knife responsible if a husband carves his wife?"

"The cases aren't parallel."

"They wouldn't concede that. They would say that they were not breaking any laws and even stipulating that there might be slavery somewhere, how can you expect people to get worked up over a possible evil light-years away? In which they are correct; you can't expect people to, because they *won't*. Then some smarmy well-dressed character will venture the opinion that slavery—when it existed—was not so bad, because a large part of the population is really happier if they don't have the responsibilities of a free man. Then he'll add that if they didn't sell ships, someone else would—it's just business."

Thorby thought of nameless little Thorbys out there in the dark, crying hopelessly with fear and loneliness and hurt, in the reeking holds of slavers—ships that might be *his*. "One stroke of the lash would change his slimy mind!"

"Surely. But we've abolished the lash here. Sometimes I wonder if we should have." He looked at the display. "I'm going to record this; it has facets not yet considered together. Thanks for coming in. If you get more ideas, come in again."

Thorby realized that his notion of joining the corps had not been taken seriously. "Marshal Smith . . . there's one other thing I might do."

"What?"

"Before I join, if you let me . . . or maybe after; I don't know how you do such things . . . I could go out as Rudbeck of Rudbek, in my own ship, and check those places —the red ones, ours. Maybe the boss can dig out things that a secret agent would have trouble getting close to."

"Maybe. But you know that your father started to make an inspection trip once. He wasn't lucky in it." Smith scratched his chin. "We've never quite accounted for that one. Until you showed up alive, we assumed that it was natural disaster. A yacht with three passengers, a crew of eight and no cargo doesn't look like worthwhile pickings for bandits in business for profit—and they generally know what they're doing."

Thorby was shocked. "Are you suggesting that—"

"I'm not suggesting anything. But bosses prying into employees' sidelines have, in other times and places, burned their fingers. And your father was certainly checking."

"About the slave trade?"

"I couldn't guess. Inspecting. In that area. I've got to excuse myself. But do come see me again . . . or phone and someone will come to you."

"Marshal Smith . . . what parts of this, if any, can be talked over with other people?"

"Eh? Any of it. As long as you don't attribute it to this corps, or to the Guard. But facts as you know them—" He shrugged. "—who will believe you? Although if you talk to your business associates about your suspicions, you may arouse strong feelings against you personally . . . some of those feelings sincere and honest. The others? I wish I knew."

Thorby was so late that Leda was both vexed and bursting with curiosity. But she had to contain it not only because of possible monitoring but because of an elderly aunt who had called to pay her respects to Rudbek of Rudbek, and was staying the night. It was not until next day, while examining Aztec relics in the Fifth of May Museum, that they were able to talk.

Thorby recounted what Garsch had said, then decided to tell more. "I looked into rejoining the Guard yesterday."

"Thor!"

"Oh, I'm not walking out. But I have a reason. The Guard is the only organization trying to put a stop to slave traffic. But that is all the more reason why I can't enlist now." He outlined his suspicions about Rudbek and the traffic.

Her face grew pale. "Thor, that's the most horrible idea I ever heard. I *can't* believe it."

"I'd like to prove it isn't true. But somebody builds their ships, somebody maintains them. Slavers are not engineers; they're parasites."

"I still have trouble believing that there is such a thing as slavery."

He shrugged. "Ten lashes will convince anybody."

"Thor! You don't mean they *whipped* you?"

"I don't remember clearly. But the scars are on my back."

She was very quiet on the way home.

Thorby saw Garsch once more, then they headed for the Yukon, in company with the elderly aunt, who had somehow attached herself. Garsch had papers for Thorby to sign and two pieces of information. "The first action has to be at Rudbek, because that was the legal residence of your parents. The other thing is, I did some digging in newspaper files."

"Yes?"

"Your grandfather did give you a healthy block of stock. It was in stories about the whoop-te-do when you were born. The Bourse Journal listed the shares by serial numbers. So we'll hit 'em with that, too—on the same day. Don't want one to tip off the other."

"You're the doctor."

"But I don't want you in Rudbek until the clerk shouts 'Oyez!' Here's a mail-drop you can use to reach me . . . even phone through, if you have to. And right smartly you set up a way for me to reach you."

Thorby puzzled over that requirement, being hemmed in as he was by bodyguards. "Why don't you, or somebody—a young man, maybe—phone my cousin with a code message? People are always phoning her and most of them are young men. She'll tell me and I'll find a place to phone back."

"Good idea. He'll ask if she knows how many shopping days left till Christmas. All right—see you in court." Garsch grinned. "This is going to be fun. And very, very expensive for you. G'bye."

Chapter   22

"Have a nice vacation?" Uncle Jack smiled at him. "You've led us quite a chase. You shouldn't do that, boy."

Thorby wanted to hit him but, although the guards let go his arms when they shoved him into the room, his wrists were tied.

Uncle Jack stopped smiling and glanced at Judge Bruder. "Thor, you've never appreciated that Judge Bruder and I worked for your father, and for your grandfather. Naturally we know what's best. But you've given us trouble and now we'll show you how we handle little boys who don't appreciate decent treatment. We teach them. Ready, Judge?"

Judge Bruder smiled savagely and took the whip from behind him. "Bend him over the desk!"

Thorby woke up gasping. Whew, a bad one! He looked around the small hotel room he was in and tried to remember where he was. For days he had moved daily, sometimes half around the planet. He had become sophisticated in the folkways of this planet, enough not to attract attention, and even had a new ID card, quite as good as a real one. It had not been difficult, once he realized that underworlds were much the same everywhere.

He remembered now—this was América de Sud.

The bed alarm sounded—just midnight, time to leave. He dressed and glanced at his baggage, decided to abandon it. He walked down the backstairs, out the back way.

Aunt Lizzie had not liked the Yukon cold but she put up with it. Eventually someone called and reminded Leda that there were few shopping days to Christmas, so they left. At Uranium City Thorby managed to return the call. Garsch grinned. "I'll see you in the district court in-and-for the county of Rudbek, division four, at nine-fifty-nine the morning of January fourth. Now get lost completely."

So at San Francisco Thorby and Leda had a tiff in the presence of Aunt Lizzie; Leda wanted to go to Nice, Thorby insisted on Australia. Thorby said angrily, "Keep the car! I'll go by myself." He flounced out and bought a ticket for Great Sydney.

He pulled a rather old washroom trick, tubed under the Bay, and, convinced that his bodyguard had been evaded, counted the cash Leda had slipped him as privately as they had quarreled publicly. It came to a little under two hundred thousand credits. There was a note saying that she was sorry it wasn't more but she had not anticipated needing money.

While waiting at the South American field Thorby counted what was left of Leda's money and reflected that he had cut it fine, both time and money. Where did it all go?

Photographers and reporters gave him a bad time at Rudbek City; the place swarmed with them. But he pushed through and met Garsch inside the bar at nine-fifty-eight. The old man nodded. "Siddown. Hizzoner will be out soon."

The judge came out and a clerk intoned the ancient

promise of justice: "—draw nigh and ye shall be heard!" Garsch remarked, "Bruder has this judge on a leash."

"Huh? Then why are we here?"

"You're paying me to worry. Any judge is a good judge when he knows he's being watched. Look behind you."

Thorby did so. The place was so loaded with press that a common citizen stood no chance. "I did a good job, if I do say so." Garsch hooked a thumb at the front row. "The galoot with the big nose is the ambassador from Proxima. The old thief next to him is chairman of the judiciary committee. And—" He broke off.

Thorby could not spot Uncle Jack but Bruder presided over the other table—he did not look at Thorby. Nor could Thorby find Leda. It made him feel very much alone. But Garsch finished opening formalities, sat down and whispered. "Message for you. Young lady says to say 'Good luck.'"

Thorby was active only in giving testimony and that after many objections, counter objections, and warnings from the bench. While he was being sworn, he recognized in the front row a retired chief justice of the Hegemonic Ultimate Court who had once dined at Rudbek. Then Thorby did not notice anything, for he gave his testimony in deep trance surrounded by hypnotherapists.

Although every point was chewed endlessly, only once did the hearing approach drama. The court sustained an objection by Bruder in such fashion that a titter of unbelief ran around the room and someone stamped his feet. The judge turned red. "Order! The bailiff will clear the room!"

The move to comply started, over protests of reporters. But the front two rows sat tight and stared at the judge. The High Ambassador from the Vegan League leaned toward his secretary and whispered; the secretary started slapping a Silent-Steno.

The judge cleared his throat. "—unless this unseemly behavior ceases at once! This court will not tolerate disrespect."

Thorby was almost surprised when it ended: "—must therefore be conclusively presumed that Creighton Bradley

Rudbek and Martha Bradley Rudbek did each die, are now dead, and furthermore did meet their ends in common disaster. May their souls rest in peace. Let it be so recorded." The court banged his gavel. "If custodians of wills of the decedents, if wills there be, are present in this court, let them now come forward."

There was no hearing about Thorby's own shares; Thorby signed a receipt for certificates thereto in the judge's chambers. Neither Weemsby nor Bruder was present.

Thorby took a deep breath as Garsch and he came out of chambers. "I can hardly believe that we've won."

Garsch grinned. "Don't kid yourself. We won the first round on points. Now it begins to get expensive."

Thorby's mouth sagged. Rudbek guards moved in and started taking them through the crowd.

Garsch had not overstated it. Bruder and Weemsby sat tight, still running Rudbek & Assocs., and continued to fight. Thorby never did see his parents' proxies—his only interest in them now was to see whether, as he suspected, the differences between the papers Bruder had prepared and those of his parents lay in the difference between "revocable" and "revocable only by mutual agreement."

But when the court got around to ordering them produced, Bruder claimed that they had been destroyed in routine clearing from files of expired instruments. He received a ten-day sentence for contempt, suspended, and that ended it.

But, while Weemsby was no longer voting the shares of Martha and Creighton Rudbek, neither was Thorby; the shares were tied up while the wills were being proved. In the meantime, Bruder and Weemsby remained officers of Rudbek & Assocs., with a majority of directors backing them. Thorby was not even allowed in Rudbek Building, much less in his old office.

Weemsby never went back to Rudbek estate; his belongings were sent to him. Thorby moved Garsch into Weemsby's apartment. The old man slept there often; they were very busy.

At one point Garsch told him that there were ninety-seven actions, for or against, moving or pending, relating to the settlement of his estate. The wills were simple in essence; Thorby was the only major heir. But there were dozens of minor bequests; there were relatives who might get something if the wills were set aside; the question of "legally dead" was again raised, the presumption of "common disaster" versus deaths at different times was hashed again; and Thorby's very identity was questioned. Neither Bruder nor Weemsby appeared in these actions; some relative or stockholder was always named as petitioner—Thorby was forced to conclude that Uncle Jack had kept everyone happy.

But the only action that grieved him was brought by his grandparents Bradley, asking that he be made their ward because of incompetence. The evidence, other than the admitted fact that he was new to the complexities of Terran life, was his Guardsman medical record—a Dr. Krishnamurti had endorsed that he was "potentially emotionally unstable and should not be held fully answerable for actions under stress."

Garsch had him examined in blatant publicity by the physician to the Secretary General of the Hegemonic Assembly. Thorby was found legally sane. It was followed by a stockholder's suit asking that Thorby be found professionally unequipped to manage the affairs of Rudbek & Assocs., in private and public interest.

Thorby was badly squeezed by these maneuvers; he was finding it ruinously expensive to be rich. He was heavily in debt from legal costs and running Rudbek estate and had not been able to draw his own accumulated royalties as Bruder and Weemsby continued to contend, despite repeated adverse decisions, that his identity was uncertain.

But a weary time later a court three levels above the Rudbek district court awarded to Thorby (subject to admonitions as to behavior and unless revoked by court) the power to vote his parents' stock until such time as their estates were settled.

Thorby called a general meeting of stockholders, on stockholders' initative as permitted by the bylaws, to elect officers.

The meeting was in the auditorium of Rudbek Building; most stockholders on Terra showed up even if represented by proxy. Even Leda popped in at the last minute, called out merrily, "Hello, everybody!" then turned to her stepfather. "Daddy, I got the notice and decided to see the fun—so I jumped into the bus and hopped over. I haven't missed anything, have I?"

She barely glanced at Thorby, although he was on the platform with the officers. Thorby was relieved and hurt; he had not seen her since they had parted at San Francisco. He knew that she had residence at Rudbek Arms in Rudbek City and was sometimes in town, but Garsch had discouraged him from getting in touch with her—"Man's a fool to chase a woman when she's made it plain she doesn't want to see him."

So he simply reminded himself that he must pay back her loan—with interest—as soon as possible.

Weemsby called the meeting to order, announced that in accordance with the call the meeting would nominate and elect officers. "Minutes and old business postponed by unanimous consent." *Bang!* "Let the secretary call the roll for nominations for chairman of the board." His face wore a smile of triumph.

The smile worried Thorby. He controlled, his own and his parents', just under 45% of the voting stock. From the names used in bringing suits and other indirect sources he thought that Weemsby controlled about 31%; Thorby needed to pick up 6%. He was counting on the emotional appeal of "Rudbek of Rudbek"—but he couldn't be sure, even though Weemsby needed more than three times as many "uncertain" votes . . . uncertain to Thorby; they might be in Weemsby's pocket.

But Thorby stood up and nominated himself, through his own stock. "Thor Rudbek of Rudbek!"

After that it was pass, pass, pass, over and over again—until Weemsby was nominated. There were no other nominations.

"The Secretary will call the roll," Weemsby intoned.

"Announce your votes by shares as owners, followed by votes as proxy. The Clerk will check serial numbers against the Great Record. Thor Rudbek . . . of Rudbek."

Thorby voted all 45%-minus that he controlled, then sat down feeling very weary. But he got out a pocket calculator. There were 94,000 voting shares; he did not trust himself to keep tally in his head. The Secretary read on, the clerk droned his checks on the record. Thorby needed to pick up 5657 votes, to win by one vote.

He began slowly to pick up odd votes—232, 906, 1917 —some of them directly, some through proxy. But Weemsby picked up votes also. Some shareholders answered, "Pass to proxy," or failed to respond—as the names marched past and these missing votes did not appear, Thorby was forced to infer that Weemsby held those proxies himself. But still the additional votes for "Rudbek of Rudbek" mounted—2205, 3036, 4309 . . . and there it stuck. The last few names passed.

Garsch leaned toward him. "Just the sunshine twins left."

"I know." Thorby put away his calculator, feeling sick—so Weemsby had won, after all.

The Secretary had evidently been instructed what names to read last. "The Honorable Curt Bruder!"

Bruder voted his one qualifying share for Weemsby. "Our Chairman, Mr. John Weemsby."

Weemsby stood up and looked happy. "In my own person, I vote one share. By proxies delivered to me and now with the Secretary I vote—" Thorby did not listen; he was looking for his hat.

"The tally being complete, I declare—" the Secretary began.

"No!"

Leda was on her feet. "I'm here *myself*. This is my first meeting and *I'm going to vote!*"

Her stepfather said hastily, "That's all right, Leda—mustn't interrupt." He turned to the Secretary. "It doesn't affect the result."

"But it *does!* I cast one thousand eight hundred and eighty votes for Thor, Rudbek of Rudbek!"

Weemsby stared. "Leda Weemsby!"

She retorted crisply, "My legal name is Leda *Rudbek.*"

Bruder was shouting, "Illegal! The vote has been recorded. It's too—"

"Oh, nonsense!" shouted Leda. "I'm here and I'm voting. Anyhow, I cancelled that proxy—I registered it in the post office in this very building and saw it delivered and signed for at the 'principal offices of this corporation'—that's the right phrase, isn't it, Judge?—ten minutes before the meeting was called to order. If you don't believe me, send down for it. But what of it?—I'm here. Touch me." Then she turned and smiled at Thorby.

Thorby tried to smile back, and whispered savagely to Garsch, "Why did you keep this a secret?"

"And let 'Honest John' find out that he had to beg, borrow, or buy some more votes? He might have won. She kept him happy, just as I told her to. That's quite a girl, Thorby. Better option her."

Five minutes later Thorby, shaking and white, got up and took the gavel that Weemsby had dropped. He faced the crowd. "We will now elect the rest of the board," he announced, his voice barely under control. The slate that Garsch and Thorby had worked out was passed by acclamation—with one addition: Leda.

Again she stood up. "Oh, no! You can't do this to me."

"Out of order. You've assumed responsibility, now accept it."

She opened her mouth, closed it, sat down.

When the Secretary declared the result, Thorby turned to Weemsby. "You are General Manager also, are you not?"

"Yes."

"You're fired. Your one share reverts. Don't try to go back to your former office; just get your hat and go."

Bruder jumped up. Thorby turned to him. "You, too. Sergeant-at-Arms, escort them out of the building."

Chapter 23

THORBY LOOKED glumly at a high stack of papers, each item flagged "URGENT." He picked up one, started to read—put it down and said, "Dolores, switch control of my screen to me. Then go home."

"I can stay, sir."

"I said, 'Go home.' How are you going to catch a husband with circles under your eyes?"

"Yes, sir." She changed connections. "Good night, sir."

"Good night."

Good girl, there. Loyal, he thought. Well, he hoped. He hadn't dared use a new broom all the way; the administration had to have continuity. He signaled a number.

A voice without a face said, "Scramble Seven."

" 'Prometheus Bound,' " Thorby answered, "and nine makes sixteen."

"Scramble set up."

"Sealed," Thorby agreed.

The face of Wing Marshal "Smith" appeared. "Hi, Thor."

"Jake, I've got to postpone this month's conference again. I hate to—but you should see my desk."

"Nobody expects you to devote all your time to corps matters."

"Doggone it, that's exactly what I planned to do—clean this place up fast, put good people in charge, grab my hat and enlist for the corps! But it's not that simple."

"Thor, no conscientious officer lets himself be relieved until his board is all green. We both knew that you had lots of lights blinking red."

"Well . . . all right, I can't make the conference. Got a few minutes?"

"Shoot," agreed "Smith."

"I think I've got a boy to hunt porcupines. Remember?"

" 'Nobody eats a porcupine.' "

"Right! Though I had to see a picture of one to understand what you meant. To put it in trader terms, the way to kill a business is to make it unprofitable. Slave-raiding is a business, the way to kill it is to put it in the red. Porcupine spines on the victims will do it."

"If we had the spines," the "X" Corps director agreed dryly. "You have an idea for a weapon?"

"Me? What do you think I am? A genius? But I think I've found one. Name is Joel de la Croix. He's supposed to be about the hottest thing M.I.T. ever turned out. I've gossiped with him about what I used to do as a firecontrolman in *Sisu*. He came up with some brilliant ideas without being prodded. Then he said, 'Thor, it's ridiculous for a ship to be put out of action by a silly little paralysis beam when it has enough power in its guts to make a small star.' "

"A *very* small star. But I agree."

"Okay. I've got him stashed in our Havermeyer Labs in Toronto. As soon as your boys okay him, I want to hand him a truckload of money and give him a free hand. I'll feed him all I know about raider tactics and so forth—trance tapes, maybe, as I won't have time to work with him much. I'm being run ragged here."

"He'll need a team. This isn't a home-workshop project."

"I know. I'll funnel names to you as fast as I have them. Project Porcupine will have all the men and money it can use. But, Jake, how many of these gadgets can I sell to the Guard?"

"Eh?"

"I'm supposed to be running a business. If I run it into the ground, the courts will boost me out. I'm going to let Project Porcupine spend megabucks like water—but I've got to justify it to directors and stockholders. If we come up with something, I can sell several hundred units to

Free Traders, I can sell some to ourselves—but I need to show a potential large market to justify the expenditure. How many can the Guard use?"

"Thor, you're worrying unnecessarily. Even if you don't come up with a superweapon—and your chances aren't good—*all* research pays off. Your stockholders won't lose."

"I am *not* worrying unnecessarily! I've got this job by a handful of votes; a special stockholders meeting could kick me out tomorrow. Sure research pays off, but not necessarily quickly. You can count on it that every credit I spend is reported to people who would love to see me bumped—so I've got to have reasonable justification."

"How about a research contract?"

"With a vice colonel staring down my boy's neck and telling him what to do? We want to give him a free hand."

"Mmm . . . yes. Suppose I get you a letter-of-intent? We'll make the figure as high as possible. I'll have to see the Marshal-in-Chief. He's on Luna at the moment and I can't squeeze time to go to Luna this week. You'll have to wait a few days."

"I'm not going to wait; I'm going to assume that you can do it. Jake, I'm going to get things rolling and get out of this crazy job—if you won't have me in the corps I can always be an ordnanceman."

"Come on down this evening. I'll enlist you—then I'll order you to detached duty, right where you are."

Thorby's chin dropped. "Jake! You wouldn't do that to me!"

"I would if you were silly enough to place yourself under my orders, Rudbek."

"But—" Thorby shut up. There was no use arguing; there was too much work to be done.

"Smith" added, "Anything else?"

"I guess not."

"I'll have a first check on de la Croix by tomorrow. See you."

Thorby switched off, feeling glummer than ever. It was not the Wing Marshal's half-whimsical threat, nor even his troubled conscience over spending large amounts of other people's money on a project that stood little chance of success; it was simply that he was swamped by a job more complex than he had believed possible.

He picked up the top item again, put it down, pressed the key that sealed him through to Rudbek estate. Leda was summoned to the screen. "I'll be late again. I'm sorry."

"I'll delay dinner. They're enjoying themselves and I had the kitchen make the canapés substantial."

Thorby shook his head. "Take the head of the table. I'll eat here. I may sleep here."

She sighed. "If you sleep. Look, my stupid dear, be in bed by midnight and up not before six. Promise?"

"Okay. If possible."

"It had better be possible, or you will have trouble with me. See you."

He didn't even pick up the top item this time; he simply sat in thought. Good girl, Leda . . . she had even tried to help in the business—until it had become clear that business was not her forte. But she was one bright spot in the gloom; she always bucked him up. If it wasn't patently unfair for a Guardsman to marry— But he couldn't be that unfair to Leda and he had no reason to think she would be willing anyhow. It was unfair enough for him to duck out of a big dinner party at the last minute. Other things. He would have to try to treat her better.

It had all seemed so self-evident: just take over, fumigate that sector facing the Sargony, then pick somebody else to run it. But the more he dug, the more there was to do. Taxes . . . the tax situation was incredibly snarled; it always was. That expansion program the Vegan group was pushing—how could he judge unless he went there and looked? And would he know if he did? And how could he find *time?*

Funny, but a man who owned a thousand starships automatically never had time to ride in even one of them. Maybe in a year or two—

No, those confounded wills wouldn't even be settled in

249

that time!—two years now and the courts were still chewing it. Why couldn't death be handled decently and simply the way the People did it?

In the meantime he wasn't free to go on with Pop's work. True, he had accomplished a little. By letting "X" Corps have access to Rudbek's files some of the picture had filled in—Jake had told him that a raid which had wiped out one slaver pesthole had resulted directly from stuff the home office knew and hadn't known that it knew.

Or *had* somebody known? Some days he thought Weemsby and Bruder had had guilty knowledge, some days not—for all that the files showed was legitimate business . . . sometimes with wrong people. But who knew that they were the wrong people?

He opened a drawer, got out a folder with no "URGENT" flag on it simply because it never left his hands. It was, he felt, the most urgent thing in Rudbek, perhaps in the Galaxy —certainly more urgent than Project Porcupine because this matter was certain to cripple, or at least hamper, the slave trade, while Porcupine was a long chance. But his progress had been slow—too much else to do.

Always too much. Grandmother used to say never to buy too many eggs for your basket. Wonder where she got that? —the People never bought eggs. He had both too many baskets and too many eggs for each. And another basket every day.

Of course, in a tough spot he could always ask himself: "What would Pop do?" Colonel Brisby had phrased that— "I just ask myself, 'What would Colonel Baslim do?' " It helped, especially when he had to remember also what the presiding judge had warned him about the day his parents' shares had been turned over to him: "No man can own a thing to himself alone, and the bigger it is, the less he owns it. You are not free to deal with this property arbitrarily nor foolishly. Your interest does not override that of other stockholders, nor of employees, nor of the public."

Thorby had talked that warning over with Pop before deciding to go ahead with Porcupine.

The judge was right. His first impulse on taking over the business had been to shut down every Rudbek activity in that infected sector, cripple the slave trade that way. But you could not do that. You *could not* injure thousands, millions, of honest men to put the squeeze on criminals. It required more judicious surgery.

Which was what he was trying to do now. He started studying the unmarked folder.

Garsch stuck his head in. "Still running under the whip? What's the rush, boy?"

"Jim, where can I find ten honest men?"

"Huh? Diogenes was satisfied to hunt for one. Gave him more than he could handle."

"You know what I mean—ten honest men each qualified to take over as a planetary manager for Rudbek." Thorby added to himself, "—and acceptable to 'X' Corps."

"Now I'll tell one."

"Know any other solution? I'll have each one relieve a manager in the smelly sector and send the man he relieves back—we can't fire them; we'll have to absorb them. Because we don't *know*. But the new men we can trust and each one will be taught how the slave trade operates and what to look for."

Garsch shrugged. "It's the best we can do. But forget the notion of doing it in one bite; we won't find that many qualified men at one time. Now look, boy, you ain't going to solve it tonight no matter how long you stare at those names. When you are as old as I am, you'll know you can't do everything at once—provided you don't kill yourself first. Either way, someday you die and somebody else has to do the work. You remind me of the man who set out to count stars. Faster he counted, the more new stars kept turning up. So he went fishing. Which you should, early and often."

"Jim, why did you agree to come here? I don't see you quitting work when the others do."

"Because I'm an old idiot. Somebody had to give you a hand. Maybe I relished a chance to take a crack at anything as dirty as the slave trade and this was my way—I'm too old and fat to do it any other way."

Thorby nodded. "I thought so. I've got another way— only, confound it, I'm so busy doing what I must do that I don't have time for what I ought to do . . . and I *never* get a chance to do what I *want* to do!"

"Son, that's universal. The way to keep that recipe from killing you is occasionally to do what you want to do anyhow. Which is right now. There's all day tomorrow ain't touched yet . . . and you are going out with me and have a sandwich and look at pretty girls."

"I'm going to have dinner sent up."

"No, you aren't. Even a steel ship has to have time for maintenance. So come along."

Thorby looked at the stack of papers. "Okay."

The old man munched his sandwich, drank his lager, and watched pretty girls, with a smile of innocent pleasure. They were indeed pretty girls; Rudbek City attracted the highest-paid talent in show business.

But Thorby did not see them. He was thinking.

A person *can't* run out on responsibility. A captain can't, a chief officer can't. But he did not see how, if he went on this way, he would ever be able to join Pop's corps. But Jim was right; here was a place where the filthy business had to be fought, too.

Even if he didn't like this way to fight it? Yes. Colonel Brisby had once said, about Pop: "It means being so devoted to freedom that you are willing to give up your own . . . be a beggar . . . or a slave . . . or die—that freedom may live."

Yes, Pop, but I don't know *how* to do this job. I'd do it . . . I'm *trying* to do it. But I'm just fumbling. I don't have any talent for it.

Pop answered, "*Nonsense! You can learn to do anything if you apply yourself. You're going to learn if I have to beat your silly head in!*"

Somewhere behind Pop Grandmother was nodding agreement and looking stern. Thorby nodded back at her. "Yes, Grandmother. Okay, Pop. I'll try."

"*You'll do more than try!*"

"I'll do it, Pop."

"*Now eat your dinner.*"

Obediently Thorby reached for his spoon, then noticed that it was a sandwich instead of a bowl of stew. Garsch said, "What are you muttering about?"

"Nothing. I just made up my mind."

"Give your mind a rest and use your eyes instead. There's a time and place for everything."

"You're right, Jim."

"Goodnight, son," the old beggar whispered. "*Good dreams . . . and good luck!*"

DEL REY SCIENCE FICTION CLASSICS
FROM BALLANTINE BOOKS

CHILDHOOD'S END, Arthur C. Clarke	27603	1.95
FAHRENHEIT 451, Ray Bradbury	27431	1.95
HAVE SPACESUIT, WILL TRAVEL, Robert A. Heinlein	26071	1.75
IMPERIAL EARTH, Arthur C. Clarke	25352	1.95
MORE THAN HUMAN, Theodore Sturgeon	24389	1.50
RENDEZVOUS WITH RAMA, Arthur C. Clarke	27344	1.95
RINGWORLD, Larry Niven	27550	1.95
A SCANNER DARKLY, Philip K. Dick	26064	1.95
SPLINTER OF THE MIND'S EYE, Alan Dean Foster	26062	1.95
STAND ON ZANZIBAR, John Brunner	25486	1.95
STAR WARS, George Lucas	26079	1.95
STARMAN JONES, Robert A. Heinlein	27595	1.75
TUNNEL IN THE SKY, Robert A. Heinlein	26065	1.50
UNDER PRESSURE, Frank Herbert	27540	1.75

LG-3

DEL REY *Catch a Rising Star!*

DEPENDENCE UPON THE LORD